"Lois Murphy's *Soon* is an exquisitely written, atypical post-apocalyptic/horror story that smartly focuses on the characters/survivors without sacrificing story/thrills/scares. Like the nightly mists, *Soon* will linger"
Paul Tremblay, author of *The Cabin at the End of the World*

"Once I started reading *Soon*, I couldn't stop. Page after page slips by and you want it to go on forever. It charms and beguiles right up to the end—with an ending that might stop your heart. Lois Murphy is a sorceress who turns dystopian on its ear"
Alma Katsu, author of *The Hunger*

"Skilfully balances genuine scares with an exploration of human obsession and grief"
James Brogden, author of *The Plague Stones*

"Disarming... I had to carry on reading through the night"
Aliya Whiteley, author of *The Beauty*

"Unsettling, exquisitely written, elevated by stark, haunting imagery and a coolly measured dread. *Soon* by Lois Murphy is, without question, one of the finest horror novels I've read this decade"
Rio Youers, author of *The Forgotten Girl*

"Stephen King can keep his maniacally grinning clowns—*Soon* made this reader get out of bed to check the windows were closed"
Saturday Paper

SOON

SOON

LOIS MURPHY

TITAN BOOKS

Soon
Print edition ISBN: 9781789092356
E-book edition ISBN: 9781789092363

Published by Titan Books
A division of Titan Publishing Group Ltd.
144 Southwark Street, London SE1 0UP
www.titanbooks.com

First published in the US and UK by Titan Books 2019
First published in Australia by Transit Lounge Publishing 2017
10 9 8 7 6 5 4 3 2 1

A CIP catalogue record for this title is available from the British Library.

Printed and bound by CPI Group (UK) Ltd, Croydon, CR0 4YY

For Joyce and Les Timmins
– better late than never

And for Peter Riley, too late

PART
ONE

April, 1999

The hardest thing, I sometimes think, is keeping track of time. With no school or shops there is nothing to define the days, and the weeks flow through the calendar like a sluggish river. You don't realise the importance of ritual, commonplace, until it's gone. One of those peripheral things that you take for granted; even if they don't affect you personally, their absence is profound. I do have the TV, though: that helps keep track to a degree. I have it on most nights, understandably. SBS is my preference – I'm most partial to those documentaries that show people suffering all around the world. It's a guilty relief to know that there are always people worse off than you are. And if I have the volume up loud enough, it drowns out the night.

I'm not into the soap operas, though. All those drawn-out plots, *Oh there's a lull, maybe we should kill someone off? No, hang on, we haven't had a coma yet this year, there's nothing like a good coma. Whatsit's been forgetting his lines, let's give him a turn.* The unconvincing actors, who think bewilderment is a good portrayal of angst. No, the soaps leave me cold.

The reality shows are a hoot. So contrived you can practically see the participants struggling to remember their scripts, forever anticipating their cues.

There was talk at one stage that some bright spark wanted to do a reality show out here. That would have been a laugh. What would they do, an eviction each week, send them out into the mist and see what they come back as? Last one left alive gets to leave.

Oh yes, highly entertaining. Would have pulled an audience, I'd imagine. They say government authorities put a stop to it, pressured the network with threats of prosecution for negligence and worse if anyone got hurt. It's always nice to know they're looking out for us.

But who knows. It was only a rumour.

*

We used to get a lot of journalists, film crews at first, when most people had fled and word had got out about the disappearances. We were flavour of the month, briefly, filling out the freak file of the current affairs circuit, but it never really came to much. I mean, they could hardly film outside at night and there's not much happening during the day: an empty town is an empty town. Some of them tried filming through the windows, but no matter how much they angled and twiddled and focused, they only ever got their own reflections – usually giving a better show of angst than the gormless soap stars – and their audio would only ever play back static.

So they'd come all this way and end up with nothing but dull daytime footage of closed shops, and interviews with litigious and angry locals – back when there were still some locals hanging in there – making unfounded and defamatory accusations against local authorities and developers that they could hardly air. I'll never forgot old Neil Jacobson's interview, he was ranting by the end, threatening to sue every state and federal government in the Southern Hemisphere. Finally he got so overwrought his teeth came out – now that would have been decent footage – but they'd called a discreet 'Cut' long before then.

Anything they managed to patch together was unconvincing, and the 'shocking true story' angle was hard to milk from a few teary mothers and dismissive government officials. One lot even tried to tie our story in with that bloody program *The X-Files* (now one of my firm favourites), which was starting its new season. They never miss a trick.

All that they ever really succeeded in doing, as far as we were concerned, was in making Nebulah – and its unfortunate inhabitants – a byword for fruitcake. You can appreciate how happy we all were about that.

Every now and then I'll get a call from some journalist with an unmet deadline, wanting to 'follow up' on our 'situation'. Lazy sods. They only ever want to interview over the phone, never to actually come out here. I always say, 'Yeah, look, can you just hang on just a sec?' and then I take

Gina for a walk or go back to the paper, or whatever the hell it was I was doing when they interrupted me. It usually stops them ringing, although I did have one guy who hung on there for over an hour (he was freelance).

Mostly now they leave us in peace. Relatively speaking, of course.

*

Peace is a great word. I often think of it on mornings like these, when the season is turning and the weather has abated to a lull, as if it's still trying to decide which extreme to adopt. The air has a hovering quality to it, expectant but calm, and it's the calmness I appreciate most of all. I often find I do absolutely nothing on mornings like this one, just sit on the edge of the porch, watching Gina snuffle after smells, and enjoy the sky, the absence of walls. I prefer to be outside during the day, it eases the sense of confinement.

Today's a Tuesday. I know that because Li's gone to town, rumbling off in her old truck just after daybreak. The Barrys at the co-op in Woodford are good people, they've never stopped taking her produce, even though she grows so little these days. Not much point when you can't get pickers to come here, and you have to do the lot on your own. And no one will buy your stuff anyway, in case it's infected with something. The Barrys don't label her produce as 'local'; better that people don't know. Li doesn't stop, though, takes a load out every week, bunking down on the floor of the co-op because there's no way she can unload and shop and get the post and pay bills and make the return journey in that wreck of a pick-up to be back before dark. She takes a sleeping bag and her and Blackie camp in the co-op's office. Even though it's safe enough in a tent out the back, we're all inflexible about being indoors after dark. I sometimes think none of us would ever feel quite safe outside at night again.

Milly and I always cook a big meal for Li on Wednesday nights, feed her up. She's usually pretty beat by the time she gets back. I'll go up to her place later and get some apples, make a pie, I'm thinking.

That's one good thing that's come of the mist, we get bumper fruit crops. Don't even have to net anymore. For all that, though, I'd rather have the birds back. There's nothing quite as unnatural as a silent dusk. Oppressive.

Eerie, Milly says. She's a retired schoolteacher, likes her words. We have this ongoing routine, where we bounce words, throw them at each other in turn. So our conversation can seem a little odd to other people, like verbal volleyball.

Stunted, you could say.

Curtailed, Milly would say back.

And off we would go.

*

My phone is ringing, an intrusion on my agreeably peaceful morning. Like an alarm going off. I stretch my legs and flex my feet and wait. It rings three times, then stops. Our little code: it means it's somebody I'd want to talk to, probably Milly or Li. As I haul myself up I notice my toenails need cutting. I'm getting bestial, now there's a thought. The hall's dusty too, I can see mites disturbed by my entry swirling in my nice calm sunlight. It's disgraceful, really, how one lets oneself go. I'll have to check with Milly about the state of my hair. When the phone starts ringing again, I pick up.

'Mornin,' I say.

There's the slightest of pauses, one that speaks of composure being regained, then Milly's voice is as steady as ever. It's the pause that puts me on edge. When you've worked in the police force you know that the calls which begin with such a pause are the ones you don't want. 'Pete,' says Milly, 'I'm at Rolf's. Can you come?'

*

When I get to Rolf's old fibro on Hobson Street, Milly's sitting on the porch, with the teapot on the step. She is calm in a way that speaks of exhaustion. Even her clothes have a limpness to them. Everything about her seems faded, except her eyes, which radiate pain.

'Where is he?'

'In his bedroom. I've called Sean. He said they'll be out here by two at the latest.'

She's shut the bedroom door. I know there's no need for me to go in, but I feel somehow as if it's my duty. The Old Cop Syndrome.

Rolf is between the wardrobe and the bed, his back to the door. It's all very simple, unadorned, a kitchen chair and cheap yellow nylon rope. I don't need to go further, or see

6

his face. The smell is enough. As I shut the bedroom door I register the dust – Rolf's hall is much dirtier than mine. Somehow this is consoling, as if it's a reassurance that I am still on safe ground. For the time being.

Back on the porch I gasp fresh air. I've left my smokes at home. How the hell did I do that?

'Shit,' I say.

Milly nods. 'Very sad.'

'Did he leave a note?'

'Couldn't see one. Can't say I looked that hard, though.'

I swig the cup of tea she hands me and draw breath. There's been a lot more added to it besides milk. Gina's got her nose stuck forlornly out of the Land Cruiser's window, while Milly's dog Felix frets below, whining. I go over to let her out and the two dogs, tails wagging sloppily, immediately make off to sniff round the weeds at the house next door, long empty. On the other side, Liz's house is now also locked and empty. There are still kids' toys on the lawn around the swing set. The grass is just starting to suggest it could use a mow. It looks as if the occupants have just gone away for a little while, on holiday perhaps. All the other yards in the street are overgrown, shrouded by weeds. Faded sheets of newspaper protrude from the shrubs, embrace the oblivious walls of vacant houses. Rolf's house was the last place in the street that was occupied. I'm glad I live out of town; the sense of desertion here distorts the morning peace, making it empty rather than calm.

'Li'll be upset,' I say.

7

Milly doesn't answer, just shoves away the teapot and pulls a small hipflask out of her jacket, pours brandy neat into our cups.

'That's the last,' she says, 'till Li gets back.'

I go back inside to check the kitchen. I notice that Rolf made the time to do the dishes, but didn't bother to dry them, just left them stacked in the rack. There aren't very many. I guess he felt that putting them away would be beside the point. There's half a bottle of Tullamore Dew in the cupboard with the spuds and onions. I have a quick look in his bin. It doesn't contain much; a rinsed-out sardine tin is on top. Some last supper. Rolf was never one for formalities.

Back on the porch Milly looks at the whiskey doubtfully. 'Won't that be evidence?'

'Yeah, it'll be evidence. They'll need to keep it on hand, probably in a filing cabinet. Your choice.'

'God, what have we become?'

*

It's a little after two when the police car pulls up. It's not peaceful anymore, a wind has sprung, causing the sheets of scattered newspaper to dislodge and billow across the empty street, turning page over page as if catering to the gusts. I'm wandering around lethargically gathering them up when Sean and a young constable haul themselves stiffly from the car.

Sean lifts his sunglasses and squints, then leans to give Gina a scritch. He is still trim and fit, his hair neat and short and only just beginning to show grey. A clutch of laugh lines reach from his eyes as he squints, but otherwise his face is unlined. I'm in ancient rubber thongs, with my lethal toenails, my arms spilling stained sheets of old newsprint. I've spent the morning slouched on concrete steps drinking a dead man's whiskey. My stubble is suddenly prickly. I can feel gloom mustering.

'Milly, how are you?' Sean nods.

'Hello, Sean,' she sighs. 'I'm fine.'

He puts out a paw, squeezes her shoulder gently, then turns to me.

'Pete,' he says, 'you're a hard man to reach. I must have called you maybe twenty times the last couple of months, you're never there.'

'Shit. I didn't think to…'

'You need to call twice, let it ring three times first,' explains Milly.

'Bit of a filter system. I should have told you. Sorry.'

But Sean just chuckles. 'Just as well I didn't make a special trip to check on you. Would've billed you for the fuel.'

The young constable stands beside him with a fixed smile. His edges are sharp and crisp, like a fresh new note. There is the smallest of flickers in Sean's eyes.

'This is Constable Greg Denham. And this is Pete McIntosh and Milly Pryor. Two of the last.'

We nod. The constable's face tries to stay noncommital, but he's not experienced enough to veil the mix of curiosity and suspicion. He will be wondering why we are still here, if

9

everything he has heard is true. He will be wondering about us, about what sort of people we must be.

He will be thinking we are outcasts. He will be slotting us away under *Dubious*. He raises his jaw from our faces to the open front door behind us.

'So old Rolf's thrown it in, you say?' Sean's saying to Milly.

'He's in the bedroom.'

They're back in only a few minutes. Constable Denham looks a little blurred on his return; he breathes deeply when he reaches the clean air.

Sean is fanning his face with his hat. Denham pauses briefly, then does the same. Sean sends him to radio for a medical team, then lowers himself onto the steps.

'Poor old bastard,' he says. 'When did you last see him?'

Milly screws up her face. 'I know Li dropped some vegies in to him yesterday morning. I was here Sunday – one of us always tries to drop in and say hello, check on him. Liz left last week and he took it pretty hard. The kids were what really kept him going.'

'Liz left? You think that's the cause?'

'Without a doubt. We knew he wouldn't cope, even if he was an old recluse. It must have been awful being there, completely on his own, but we couldn't persuade him to come to one of us.' She looks hunched in sadness.

'It would have gloated,' I say.

She looks up. 'Celebrated.'

'Performed.'

'Tormented.'

Sean butts in. 'What made Liz leave?'

We look at him in amazement.

'Okay,' he acknowledges. 'Where did she go?'

'She said maybe Perth. I don't think even she really knew. She thought she might have more chance of getting a place there, through Social Services.'

Sean looks doubtful. 'Who knows.'

'I think the main thing was to just get the boys out,' Milly says. 'It really got to her this time, she was pretty fraught.'

'I'm amazed she kept them here at all.'

Milly gives him a sharp look, her best schoolteacher. 'When you have no money you have no choice.'

Sean sighs, nodding. 'I'll need a statement before I go. Any chance of some tea?' Already he's looking older.

Later, while Sean's coordinating the removal of Rolf's body, I corner Milly.

'You gave Liz your savings, didn't you?'

Her arthritis is bad from sitting out on the concrete for so long. She rubs her elbows with cupped palms, always a sign of pain. 'More use to her.'

'But what about you? You're cutting off your options.'

'Options?' She laughs. 'I don't have options. I won't be dying anywhere other than here.' She shrugs and limps away, elbows cupped, her back to the stretcher being manoeuvred down Rolf's narrow, dusty hallway.

*

At home I fill Gina's bowl with water, but go to the fridge for beer for myself, even though I know it's unwise. After giving our statements, we called the others. They should be round soon. A saucepan of stew simmers fragrantly on the stove, a pot of potatoes peeled and ready to go.

There's still a bit of time before it'll start to get dark, and I drop into the old couch on the porch with a sigh that comes from my bones. My tobacco pouch is almost empty. I can't remember whether I asked Li to get me any more.

I've just lit my cigarette when the phone rings. It keeps ringing. I decide, under the circumstances, that I should probably answer it.

'A book, eh? Look, can you hang on half a tick, I've just got to grab something on the stove.'

I put the phone down on the table and go back out to the couch and what's left of the fading day. The wind has ebbed to a breeze; the trees sway lightly, giving the illusion of life, as if birds were flitting through them. At any other time of day it would be comforting.

The others had better get a move on if they're coming, the mist will start soon, tendrils winding through the evening breeze. I give them half an hour at the most.

*

Have you ever seen that movie *The Omega Man*, with Charlton Heston? Where he's holed up on his own in some penthouse apartment in a ruined city, and every night all these scabby people with white eyes and black robes crawl out and spout tracts and try to blow him up? He's got this armoury full of weapons, and he spends his nights playing target practice, gleefully picking them off, bam-bam. Bam!

If only it were that simple. Something tangible. Something to take aim at.

And then he meets the hippie guy with no shirt – Dutch, he's called, it's all so seventies – and ta-da! Between them they cook up an antidote to the plague, so the survivors are all saved, just like that. Except for poor old Charlton, the obligatory martyr, who bleeds to death in a fountain, the saviour spread as if crucified, while they all pile into their old cars and drive off into the sunrise.

Ah, the sunrise. At least we have that in common.

The others arrive in short succession, one eye always turned to the sky and the approaching dusk. Bedding is yanked from back seats, and dogs encouraged to roam before being confined for the night. We are experts at these slumber parties, geriatric get-togethers. Misery loves company, they say – add to it a shot of fear and you have the perfect cocktail for ongoing social whirl.

I'm morose tonight, savagely so. It's not just the booze; we are all glummer than usual, huddled within my small, hastily tidied lounge room, the curtains drawn, like the sheet draped over a birdcage at night. With Liz and the kids gone it's too quiet, there're too few of us left. The children were like a good behaviour bond, an unspoken restraint in the presence of innocence. We'd make the effort to be jolly: *Here we all are, isn't this fun, what ho!* We've lost our pretence now; we are teeth rather than smiles. We don't bother covering our stains.

And we're all getting old, except for Stick, who could be anything from thirty up. One of those people born grizzled. The kids were a bit of noise, necessary energy. Sods that they were, at least they were lively. Without them we're like a funeral party. Which tonight, I guess, is what we are. That knowledge doesn't help.

Gail's managed to rustle up a bottle of wine, she pulls it from her overnight bag, a generous and rare gesture. How she's kept it out of Tom's clutches is beyond me.

Already he's bleary, tottering, but I guess I can't really talk today, belly full of whiskey from morning tea. I manage to locate four wineglasses, and make do with a tumbler myself. It's not often we're all here. I'm used to Milly and Li; the others seem an intrusion, cluttering my space, disturbing my dust. But necessary under the circumstances; I need to be gracious. Or I'll end up like Rolf.

As if on cue, Gail calls a toast. Her eyes are already brimming. 'To Rolf.'

'Rolf,' we all echo, glasses raised. It's interesting, the personalities revealed in the motions: Gail's toast is overdone, melodramatic; Milly's is graceful, her glass raised with dignity; Stick's and Tom's efforts are perfunctory, barely a tip to formality. There's a brief pause while we sip – a good New Zealand white, very nice – then Tom's got his glass up again.

'And then there were...' he booms. As if we needed reminding. Beside him Gail heaves and sobs.

Six. And then there were six.

We're dwindling. Down to dregs. Yesterday we were seven. And last week, before Liz threw the kids and whatever she could fit into the station wagon and fled, we'd been eleven.

At winter solstice last year, the day it all began, we'd been a typically dying, but nowhere near dead, country town of 547 residents. Nine months ago.

How time flies. Only nine months since the convoy of silent grey vehicles drifted along the main street of town, anonymous dark-suited men immobile within them, and disappeared in the direction of the cemetery.

The cemetery. It seems we all have the same thought at once. It's too horrible to contemplate.

'Jesus,' Tom's saying, 'they wouldn't bury Rolf there, they couldn't do that to him.'

And then we're all quiet, trying hard not to look at Milly, who sips quietly at her wine while one cupped palm rubs a throbbing elbow. Outside the whispering is starting, curling round the house with the wind.

I stand up; it's time to serve some food. Once the whispers build it can be challenging to eat anything. On my way to the kitchen I switch on the television, loud.

There's been an earthquake somewhere, thousands of survivors destitute, stranded without food or water. I hum as I dig out the plates.

*

It's a quiet meal, unsurprisingly. It's only a passable stew, but we tuck in, always appreciative. Food is a wonderful

15

distraction. Stick's eating with gusto, he usually does. I think he mostly lives on packet noodles. And spliffs, of course, that's the only real reason he's still here, where else could you grow a crop so undisturbed? He keeps half an eye on me, though, never quite sure how much I know, how safe he is. I couldn't care less, but I like to keep him on his toes and, truth be told, at a bit of a distance. How anyone could stand being stoned under our circumstances is beyond me.

It'd be enough to drive anyone mad. Stick's living proof of that.

He's pretty quiet tonight. Has been since Liz left. I think he managed to share her bed every now and then, so he'll be feeling the loss. She won't be, though; she may have been a bit of a flake in some respects, our Liz, but she knew a dead loss when she saw one. Some nights he was lucky, but mostly he wasn't, and she would never have shared anything more than the occasional stress relief with him. She wasn't all that keen on him being around the kids, and old Rolf hates – hated – him with a passion, would always have his teeth bared.

It amazes me that in a community depleted almost to nothing, we can still find the motivation to dislike each other.

But then Stick is a special case. It's his eyes, something in the set of his jaw. He has about him the gleeful, shrewd brutality of a crocodile. One day I might mention his crop to Sean. For now, though, he's number six, and that's all that matters. We can't afford to lose any more. It makes the focus too intense.

Though, having said that, Gail's starting up. There

are some things, no matter how desperate you feel the circumstances, you could do without, bugger the numbers. It's usually about now, when the wailing outside's starting to gain force, and everyone's finished eating except her – she never gets through a meal, it adds to the dramatic effect.

Like clockwork. She gives an elaborate shudder – her idea of an introduction, like the raising of stage curtains – and places her cutlery carefully, elaborately on her plate, which is pushed ever so slowly away, as if with deep, deep regret at not being able to eat another mouthful. The tears well at this point, the mouth quivers. She has the routine down pat, gasping sobs to accompany the first of the wails outside. A duet: drawn-out, turgid theatre perfected over time. Faded grey wisps of hair wave from her clips, small escape attempts: *Let us go!*

'I can't…' she starts. Tom, just as predictably, has fetched a bottle from his bag and started work on it. No escaping strands on his head: what's there is well and truly flattened. He ignores his wife, effortlessly.

Milly is up, gathering the dishes, the purpose in her movements singing clearly, *here we go again*. The dogs follow her into the kitchen.

Gail eyes Milly's back as she retreats. 'It's not as if we *have* to stay. Jon…'

'Be quiet, woman!' barks Tom.

We disperse at this. Jonathan, their only son, took off for New Zealand the minute he could get away. Not many cross the Tasman in that direction, but a drunken disgrace of a father and a mother perpetually soggy with brimming tears are a pretty good impetus. Apparently he moves a lot, they don't always have his current address. Good on him, I say. I do not think about my own daughter.

*

In the kitchen Milly stacks the dishes and I retrieve the remainder of Rolf's Tullamore Dew and attempt discretion by using mugs.

'She's off,' I say as I hand Milly hers. 'The Greek Chorus.'

'Tragic.'

'Predictable.'

'Typical.'

'Pathetic.'

We stop and raise our mugs.

'Woeful,' Milly says. 'To Rolf.'

'Rolf,' I reply.

I've just swigged a large gulp of my drink when the kitchen door creaks open, and Stick sidles in, holding a tin of dog food and a bowl. Gina and Felix raise their ears and sit at casual attention on their haunches.

'Just got to feed Elvis. You wouldn't have a can opener, would you, mate?' Elvis is Stick's staffy, a mad thing that has to be shut in the laundry, to stop it attacking the other dogs. I cross to the top drawer, but Stick doesn't take his eyes from the mug I've placed on the table.

'Cheers,' he says when I hand him the can opener. I have the feeling that it wasn't really what he was after.

*

It's a strange, and I think inherently human, trait that no matter how few members of a group there are, it will always divide itself into alliances, never stay completely homogeneous. Like oil and water. Even we, the pathetic remnants of what used to be a town, are evidence of this. While it isn't exactly uncommon for us to be all together like this, it isn't usual. It's been more so since we lost Liz, and now Rolf's death has brought us together again, but it'll only be temporary. Tom and Gail aren't really welcome anywhere, truth be told, which is why they are still in Nebulah. Lucky us.

Stick usually sticks with them, though – shifty little bugger knows that Tom'll be generous once he's had a few, and there's nothing like a free drink. Gail's whining doesn't seem to get to him, and he finds Tom's drunkenness amusing rather than frustrating. He'll put up with most things. Most leeches will.

Liz often spent her evenings with them: the kids were more indulged there, giving Tom an excuse for stupidity and Gail something to cry over. But Milly and Li were closer to Liz; the three of them formed a practical female bond around the children, free of the dripping sentiment of Gail. When the school ground to a close, Milly took over from Liz's laughable attempts at home schooling, although the discipline side of things was always a struggle with those boys. They were always a little wild, and with the instinctive cunning of unruly children, they recognised that the situation

19

was beyond any control of ours. You can't get kids like that to respect authority when they perceive it to be powerless.

'I *hate* you!' Dylan, the middle one, screamed at me once when I caught him throwing rocks at the windows of the empty houses down on Middle Street. 'I'm going to come round to your place one night and *open a door.*'

'They're just kids,' said Milly, 'they don't understand. It isn't healthy for them, being here, there's too much threat. And they need to grow up with other kids their own age.' She paused. 'Hell, if they just grow up they'll be doing well.'

Rolf was the self-imposed exile, our recluse. He was your archetypal old codger, kept himself to himself. He'd emigrated from Scotland as a young man, with barely more than his fare, and travelled the country on foot or by thumb, working as a roustabout till his back collapsed and he became sedentary. He settled in this district for no particular reason – he was someone who didn't require anything. He'd no relatives or family, and when Liz and her sons, more or less just toddlers then, moved next door to him, instead of there being hell to pay, he'd uncharacteristically taken to them in a fiercely loving, grumpy-old-man kind of way. He'd scowl at Liz's outfits, shaking his head as she laughed at his expression, and it was him who christened her Swamphen, in acknowledgement of her braying bursts of laughter.

'I s'pose ye wanna help paint?' he'd growl with resigned reluctance at the boys' eager faces, and they'd scurry over the fence to find old shirts and paintbrushes laid out ready for them. They adored him, were always following as he limped around his place, fetching him hammers, nails, screwdrivers, with delighted self-importance. He was the only one they'd listen to – had it been Rolf who'd chastised Dylan for breaking windows, he would have been crushed with remorse.

While he'd kept his distance, Rolf'd always treated Milly and Li with the utmost respect, particularly Li. Their independence and refusal to give up, and Li's unfailing commitment to her farm, appealed to his own values. He treated them with the outdated courtesy that comes of old men whose contact with women over the course of their lives has been at a distinct remove.

But Stick he'd detested, and Gail and Tom had infuriated him, with their amused and painfully indulgent condescension, as if they bestowed favours.

When Liz took the boys, the cloak of his isolation, previously a comfortable fit, had shrunk around him, to become as constrictive as a shroud. Instead of solitary he'd become lonely, the whole tenor of his existence distorted, out of tune. He knew he could have come to us – we invited him every day – but the awkwardness of inclusion for someone of his age and solitary habits would have been more painful than the loneliness.

It was typical of him to have died as he did, without ceremony and without a note. He owed us nothing.

*

I've discussed this with Milly before, this tendency to split into camps, even in the most dire of circumstances. She's had a lifetime of watching it in the schoolyard. She says at heart human beings aren't really far removed from poultry, that William Golding should have called his classic book *Lord of the Chickens.*

I can see her point, but it doesn't really have quite the same ring to it.

We dawdle in the kitchen as long as we can manage. In the lounge room Tom is snoring in a chair, and Stick is setting up his swag between the sideboard and the dining table, in the corner of the room furthest from the windows. The faint odour of dog sausage clings to him.

Gail will have Li's bed, sharing my spare room with Milly. She is sitting tensely on the couch, wanting to turn in. The dogs, who usually spend the evenings on the couch, sprawl resentfully on the floor at her feet. She looks up with a pained and accusing air when we come in, as if it's Milly's fault that she isn't capable of going off to bed on her own. I can feel Milly's irritation. There is something in Gail that provokes this, even in the most patient of people.

'I think I'll have a cuppa,' says Milly suddenly.

'Yeah, me too,' I say. 'Might be a movie on.' Gail sags.

'You go on to bed,' Milly tells her. 'I won't wake you.'

Gail's face turns grey at the prospect of leaving the room on her own. Even after all these months. She is not a personality to adapt.

'No, no,' she says, without enthusiasm, 'I think I'll have a cup of tea too.' So here we are, our big jolly slumber party. What ho, indeed.

22

Outside the mist responds, in the disturbing way it has of sometimes picking up our thoughts and moods and throwing them back at us, distorted and mocking, the most intimate and unsettling of intrusions.

What ho? It shrieks in at us now, *what ho?* Like a rapist asking his victim, *Is that good?* The windows rattle with the force of its laughter.

I settle close to the TV and concentrate on keeping my teeth unclenched.

*

I came to Nebulah twenty-two years ago, transferred over from the east when my marriage stopped sputtering and came to a grinding, unavoidable halt. I wanted to put as much ground between me and Mildura as I could. I always blamed Gina, my ex-wife, for the move, citing the need for distance from her breakdown and her bewildering raft of accusations, but the truth is that she was only ever just a part of it. I've never really been much of a cop, only joined the force to spite my old man, coveting the chance to display a bit of authority. But authority has to be innate to be effective, it isn't just magically bestowed on you with a uniform. I never really had the right mindset for the job, and I've always hated violence, which was unavoidable in that line of work. After a night-shift beat I could shake for days. They knew it, too. I started drinking pretty early on.

When the opportunity came to transfer to Nebulah, a two-bit town in the middle of nowhere, a career dead end if ever there was one, I grabbed it, had the removalists in before my uniform was back from the cleaners. Gina had made our divorce proceedings both bitter and public, so the professional indifference behind the transfer was pretty well camouflaged by personal drama, and there were no obstacles. And anyway, they were pretty desperate to get someone – most cops would despair of days spent warning kids on unregistered trail bikes or slapping farmers' wrists over inadequately secured loads. It wasn't considered a desirable position.

For me it was perfect. I cut my drinking back to a few beers, gave up smoking (again), got myself a heeler pup that was obedient and loved me unconditionally. I couldn't resist calling her Gina, relishing her adoration, and her obedience. A much more satisfying arrangement. She was a beautiful dog; I had her for fourteen years before a snake got her in the long grass out at Dawson's place.

The current Gina is an Alsatian, another comfortingly affectionate companion.

We all have dogs, of course. (Except Tom and Gail – Tom, drunk, had let Nelly, their Jack Russell, outside one evening when she was barking. I'd had to deal with the remains the next day, Tom maudlin with self-pity and Gail in hysterics. Rolf never did: he had always been indifferent to animals, and refused to have any kind of dependant.)

Most residents who didn't have a dog before the mist soon procured one – thinking, for some reason, that they would be protection. Before long people just got too spooked and shot through, and a lot of them left the dogs behind – hard enough to find a new place as it is without a dog in tow. And you know how dogs are, they soon formed into packs. So, as if we didn't have problems enough, we found ourselves in a town empty of people but full of half-wild dogs.

It had to be dealt with, of course, but it was a sorry task. I hate shooting dogs. The pregnant bitches were the worst. That's where Stick turned out to be useful; he followed the echo of my shots one day and tracked me out to Aliceson's Corner, to see what was up. I had my doubts about the wisdom of letting him help, but he was a relentless hunter, with no visible qualms about shooting anything. To see that intensity so focused could be disturbing. He didn't get excited or celebrate a success, he just killed, methodically and emotionlessly.

Frankly, it was easier just to give him the bullets and let him work off whatever it was that was driving him. His girlfriend, a cowed and pudgy woman with badly dyed hair and tatts, had shot through when the mist started, I suspect with a considerable portion of Stick's stash, and his eyes had taken on a smoldering glow that I was finding worrying. Much better that he work it off on the dogs.

I had noticed then for the first time his fingers, long and slender, like a pianist's. He'd wrap them round the rifle's trigger with artful and fatally effective grace. It was the only time I ever had any inkling of his attractiveness to women, in those moments as he took aim, deliberate and skilful over his shots.

*

Breakfast is protracted in the morning, after our late night watching movies; people wander to the toaster at their leisure. No one is in any hurry. Tom decides he wants eggs; Gail shuffles to the stove with a tight scowl and ringing bad grace. Obviously I'm meant to play host. But that sort of formality went out the door nine months ago, when clustering became a necessity. They just happen to all be at my place this time; far as I'm concerned, if Tom wants eggs he can cook them himself. I stare preoccupied out the window, inserting distance. Gail pointedly bangs pans in Milly's direction, expecting her, as the other woman present, to help. Milly chews her toast slowly and with relish, delightfully deaf.

The phone rings three times, and stops. Gail looks over her shoulder towards it, eyebrows arched. She is not a morning person. Or an afternoon or evening, you could say. The phone starts ringing again.

'That's strange,' I say, casually stretching.

It's Li, about to leave Woodford, checking last-minute orders. I had forgotten the tobacco, but she's already bought me two pouches, knowing me far too well. I choose my words carefully, playing jolly, catching Milly's cautious eye. It's not too hard – Li is abrupt and businesslike, keen to get out of town and back to her farm. Evidently news of a Nebulah suicide hasn't reached her in Woodford, but the story will soon be spreading rapidly. With luck Li won't hear of it before she's back and Milly and I can break it to her.

Stick emerges after the disturbance of the phone,

26

crawling from his swag when everyone else is already dressed and the breakfast dishes are piled in the sink. He smells sour, had only removed his jeans and boots when he turned in. His hair is both thinning and straggly, accessorised with several days' worth of stubble. He scratches at an armpit with distraction and grimaces at the offer of breakfast, saying that he'd better shoot through. I can guess what his breakfast will be. He collects Elvis from the laundry, leading him by the collar past the other dogs, releasing him once they're clear of the house. The big dog stretches, flexing dangerous muscles, then squats to relieve itself by the car's back wheel.

Stick leans from the driver's window. 'Reckon I might take a drive up Aliceson's again, see if there's any dogs hanging bout.'

'I don't have any shells left,' I say, knowing what he's after. 'Meant to ask Li to get me some in town.'

The look he gives me is not fast enough – I see the glare before it adjusts to indifference. He can't pretend he wasn't after bullets. He shrugs.

'S'okay. I still got some.' A sharp glance. 'Not many. Enough to make it worthwhile, but.'

His engine starts with a high-pitched rattle; dirty diesel fumes like city smog. Still, at least he's gone.

Back inside I make a big show of having things to do out at Li's. Although they're sceptical, Tom couldn't really care less whether he's on the couch here or at home, so by late morning they've cleared out. Gail holds back on the porch, wanting to make their exit ceremonial, vaguely formal, our gathering-together ritual, by invoking again the loss of Rolf, his terrible absence, but Tom is firing up the engine and is perfectly capable of driving off without her, so she's forced to break off and stalk to the car without managing to pin us down for future get-togethers.

Milly stays to help wash up, then for an early lunch, tomato sandwiches on the porch, the dogs sprawled dustily in a stretch of late morning sun. The heat of February has long faded into the languid warmth of autumn. April is usually my favourite time of year, but this year its shortening days have the feel of a collar that is too tight, the early evenings claustrophobic.

'We're not much better than the dogs,' I say, as we slump lazily on the old couch, cherishing every minute of daylight, of sunshine, of being outside. Milly barks with laughter, but shortly rouses herself, shaking herself free of sandwich crumbs, and says she's going home to have a kip.

'On top of everything else, that bloody woman snores!'

*

Li's farm is south of town, only a ten-minute drive from my place. I've picked two bags of apples and am just checking the state of her grapevines when I hear a vehicle turn into the drive. Sean pulls in behind the Land Cruiser and pauses to stretch his neck and shoulders before wandering towards me. Gina appears from wherever she's been snoozing and escorts him over, keen for a pat.

'Milly said I'd find you here.'

I shade my eyes from the sun, squint towards the car. 'Where's your offsider?' Sean's smile is tight but amused. 'Wednesday afternoons he devotes to the coaching of the junior cricket team. Couldn't possibly make him miss training by dragging him out of town. Such a long drive.'

'Want a beer?'

'On duty.' The briefest pause. 'Wouldn't say no.'

Li's not much of a drinker herself, but she always has beer in the fridge for me – I often spend afternoons there, helping out.

I hand him a stubby. It's lite. He grimaces.

'So what's up?'

'Nothing, really – I needed Milly's signature on her statement, thought I'd bring it out and save her the drive to town.'

I nod. He was always thoughtful like that, a socially minded cop. Distressingly rare these days. Constable Denham may devote an evening to a bit of competitive community sport, but it's unlikely he'd put himself out to save an arthritic woman a six-hour return drive.

'Any problems?'

'Nah, nothing. It's a pretty straightforward suicide, poor old sod, no suspicious circumstances. Hell, no suspicious people! You haven't noticed anyone around?' It's more of an afterthought than a serious question.

'Just the occasional handful of tourist gawkers. Caravans passing through – not many make a special trip anymore.'

There had been talk, would you believe, of trying to make

29

us a tourist attraction, especially when the initial interest in us was waning and some turds on the shire despaired at a missed investment opportunity. They'd already tried to elbow Nebulah onto the tourist map before the mist came, hyping up the town's historical significance as an old mining centre. A rack was installed outside the post office, where badly written brochures sagged and discoloured over the summers, encouraging visits to the 'museum' – an unimpressive collection of rusty tools in display cases, and some woefully moth-eaten stuffed animals that Wally Todd managed to pick up at auction somewhere. But any visitors who did wander through, more often than not, after a limp toasted cheese sandwich at Tailings Café and Tea Rooms, were back in their vehicles and gone long before their two-hour parking had expired.

There were never many parking fines issued in Nebulah.

So the mist was promoted as an 'opportunity'. We were to be sold as Australia's premier 'haunted town', with information placards around town – and, of course, tasteful memorials – and brochures for self-guided walks. Visitors who didn't get out before nightfall could stay at The Visitation Bed & Breakfast (*Let Us Guarantee You A Sleepless Night*).

It was the councillors with business interests in Woodford behind it all, of course, there being no businesses left in Nebulah, the shops all boarded up and long deserted. That fat slug Marty Cartright, who owns the Woodford Chalet Park, was the driving force, apparently had already been sussing out the purchase of a minibus for running tours out here before the 'opportunities' were even put before council.

We managed to quash it. There were still about forty of us in town then, and we banded together to say that we weren't going to put up with the exploitation of our misfortunes, when the council should be helping stranded residents who lacked the resources to get out. We said we'd withhold our rates if they cashed in on our miserable situation with money-grubbing ventures. There was already a lot of suspicion and accusation floating around; people were convinced that the mist was the result of some dodgy shire activity, and even those in local government weren't sure how much truth was buried in the rumours, so they didn't want to push too many buttons. There was always the worry that something best left hidden would be exposed.

Sean spoke up and said that he didn't have the resources to patrol Nebulah regularly, and it'd increase the potential for looting and vandalism, not to mention the danger to the irresponsible public who thought it was all a bit of a joke. We jumped on this and said we'd bill the council for any and all damage. We couldn't and they knew it, but they knew they'd need extra security resources to keep people safe – the potential for lawsuits was huge. Then Lonely Planet said it'd be mentioning the town in its new edition – its first inclusion! – but only as a warning, not a destination.

They backed off. Cartwright pushed for a while longer, but a few of us, acting as Nebulah 'representatives', gave him an unconditional, 100 per cent guarantee that his minibus would attract vandals. Our word on that. He blustered a lot, but pulled his head in. Sometimes it's useful being an ex-cop.

*

'Any word on Rolf?' I ask.

'Haven't heard. The will's lodged at Boswell and Trent. I'll let you know.'

'You don't know his wishes?'

'Too early. Apparently there's some long-lost cousin in Wales they're gonna have to try and locate. Knowing Rolf, I'd guess his instructions would be to cremate him and chuck him in the compost. Why, what's up?'

'Just worried about the possibility of him being buried out here.'

'No way. Your cemetery is well and truly closed for business. In a manner of speaking.'

I had figured as much, but councils are funny about giving up land. With any luck they'd find the cousin, who would have his dust sent back to the mother country. Anywhere's fine, as long as he's out of the mist's reach.

'How's Rachael?' I ask.

'Good. Busy. Working herself into the ground, pretending there's no such thing as empty-nest syndrome. Usual stuff. How're you?'

I shrug, start patting my pockets for my smokes. Sean watches me roll with pointed attention. I light with a flourish.

'Still running?' he asks.

'You bet. Broke the four-minute mile last week.'

'I'll take that as a no.' He puts a finger into the neck of his stubby, swishes it around to pep up the foam, and says, eyes not lifted from the bottle, 'You look tired, mate. I got a shock when I saw you yesterday.'

'I'm getting old.'

'Not old. Worn. Worn out.'

'Well, the nights aren't exactly peaceful.'

Sean grunts, shakes his head. 'No change?'

'Unless you call a reduced target change. There aren't too many of us left to share the load now.'

'What happened to shift Liz?'

Oh, poor Liz, with her messy ponytail and wrinkled dresses, her braying swamphen laugh and her brittle determination not to be forced into shelter housing. I need another smoke for that, but I hold off.

'She looked out the window. It'd taken on the form of the boys and was calling and she fell for it, thinking the kids had snuck outside.' And that's what unhinged her – she said when she thought the kids were out there it was like her insides liquified and she realised she would never have the courage to go out after them. That if she didn't have it in her to protect them when it came to the crunch, having them there was more than just a risk. What she saw scared the shit out of her, but it was what she discovered about herself that defeated her.

'It was pretty awful. She went to pieces. They were at Milly's for two days before she was capable of driving. She couldn't eat, couldn't even keep soup down. Milly tried to get her to stay longer, till she was a bit calmer, but she was terrified, just wanted out. Left everything, just took the dog and whatever else she could fit into the stationwagon.'

Milly and I had been there to see her off, watched her cram hastily packed bags in the wagon till she almost couldn't get the tailgate closed, her back resolutely turned to her vegetable patch, the garden she had nourished with such enthusiasm and been so determined not to lose. The kids, bewildered, not understanding why everything was such an uproar; Josh, the youngest, snivelling in the back seat for his mother's attention. And Liz, the air crackling with grief around her, barely able to look at them for fear of what she might see again.

Rolf had hung back till the end, but appeared as Liz turned the engine over, giving a final admonishment to the boys and rapping his knuckles on the roof of the car, in the gesture of care made by inarticulate men. They drove out of town just after three. We watched the laden car till it turned left for the distant highway, the empty house behind us suddenly slumped with lack of life.

Rolf declined my invitation for tea, or a meal. He was gruffly self-sufficient, as always, but his breathing was laboured as he struggled for composure, and his eyes, as he turned away, were distant with distress. He shuffled up his driveway and closed his door on the absence next door. We suspected then that he was in trouble.

Sean's nodding sadly. 'Do you know what she saw?'

I can't help wincing. 'The usual sort of thing. The two older kids had disembowelled the youngest and were eating him alive. Lots of laughter.' The sort of image that is never forgotten, never escaped. 'She didn't even have anywhere to go.'

But at least she had Milly's savings.

'Do the others know about it?' asked Sean.

'Only Milly, it was her that told me. Rolf closed off when Liz broke, he was too bewildered – he didn't ask, didn't want to know. Li doesn't care to know details either, she's seen enough chaos in her lifetime already. And the last thing we wanted was for Gail to be any worse than she already is.'

'Someone should give Tom a bloody good kicking.'

I grin. 'You're the one in uniform.'

He lets that one slide and looks away, all casual. 'Stick still got a crop going?'

'You know about that?'

'Oh yeah. He's been seen a little too often in Woodford, moving round the pubs. Spends a lot of money for someone on the dole. His days are numbered.'

'Stupid prick.'

Sean nods slowly. 'Take a while, though. He watches his back pretty carefully and knows his rights. We've got bugger-all resources for surveillance, and he's careful not to give us any reason to pull him over and search. Drug squad couldn't give a shit, too small.' He flexes his fingers. 'Surprised you haven't mentioned his horticultural interests.'

'Been considering it. I hate to say it, but survival's my

35

new priority. As far as I'm concerned, take your time busting him. We're thinning out – if we lose him, the only other male will be Tom and he's worse than useless. Stick'll only be selling to a handful of his deadbeat mates, nothing too significant.' I sigh, it can't be avoided. 'The crop's out at Paddy Simms's old place.'

Sean nods again. He knows it's as much as he'll get, wouldn't ask for more. I retired years ago. He stretches. 'When do you expect Li back?'

I squint into the sun. 'Anytime bout now, really.'

'I'll let you get on.'

We stand up and I grind my butt underfoot. He gives a small smile, almost a grimace. 'Those fags'll kill you, you know.'

'Jesus, I bloody wish!'

*

It was the cancer that started me smoking again. I'd given up early on, started again when Gina went haywire, then stopped again as part of my Nebulah New Start makeover, jogging with the dog in the early morning before work. Nebulah was all I'd hoped: sleepy, uneventful. I'd spend my days chatting to elderly women and young mothers, and quiet evenings at the pub (amazing the positive effect the local copper watching consumption has on drink-driving – takeaways soared in popularity). The old-timers would stay on for a skinful, not much else for them to do, but they tended to live within the town boundary and would stagger home peacefully enough, their only offence being to water someone's bushes along the way.

I'd been accepted fairly readily, although it took a while, as it does for any new face. The oldies held on to their ownership of the town and all its history, the vital local knowledge that serves as the invaluable social guidebook to a place like this, until they established that I wasn't some authoritarian prick come to sit on them and interfere. And there'd been a danger of the station closing when they couldn't get anyone to staff it after Doug McAllister, who'd been the entire Nebulah police presence for thirty-five years, retired to Surfers. There's always some little whiz-kid in the wings, with a degree in business administration, dying to cut costs by dumping workloads onto shoulders already sagging, so as to justify his indecent salary.

Which is exactly what ended up happening twelve years later, when all my reformed habits and quiet life resulted in a cancer diagnosis. Early, treatable, but like all cancer ops, no matter how successful they are, the scars are permanent. I'd emerged from the treatment with no permanent health issues, just the constant ill ease, the endless suspicion that comes with the sense that your body is an unknown; the possibility that it is self-destructing beyond the barriers of your awareness. It causes a separation, a severance from your own being that you never quite recover from. For the first year after the treatment I found myself moving gingerly, like an old man, protecting myself as if my body were a piece of fruit that, once bruised, would decay from within. Damaged goods. The irony that it was bowel cancer, and not lung, where I would have expected it – at least felt I'd earned it – wasn't lost on me. I started smoking again. Why the hell not?

And I stopped working, took early retirement, made some bean-counter kid somewhere happy as Larry. Nebulah police station was closed, the resources to keep it manned funnelled off into executive pay rises. The nearest assistance became poor old Sean in Woodford, over three hours' drive away. I came out of retirement a couple of times to help out at the annual Woodford race carnival, but by then I'd given up any pretence of caring much about what was going on around me, so I was a disgrace to the uniform, and finally gave it away completely.

I sometimes think my whole life has been an ongoing sequence of stops and starts. Until, last June, I arrived at where I am now.

Limbo.

*

Li isn't back by the time I've had enough of pruning the grapes. When I call her mobile she's pissed off, has had a flat tyre on the highway 50 kilometres from Nebulah, as well as the truck's usual routine of overheating. She'll be another half-hour at the least.

'Bloody piece-of-crap shit truck!'

I'm impressed. It's taken me a long time to convert Li to the fine Australian art of swearing. Unfortunately, though, she's such a sedate woman that she has to be really, seriously incensed before she'll let loose, and this loss of control causes her accent, as vernacular as mine or Milly's ordinarily, to revert to strangely Asian characteristics, so her cussing never has quite the intended effect. Like now, her 'bwoody piece-of-cwap shit twuck'. Somehow it adds a touch of Tweety Bird, perpetually entertaining rather than effective.

There's still a couple of hours of daylight left, nothing to be overly concerned about. But even so, the muscles in my back are tightening, and won't unwind till she's back.

I stay to prepare the apples for my pie, then head home for a shower. A hot one, long.

*

Milly's ute is the only vehicle at Li's when I get back. Felix is sniffing round by the herb pots, and lopes over to the Land Cruiser as I pull in. I lean over to let Gina out, and the two dogs immediately start tussling playfully.

Milly has come onto the back porch, and the smell of roasting lamb follows her from the house. There's still no sign of Li's truck. It's over an hour since I spoke to her. I leave the Land Cruiser's engine running, then change my mind and switch it off. She would have called if she was in trouble. I'll give her another fifteen minutes. I sometimes think the worst part of the way we live is the agony involved in the decisions we make, the terrible potential always hanging over the consequences.

I'm just starting to change my mind again and am reaching for the ignition when the dogs stop wrestling and raise their heads, bursting into watchdog barks. And yes, I can hear it too, the approaching grind of a worn-out, piece-of-crap shit old truck.

On the porch Milly smiles calmly, but I see the relief in her eyes, which had been carefully distant. She frees her hands from her old jumper, where she had wound them. I hunch my shoulders forward to stretch my tight neck muscles. The noise of the approaching truck swirls around us, diffusing the tension. The air seems to sigh with sudden domestic peace, and the scene, previously edgy with clamouring possibilities, becomes benign.

When Li's truck turns finally from the road, the smell of burning rubber is overpowering. Behind the wheel her face is fatigued. Even Blackie, tongue lolling, on the back of the tray, looks relieved to be home. Li climbs slowly, stiffly from the cab, leaving the engine running to cool it. She reaches over to unhook Blackie from his chain.

'What time do you call this, then?' I call out. 'Cutting it a bit fine, aren't you?'

'It's all your shopping,' she shoots back. 'Bloody fags and booze, running round like a mouse with a cat up its bum, all to help you kill yourself.'

'It's criminal.' Milly nods.

I reach into the cab and turn the truck's ignition off. As it ticks to a halt the sound of boiling water is audible.

'The only crook thing round here is this truck. Listen to it. You're lucky you got back at all.'

Li grimaces. 'I had to rest it every twenty minutes or so, but it was getting so late I pushed it a bit towards the end.'

She and Milly start unloading bags from the back. I raise the bonnet and prop it, watching steam curl threateningly round the radiator cap. There's nothing I can do till it cools down. I glance automatically at the lowering sun. It'll have to wait till morning.

I heave the last of the supplies, a milk crate full of bottles, off the truck, and dump it by the porch steps. There's time for a last smoke. I don't smoke inside, so once it's dark that's it. And it'll give Milly time to break the news about Rolf to Li. I dawdle over my cigarette, like a coward, kicking at a scatter of dandelions and listening to the murmur of the women's voices inside, Li's momentarily raised in distress before settling back to her usual tone. Above the orchard the sun hangs, sinks, hangs, then plunges through a plume of colour, like a richly velvet stage curtain drawing to expose an orchestrated tragedy, the poignantly beautiful end of another day's freedom. I can't delay any longer. I lumber up the steps, grabbing the milk crate on my way past.

Blackie is lapping loudly at his water dish; the other dogs are already inside.

'Blackie!' I call from the back door, and he lifts his head, then ambles across the porch and into the house. The sun is lost below the horizon now and already the mist is rising in the gathering dark. I close the door behind him and lock it.

Inside, Milly and Li are double-checking the window locks and pulling the curtains. The metaphorical curtains have been opened, now it's time for all others to close, as tightly as possible.

41

My pie is good. I'm no cook, but I have a small repertoire of specialties, spaghetti bog and the like, the usual suspects, which I pull out at regular intervals. Apple pie is one of them. The regular intervals may be a little more persistent with that one – among the remains of Nebulah it is known as Pete's Pie.

Dinner is a fairly silent affair, under the circumstances. Li is bordering on exhaustion – everyone's supplies are piled by the laundry door. If Liz was still around she would have phoned by now to make sure Li had got back okay. None of the others seem to have even considered this courtesy. We'll be feeling the Swamphen's loss for some time.

Li's flash of distress at the news of Rolf's death has been quickly contained into a composed and accepting regret. 'Alone is not good,' she'd said, shaking her head sadly. Outside there is a sense of movement, and a tiny, chilling tapping begins at the kitchen window, a snigger.

With a sigh Li wanders into the lounge and turns the television on and up.

We sit for a while, listening to a politician bluster threadbare reassurances as Kerry O'Brien tears him to shreds.

'I'll have another look at the truck in the morning,' I tell Li. 'But I reckon its time's up, it's rooted. You'd be crazy to keep relying on it, it's too dangerous.'

Li twines her fingers and examines them intently. She has working hands: no rings; short, blunt nails. The sort of hands you'd expect Stick to have. 'You think it'll go another month?'

'At the very most, possibly. But we have to sort out something else.' I glance at Milly. 'We were wondering about a trailer, with Milly's ute it should just about do.' There is no response from Li, who just looks grim and preoccupied.

'What do you think?'

She shrugs. 'I reckon a month, tops, will be enough. There is wall writing at the co-op.'

Milly frowns. 'Graffiti?'

'No. The writing that tells.'

We realise together what she means: the writing on the wall. Li has muddled the phrasing, a sign of her exhaustion.

'They are waiting to hear on a loan. If they get it, they can last the year, till the new subdivision is more established and things hopefully pick up. Otherwise…'

Otherwise. She doesn't have to continue. Otherwise there is only the IGA in Woodford, and Jed Pearce, who owns it, also owns shares in his brother-in-law's wholesalers in Perth. There's no way he'd sacrifice his own business to support her. Even the co-op does it largely out of charitable intentions. Without them she'll have nothing.

The borders of all we have left seem to be disintegrating. It is turning into a week I'll never want to live through again.

*

The truck has had it. I flush the radiator – again – but that isn't the problem, the engine is shot. It might scrape one, maybe two, trips to Woodford, but even that's a risk. Milly's ute isn't big enough on its own, she wouldn't be able to take enough produce to cover the cost of the fuel, let alone turn a profit. There's no point forking out for a trailer under the circumstances. And renting one isn't viable either.

I wipe the grease off my hands and rub the sore spot in my belly. It's not quite one o'clock and I'm not particularly hungry; I decide to take the truck for a test drive before lunch.

Nebulah's not a big town. The majority of its small population used to live among the sprawling blocks that stretch listlessly from the town's main street. Large scruffy lawns adorned mainly fibro houses, giving little visual credence to the council's attempts to ennoble the place with historical value. Yards embraced weeds and worn-out cars, which briefly sported P-plates before subsiding permanently under tarpaulins. Wilted lawns spawned children's play equipment or obsessive vegetable patches, depending on the demographic. It was a town without money; there was rarely any trouble beyond squabbles.

About a third of us lived beyond the street signs of the town's centre, on modest acreages that were little more than personal indulgences. The larger holdings had long since decided there was more profit in real estate: farms were carved up, like carcasses reduced to the manageable packages of meat on supermarket shelves. There were a handful of hobby farms, a small amount of livestock, but apart from Li only Tom Reid had retained a holding big enough to support any serious agriculture, working land that his great-grandfather had cleared. But once his flocks perished in the first outbreaks of the mist, he gave up, and cleared out to try starting from scratch further north. But it takes capital to start again, as any previous resident of Nebulah well knows; last I heard of Tom he was working at the abattoir in Harvey.

It's said that the skeletons of his flocks still roam the paddocks, mournfully grazing the muddy fields, while the *For sale* sign hangs pointlessly on the main gate, but I haven't ever been out there after dark to establish whether or not this is true.

All in all, Nebulah was a lethargic town, peaceful through its lack of prosperity. A place for retirees and families on welfare, where you could live cheaply out of the fast lane, but where there was not nearly enough work to keep the younger generation around. Most of our young ones would have cleared off up to Perth or over east anyway, with or without the mist.

It was typical of a country town in that everyone knew everyone – or at least their business. Everyone followed – and eventually yawned through – the dreary battles going on along McKenzie's Rise above the falls, over kids on unlicenced dirt bikes, a problem long redundant now, as the bikes are either gone or rusting in the sheds of empty houses.

And the silence, so long fought for, is as empty as the echo of lost life.

*

I head towards Pearson Street, the main drag of town, gunning the truck hard, listening for telltale rattles from the gasket. Both Gina and Blackie are on the back, Li despairing of a dog that would always choose a ride in the truck over the company of his owner.

On the outskirts of town the deserted primary school is starting to show advanced signs of decay, weeds reaching up the flimsy walls of the portables, and sprouting defiantly from the tarmac of the netball court. The huge old pepper tree at the junction of Mason and Pearson sits unmolested at last, liberated from decades of kids clambering up its branches or scratching initials into its trunk.

Once I've turned into Pearson, I cruise along the empty road, the two-hour parking signs uselessly guarding the steeply kerbed roadsides, which are gradually disappearing under drifts of debris.

After a block of wilting houses the shops begin, boarded-up and smeared, a handful of token *Business for sale* and *Commercial premises for lease* signs still propped crookedly on the shuttering.

I try to come down here about twice a week, to check that there hasn't been any unwelcome attention. Although we've had surprisingly little trouble. Looters and vandals tend to prefer the cover of darkness. The government managed to post a cop out here on temporary assignment for a few weeks when there were some 'mishaps'. He was a useless prick no one wanted elsewhere – made me look dynamic – but nevertheless he was a deterrent, as were the few remaining locals still trying to stay in their homes, who didn't treat any of the window-shoppers they encountered with gentleness. Gordon Toms and his boys used to escort them out to the cemetery, where they'd relieve them of their mobile phones and chain them to the gates.

Gordon would give me a call and let me know they were there, and I'd 'happen' to turn up later on, pretend to stumble accidentally over the poor sods, who, after a stretch of the cemetery's isolation, reflecting on the stories going round of what happens in Nebulah after dark, would be literally crapping themselves.

I'd give them the routine: *You're bloody lucky, I don't normally come this way. Hate to think what would have happened to you out here, holy shit.* Etcetera. By now the guys would be blubbering with relief, all thoughts of rummaging through the garages of empty houses, or squeezing through jemmied windows at the back of bolted shops, long gone.

But the padlocks! I'd need keys to free them, did they have any idea who'd chained them up? I'd need to find the guys responsible and persuade them to hand over the keys (Gordon's spares in my glove box). Could they describe the men who did this? *Mmm, that could be… maybe so-and-so – hope it's not him, for your sake, I passed him heading out of town on the Woodford Highway, twenty minutes ago.*

Mmm, it's tricky. I'll have to ask around, see if I can find out. Worried look at the sky. *Not much time, though.*

Bugger that, get a saw, cut the fucking chain, for fuck's sake! They were usually a tad stressed by this point, as predictable as Gail's tears.

Well, all the good saws have been pinched. Bloody looters, you wouldn't credit it, would you, putting people's lives at risk.

Only got a crappy hacksaw left, pretty blunt. Don't reckon there's enough time for that. Still, better than nothing, I suppose.

And I'd leave them snarling and ready to throttle each other for the single hacksaw blade. In about half an hour I'd return: *Wow, how lucky are you? I managed to convince the guys responsible that they'd be hit with felony charges if I couldn't get you out. Just in the nick of time, I'd say.*

They would extend wrists shallowly shredded from fumbling efforts with the hacksaw. *Boy, you're gonna have some scarring there, what a mess! People will think you tried to slit your wrists when they see that. Permanent, I'd reckon.*

Then I'd helpfully point out that they only had about twenty minutes before sunset to get out of town. Their vehicles would still be back where they'd left them, usually at a distance out of sight. Of course there wasn't time to get to them on foot, but no way would I drive them, no, no – my place was in the other direction and I needed to get myself home before dark.

Some would get threatening at this point, but a snarling Alsatian is a pretty effective sidekick, and I suspect Gina enjoyed these routines at least as much as I did – she never missed her cue. And Gordon's boys would be on stand-by at the turn-off, just in case of trouble.

After a protracted period of refusals – the sun menacingly lowering as we argued – I would reluctantly relent, and accept the generous offer of the contents of their wallets as compensation for my personal risk.

I'd usually split fifty-fifty with Gordon. It was a strategy more effective as a deterrent than the useless slob of a cop they'd sent us. No one had missed the irony of his presence. When the town was fully populated, the station was closed down – we only got another cop when there was hardly anyone left. Money will always be found for the protection of property.

So we justified our own little form of justice. And it was great stress relief.

That was while Gordon was still around, though, before he followed his boys out to Hedland. *Shit of a place,* he'd said, last time he rang, back when I was still answering the phone. *$1500 a week for a dogbox that's barely livable, but you have to be grateful for anything at all. At least you can spend your evenings outside, have a fire or a barbie. Not shut up every night like a flock of goddamn chickens with the foxes circling. You can't do that to people, drives them insane.*

There was a protracted pause. I know he meant well.

*

Apart from the usual tattered cardboard boxes blowing round the shopfronts (God only knows where they come from), Pearson Street is unchanged. The pub bolted and the post office security-shuttered; the rest a medley of broken windows and sheets of warped untreated pine.

So far the truck's behaving itself, but I haven't covered much distance. At the end of Pearson I turn left for the highway, thinking that a twenty-k jaunt and back should give a fair indication of its capabilities. I've only covered about eight k's and I'm concentrating on gunning the engine and watching the temperature gauge, so when the blue Camry passes me I'm taken by surprise. I don't get time to take down the rego or note anything more than the fact that it only seems to contain one person.

A woman. Heading into town.

I keep driving, watching the gauge which has started to rise steadily, the Camry's presence an added ripple of concern.

After another five k's I turn back, unable to shrug the car's presence off as someone who's just taken a wrong turn. Usually sightseers, if they bother to come at all, are in groups. Nebulah's not the sort of place people tend to visit on their own.

Something about the car has me worried – you don't spend as much time on the force as I did, albeit with my head in the sand, without learning to follow your intuition.

Which isn't always fail-safe. I've left it too late; the temperature gauge's needle suddenly stirs from its usual position, hovering just over halfway, and creeps towards the red zone.

To keep driving would be madness. I have to pull over. And wait.

I let the dogs down and lift the bonnet, listening to the ominous sound of water boiling in the radiator, the engine's unhappy tick. I have a smoke, then cover the cap with a thick towel and slowly release it, liberating a geyser of steaming liquid. When it's subsided I start the engine and top up the radiator, willing myself to take it slowly and not become careless in my haste to get back to town.

The drive back is agonising. I have to cruise at around thirty, the needle shivering about three-quarters of the way up the gauge. Finally I turn back into Pearson, my shoulder muscles by now curled rigid with tension. There is no sign of the Camry. I take the first left and start to slowly cruise the blocks that run parallel to the main street. I haven't got far before the gauge is up in the red. There's nothing for it. I have to rest the truck again.

This time I tell the dogs to stay. When I lift the bonnet, steam is hissing from the radiator cap. It needs a substantial rest, not just a cigarette break. Cursing, I reach into the cab for a water bottle and call the dogs down. They immediately lope from fence to fence, stopping to inhale gateposts and patches of weeds. Fingers crossed they're old scents. At least it's not cold; the sun is enough to keep the air temperature up. At another time, in another place, it could be considered quite pleasant. I head off in the direction of Mason's Reserve, off the other side of Pearson, thinking to give the dogs a good run.

I've just reached the main street and am lighting a smoke in my cupped hands when I hear the car. I look up instantly, but even then I'm too late, it's turned left out of Middle Avenue, several blocks away, and is driving slowly away from the shops, towards the east of town. The cemetery. And the significance of it coming out of Middle Avenue isn't lost on me, either – it's the through road to Hobson Street.

Rolf's place.

Sean answers his mobile on the second ring. He doesn't

know of any official visits to Rolf's, a blue Camry doesn't sound like anyone he's aware of.

'Got the rego?'

'Didn't get close enough. Just thought I'd run the vehicle past you, see if it rang any bells.'

'Not with me.' There's a flurry on the other end of the phone, voices. 'Sorry, I've got to go, mate. Keep me posted.'

I've only been gone from the truck for twenty minutes. I turn the ignition, just in case, but any optimism is ill-founded: the gauge is straight back into the red. It's a forty-five minute walk to Li's, where I've left the Land Cruiser. I reach for the mobile again, but then feel, in my pocket with the phone, my car keys. There's no point phoning Li to drive down and get me.

I can leg it there or stay with the truck and try it again in half an hour or so. The truck's clock says it's now after three. There's no guarantee that half an hour will be long enough to cool the engine. My shoulders are aching something shocking. The idea of sitting here, not doing anything, is unbearable.

I don't bother locking the truck behind me.

The dogs enjoy the walk, weaving around the streets following scent lines, any training regarding the crossing of roads long forgotten. The walk is helping me loosen up too. It's probably nothing, the first ghoulish sightseer from Woodford since news of Rolf's suicide broke. There's nothing to suggest that there's any more to it than that.

When I finally reach Li's place out on Dickson Road it's well after four o'clock and I'm dismayed at the way

I'm puffing like an old man. I've really let myself go. I am reminded of Sean's concerned comments the day before. Tomorrow I will go for a jog, something short and not too strenuous, but a beginning. For now, though, I need to get my breath back and have a smoke.

There's no sign of Li when I reach the house – I can see her wheelbarrow over at the third shade house. I'm too concerned with the passing time, I pause only to let Gina have a drink, and grab a glass of water myself. Li appears from the shade house when she hears my car, shielding her eyes from the sun, but I don't stop to explain about the truck. I'll call her later.

I'm halfway back to town when I see Tom and Gail's Honda approaching, heading out to Li's. Typically, they've left it to the last minute to pick up their supplies, obviously expecting to have their stuff delivered. Tom slows and waits for me to reach them. As I draw up to a reluctant stop he winds down his window.

'Li get back okay?' he asks, beer already evident on his breath. I want to say that it's a bit bloody late to be asking that, but instead I just tell them they'll find her in the shade houses.

'You haven't passed any vehicles on your way out?'

Tom shakes his head no, uninterested, and beside him Gail is fidgeting, impatient to get back home.

It's already almost five when I get back to the centre of town, and it occurs to me that I've forgotten my own supplies – they're still lined up by Li's back door. There's still about an hour of daylight – if I spot the Camry early and there's nothing untoward going on, I should have time to get back for them.

I swing by Rolf's place first, and do a quick circuit of the outside. The house is locked and there's no sign of any attempt to get in. There's nothing to suggest anyone's even been there. Already the place looks as if it's been empty for years; it and Liz's place next door are mournful with loss of life, like cluttered rooms suddenly cleared out and reduced to walls, devoid of intimacy. I decide I'll make a point of avoiding this street from now on.

I'm just turning back towards the car when I catch a glimpse of unexpected colour nearby. A blue straw hat is lying in the garden, to the side of the porch steps. It's as if someone had been sitting there and taken the hat off, laid it beside them and either knocked it off or it blew away unnoticed. It's a woman's hat, battered and unadorned. It's not Milly's. I toss it onto the back seat of the car.

There's no way Rolf's name or personal details would have been publicised with the news of his death, and aside from Ernie Rogers, Rolf's GP in Woodford, I couldn't think of anyone else who would know his address. As far as I know, Rolf barely ever went to Woodford. Could Liz have asked someone to check on him for her? I decide that's unlikely: if she was at all concerned for him she would have contacted one of us. I couldn't think of any reason a stranger would be visiting Rolf's empty house, or any means of them knowing where it was.

I ring Sean again. 'Rolf's address hasn't been made public, has it?'

'Not that I'm aware of. Rudy Clements from the local rag wants a brief, but he's out of town for now so I haven't spoken to him yet.'

'The lawyers?'

'Confidentiality clause. Against their code of conduct to give out information like that. Nick's pretty professional about these things.'

'How green is Denham?'

Sean barked. 'As fucking astroturf. But he's a complete by-the-booker – reckon he sleeps with the frigging training manual. He wouldn't have given anything out to anyone.'

'Someone's been at Rolf's. A woman.'

'The blue Camry?'

'Reckon so.'

'Beats me. As far as I know, they haven't even begun to trace the cousin.'

I check my watch. This can wait. 'I'd better get going.'

'I'll ask around. Holler if you need anything.'

The cemetery is only minutes from town. When I turn into the parking area I'm geared up, ready for my approach, but I see immediately that the car is not there. This is not a relief. I can't just assume the woman has left.

I stop the Land Cruiser by the chained gates, which hang, rusty and sagging as if they recognise their defeat, and the heavy chain is just another weight pressing down on them. They might stop people getting in, but they certainly have no effect on anything coming out.

I rest my elbows between the spiked points of the fence and scan the area. It's a typical, fairly nondescript country cemetery, not even particularly old. The old miners who keeled over before the thirties tended to be planted out beyond Mackenzie's Rise. Most of these graves are from around the fifties, when Nebulah had a more substantial population, before the mining ceased and the services were gradually whittled away and relocated to the larger centres.

An unkempt gravel path divides the area in two, Catholics in a smaller plot to one side. A large plaque stands at the end, a memorial to those lost in the various wars. Carved names in rows like a library catalogue, as solemn and soulless as the museum's mouldy taxidermal offerings. Of recent graves there are only a handful. Once the hospital closed, elderly residents who became infirm would be shipped off to nursing homes in urban centres – if they were lucky, close to their kids, who would prefer to have them eventually buried where the Mother's or Father's Day graveside visit wasn't such a trek. Sun-faded pots of dead plants and dirt-coated plastic flowers dot the scene, adding to the sense of neglect.

I can't help looking towards a simple green stone, veined marble, although as always it gives me an awful creeping chill. It is elegantly understated, its unadorned letters reducing an entire life, all its experiences and energy and emotions to a tiny, plain: *Gavin Pryor. 1934–1982. PEACE.*

Five letters. So little to ask. If only they'd known.

Poor Milly.

*

I'm still leaning on the fence, lost in my drifts of thought. Somehow, in spite of everything, I always find this a peaceful spot, hard to understand in a place so diabolical. But when all that has dissipated, while the sun is up, it's strangely calming to stand at the core of so much danger and know you are safe, at least for now. There is such a flatness to the place, accentuated by the absence of birdsong, and its sheltered position protects it from the extremes of storms or strong sun.

It's easy to get lulled here, to hang upon the gate till the sun just begins to slide beneath the trees and suddenly you realise that the twilight has crept upon you unnoticed, like the darkening of a room when you are engrossed in a book.

Even though the surrounding gums are quintessentially Australian, sprawled to the sky like unbound floral arrangements, they always put me in mind of that Enid Blyton book, the one about an enchanted wood, in which the trees sing to each other: *wisha-wisha-wisha*. It's a horribly twee English book, full of well-behaved children and bread and jam, but I used to love reading it with Julie, my daughter, when she was little, just for the sound of those trees, the peace it evoked. One of those little things that sneak into your psyche, speaks to you somehow. I often think of it out here. Although I can't imagine Miss Blyton's wood was ever shattered by the shrieking cries of Australian corellas, swirling through the landscape like dervishes, as rowdy as toddlers full of sugar.

I stand straight and flex my shoulders; they're still tight. I've been dreaming too long –I'm cutting it fine, probably have less than fifteen minutes to get home. I had last seen the car heading out here, and the fact that it's not here now means the woman has probably left town: I hadn't seen the Camry on my way through Nebulah, so it's unlikely to still be around. And if it is, really, it's hardly my responsibility. I've made enough of an effort to find her, warn her off.

I'm carefully not thinking of the alternative scenario, that the blue car has disappeared out here, dissolved into the unrecognised, unidentified void that swallowed the men in their solemn convoy and gave us the mist in return. Even recognising the possibility at the corner of my mind is enough to make my shoulders stab with pain, and the pain in my stomach is already distinct rather than shadowy.

But it seems unlikely. An old Toyota and a battered blue straw hat don't seem to carry the same formality or threat as the anonymous suited men in their unmarked cars.

I stretch a final time and rouse myself. I'm tired and stiff. It's been a bad few days. A long, hot bath with a new bottle for me. And then I remember my supplies, languishing in Li's kitchen. It's far too late to get back there now – in fact it's almost too late to get home, I realise with a jolt. I'm dawdling far too long, must be my mood. Being out here this late is a helluva risk.

I turn to leave, and my heart seizes on me.

Standing between me and the Land Cruiser, barely twenty feet away, a bareheaded woman is watching me. Her eyes are piercing.

She has given me such a fright I feel winded; I can barely speak for a moment. She waits briefly, then breaks the silence. 'Isn't it dangerous to be out here at this time of day?'

She smiles. Behind her the sun drops towards the horizon.

PART
TWO

It was a very close call; never again will I risk cutting it so fine. As I stand at the sink I realise how badly my hands are shaking. The aftermath of fear has made my arms limp, the muscles weak. It's all I can do to lift the kettle onto the stove.

The woman too is badly shaken, she stands rigidly beside my kitchen table, as if sitting would require a degree of relaxation currently beyond her. In her hands the blue straw hat is now twisted out of shape, perhaps completely ruined.

We only just made it, the accelerator indifferent to the weight of our fear. The mist had already risen enough to surround the vehicle; at home I did not even stop to lock the Land Cruiser, just bellowed at the stranger to move, and yanked Gina out behind me. We'd run for the house as the mist around us started to transform itself into figures, howling faces and reaching arms, elongated grasping fingers snatching at us, gleeful. Thankfully it was still hazy enough to evade – we wrenched ourselves through it and I slammed the door as it streamed after us up the porch steps, screeching with delight at this unexpected opportunity. As I flicked the locks it was pressed against the windows, a chilling kaleidoscope of bones and teeth against the glass.

I barked at the woman to get the curtains while I ran for the back door, and my tone was enough to launch her into action. We did a frantic circuit of the house, checking locks and wrenching drapes against the cacophony outside; the appalling vision of humanity, its very essence, unfettered and corrupt. And in the midst of our frenzy, the phone started to ring – three times and then again, its shrillness adding to the turmoil. I knew I had to answer it – if I didn't, after dark, it would cause panic. I grabbed it in passing and cut Li's concern short with a curt reassurance that I was okay and would call her tomorrow, while the terrible faces leered in at me through my windows, and tomorrow seemed just a hollow bluff.

At last the curtains were closed on the final vision: fingernails, long and hideously sharp, scraping across what suddenly seemed a ludicrously thin and fragile piece of glass. We came to a sudden stop, gasping, realising that we'd been barely breathing in our panic.

I'd reached for the kettle and my hands' shaking would have shamed me if I hadn't been beyond the point of caring.

I need to calm, I'm thinking now, my mind rolling through a sea of images, as if it has fallen overboard into a heavy swell. *I am alive,* I chant to myself through the tide, the words taking on the solidity of a life jacket, keeping me afloat and clear of the tumult. I try to deepen my breathing, slow it down, the match quivering above the gas burner before it bursts into life. As it fires I take a deep, long breath and turn to face the stranger standing, bewildered and terrified, in my kitchen.

As if in answer, the woman unlocks herself, reaching carefully for the table and lowering herself slowly into a chair, as if she is scared of bruising herself on surfaces. She doesn't sag once she is seated, but raises her hands to her cheeks, which are faded with fright. She traces her glowing eyes, runs her fingers the length of her eyebrows, then down her nose and across her lips, as if checking that she is still all there, grounding herself in physical reality.

'I'm Alex,' she says quietly, 'and I'm sorry, I'm a bit shaken.'

'Pete, and if it's any comfort, I'm a wreck myself.'

She smiles weakly, but is disconcerted by the noise outside, the scrapings at the window. 'Are we safe?' Her words are little more than breath.

'As far as I know. Don't ask me why, but it doesn't seem to be able to get past the locks.'

She nods. 'Like the old vampire legend – it has to be invited in before it can cross the threshold.'

'No chance of that. You'll have to excuse me a minute, I've got to see to my dog. The tea's in the left-side cupboard, if doing something helps.'

I leave her rinsing cups and locate Gina in the front room, where she has crawled beneath the dining table and is huddled, shivering uncontrollably. The smell alerts me to a large wet patch beneath her.

She whimpers when I reach for her, her ears flat. Gently,

I stroke her head with just the tips of my fingers, reach behind her ears and scratch her neck, rhythmically, slowly urging her out. Eventually her panting lessens and she begins to settle, and I croon to her, reassuring. When I have her clear of the table she is still trembling, her back legs twitching with nerves. I pull her head close, holding it to my chest so that my heartbeat will quiet her, all the time gently stroking her side. Finally, her muscles respond and she slumps against me.

This is not a cowardly dog. I have seen her bailed up by a pack of wild dogs, once when the rifle jammed on me. While I desperately fought to release the firing pin, they surrounded Gina, who stood her ground between us, facing them squarely with bared fangs, answering their bloodlust with a determined menace that held them off until the gun's mechanism finally slid into place.

I've seen hunting dogs reduced to this state by a mere clap of thunder, nothing more than the sound of nature at play.

Once she's quieter I urge her gently in the direction of the bathroom. Alex is standing in the doorway, watching. When I return with Gina washed down and towelled, Alex is on her knees under my table, sponging at the wet patch.

'You don't have to do that,' I tell her.

She uses the table as a support to pull herself up. 'I think,' she says, 'that it's the least I can do. Tea's brewed, if you want some.'

I flick on the mask of the TV. In the kitchen Alex pours tea while I feed Gina, who eats only a token amount to acknowledge the food before lurching onto her blankets by the stove.

The tea has been brewing for some time, it's good and strong. We both add several spoonfuls of sugar. I rummage under the sink and find the measly finger of whiskey left from the other night.

'It's all there is, sorry. I forgot to bring my supplies home. Not going out for them now.'

At the window fingernails are still scraping, tapping at the glass. I glance at Gina; she's already asleep, snoring and twitching. Alex sips at her drink gratefully, but with trepidation. It's clear she's not usually a drinker. She replaces her glass carefully on the table. Her eyes are striking, an unusual green that speaks of beginnings, of life about to unfold, like the uncurling of new leaves. A colour both pure yet jaded, bathed in the pull of nature's secrets. Her gaze, even under these disturbed circumstances, is disquieting.

'I believe,' she says, 'that I owe you a huge debt.' She gives an embarrassed smile. 'You must think me an imbecile.'

She had told me, as we raced for home with the sky plunging into darkness around us, that her car, parked out at McKenzie's Ridge, had refused to start. She had heard me drive past and followed me on foot to the cemetery, praying I would stop.

She lowers her gaze back to her tea, which she grips with both hands. Her hands are slight and bear a single ring, a plain silver band with a small amethyst. Around her neck on a chain is a silver pendant, some symbol I'm not familiar with. Her hair is dark, only loosely secured, and her face bears the lines of character that denote experience. I estimate her to be in her late thirties or early forties, not that much older than Liz. But her eyes, their unnerving gaze, make her seem much, much older. They put you in mind of a conjuror's hands, or a pickpocket's movements; the effect is one of being diverted while explored, probed. It is a strangely intimate feeling, although not from anything apparent, more from the sense it leaves you with – like that of a disquieting dream.

'You were very lucky,' I tell her, and feel a little shamefaced at the number of times I've used the same line in my performances out at the cemetery.

'Believe me, after that experience I can appreciate how lucky I am. It was far worse than I'd imagined. Far worse,' she repeats after a moment of distraction, gazing without focus beyond my shoulder.

So there we are – a sightseer after all. I should have known. I should have left her there to fight her own way out of the mist, since she was so keen on experiencing it. I could have just gone back to Li's for my stuff and cooked myself a decent meal, instead of risking my life and my dog for a bloody tourist. I push back my chair. 'Well, I suppose I'll have to try to feed you now that you're here.'

She is looking at me, anxious. 'I really am very grateful to you,' she begins again, 'I honestly didn't mean to cause any problems.'

But I'm pissed off and drained, petulant about my

forgotten shopping and my exhausted dog. 'You do, though,'
I tell her, keeping my back turned, rummaging in the
cupboard for food. 'Whenever someone like you comes here
it causes problems.'

'Someone like me?'

'A tourist. Sightseer. Come to see the haunted town, like
we're some kind of sideshow. As if it's entertainment, then
off you go, full of thrills about your daring, and no one ever
actually gives a shit about what it's like for us, having to exist
like this.'

I turn around. She is rigid. 'That's not why I'm here.'

'Right, you just thought you'd drop by for the hell of it.'

'No. I came to see the old man.'

Rolf. After the commotion of the evening I'd forgotten
about her visit to Rolf's.

'You knew Rolf?'

'Is that his name?' she says. 'No, I didn't. It's hard to
explain.'

I want to know. I put the onion and the can of tuna I'm
holding onto the table and sit down. 'We have time. It'll be a
long night, you can be sure of that.'

It is Alex who is unnerved now, not quite sure of her
ground. I get the impression she's used to listening to
other people, not opening up about herself; she is clearly
uncomfortable. After a moment of thought, again those
eyes digging into me, assessing, she begins. 'I am on holiday,
I'll give you that, but this place wasn't on my itinerary. I
was headed to Dongarra to visit someone. An old friend,

someone I've known since my childhood. He used to live next door to us when I was little, and he was kind of like a surrogate grandpa. He's in his nineties now and isn't well, he hasn't got much longer. I'm going to say goodbye.'

She stops to take her cup over to the sink and run some water. When she's had a drink she sits opposite me again. I get the impression that the break was so she could collect her thoughts, rather than from any abiding thirst.

'I live in South Australia now, the Yorke Peninsula. I decided to take some time off and make a holiday of the trip, seeing I was coming so far. So once I crossed the Nullarbor I started making my way round the coast, spending a few days here and there, whatever took my fancy.' She pauses again.

'About a week ago I was in Bunbury. I was lost, I was looking for the turn-off to Mandurah and I wasn't watching the traffic and I ran into a woman. Literally.' She winces. 'I ran up the back of her. There wasn't much damage to her car, but her reaction was very strange. She just didn't want to know. It was as if she just wasn't there at all.'

She pauses again, looking into my face as if watching for something. I wait. She nods slightly, as if she's heard what she needed. 'I don't usually announce this to people, especially strangers, but I'm a clairvoyant. Professionally. A reader is what I prefer to call it.'

I stay immobile, expressionless. She smiles. 'Sceptical?'

I reach for Rolf's now-empty whiskey bottle, twirling it on its rim. 'We've had quite a few turn up claiming to be psychic. To be honest, all full of shit, just looking for easy publicity. But living here you can hardly afford to be close-minded about anything.'

'Good – I only ask a fair hearing.' Suddenly she looks sheepish. 'Actually, I'll also ask for a cigarette, if that's okay.'

'So you know I'm a smoker?'

'I can see your tobacco. Top left-hand pocket. Hardly psychic.'

I pull out my pouch – under the circumstances I'm hardly going to enforce the Outside Only law. It seems hours since my last one.

When we've rolled and lit, we settle again, more relaxed this time, some kind of boundary crossed.

'This woman I hit,' Alex continues, 'was a real mess, psychically distraught, an absolute shambles. She'd obviously just been through something awful, and the air around her was screaming with it. She couldn't have given a shit about the damage to her car, it was way beyond her care factor.' She's rolled her cigarette too thin and it has already gone out. 'She'd come from here.'

Liz. She has my full attention. 'What did she say?'

'She didn't say anything. Barely glanced at the car and waved me away. Wouldn't even take my details. But this place surrounded her, she was drowning in it.'

She frowns at the extinguished cigarette, reaches for my lighter. 'A lot of psychic reading is simply down to wavelength, to put it fairly crudely. It's like radio waves, you have to be tuned in to the right station to pick up anything. Cooperation is a big part of it. Cooperation or shared experience. Professionally, it's about people's willingness to be read. Personally, it's about shared experience. That's what this was a case of. She was worrying about an old man, someone she had left behind, while I was keen to see Cliff – my friend – another old man in trouble. To put it simply, we connected.'

'She didn't say where she was going?'

'I don't think she knew. She was very traumatised. I have to say, it was a highly disturbing encounter. For me, anyway.'

I didn't doubt that. Liz had bordered on excess in all her moods, it was just fortunate for everyone around her that she tended towards the joyous side of things.

'Sometimes,' Alex continues, 'because of the depth a psychic link taps, it can be very hard to disconnect, to break free. It's like an entanglement. I found it was very hard for me, once we'd "collided"' – she waves her fingers in the air, to distinguish the word with quotation marks – 'to let go. Her fears for her old man tangled with mine, and it seemed, if her emotional state was anything to go by, that he was in some kind of danger. I went on to Mandurah for a few days to see a cousin, but I couldn't relax. I just couldn't shake myself free.' Her cigarette is already out again. 'It was something I just couldn't ignore. I finally accepted that I needed to try finding her old man.' Although her expression and her tone of voice haven't changed, somehow the lines on her face seem to have deepened. 'But I got cold feet. Or, to put it bluntly, I got scared. I stopped at Dwellingup, hung around there. I know, probably better than most, that there are elements that are dangerous to encounter, and the damage to the woman I'd run into seemed to be pretty severe.'

As if to punctuate her point there is a howling shriek outside, tapering off into grotesque gurgling. Alex shudders. 'I'm not going to pretend to be a brave person. I'm not exactly thrilled to be here.' She smiles wryly. 'Anyway, I got as close as Satrini, booked into a motel, and changed my mind about the whole thing. What was I doing? Too hard, not my business. That night I was full of relief, but then as I was drifting off to sleep, I found the old man.'

She breaks off to check my expression, make sure I haven't moved away from her. She notices her cigarette is out again and crushes it into the ashtray with a gesture of irritation.

'When I say I found him,' she resumes, 'I mean I could hear him, so to speak. It was awful. Such dreadful sadness. And so much background interference, which I realise now was...' She waves her hand towards the kitchen window. 'It was stifling, such suffering. Like being choked. I knew I wouldn't be able to forgive myself if I didn't try to help him.' She sighs. 'But I left it too late. I was so sick that night, I could barely breathe. The next morning the constriction was gone, but I was exhausted, completely drained. It was as if I'd returned from the dead. I was physically incapable of travelling anywhere. I decided to stay another night in Satrini. I did try to reconnect with him, but there was nothing. He was gone. When I arrived today it was only to confirm what I already knew.'

She has spread the fingers of both hands across her

forehead, from temple to temple, and is pressing gently, as if to massage – or soothe – the sense that she has been talking of.

'How did you know where he lived?' It's a stupid question I immediately regret.

'The same way I knew he existed. But when I got to the house there was nothing there.' She shrugs.

'He hanged himself the day before yesterday.'

She nods. 'I thought it must have been something like that.'

'You're right, you know. Everything you said. The woman you ran into must have been Liz. She was driven out a week or so back. She was only here at all because she had nowhere else to go.' I roll her another cigarette. 'Walking away from her house meant losing everything. She only has a single parent's benefit, so there's no way she can afford today's rents. She doesn't have any other family, the kids' father took off when the littlest was still in nappies. Social welfare offers nothing but a waiting list. She'll have to impose on friends, rely on charity, with three little kids and a dog in tow.' I light the cigarette for Alex and pass it over. 'She was a mess when she left – we haven't heard from her since. And her kids were all Rolf had. They were the first time he'd ever had any kind of family. Up till then he'd always been right enough on his own.'

Alex is nodding. We are talking as if this is all commonplace. A woman is sitting at my kitchen table telling me she reads people's minds, and I am chatting with her as if this is nothing out of the ordinary, as everyday as a bowl of cereal, or world events contained in a newspaper rolled in plastic and launched over the front fence. A year ago I would have humoured her and hustled her out the door at the first opportunity. I'm too tired now to give this fact anything more than a sardonic mental wink.

Alex winks at me. It gives me a start. I have a terrible feeling she knows exactly what I've just been thinking.

*

I cook a Joyce Special for tea. Joyce was an old friend from many years ago, the wife of a colleague in Mildura I used to go camping with. She was a wizard, this woman – she could look at half a packet of stale Cornflakes and transform it into a feast. My cupboards are pretty bare, but there are the makings of one of her creations: eggs, a can of tuna, half an onion and soy sauce. A Pacific Island omelette, she'd called it, but I reckon that was a bit of a furphy.

Alex looks dubious when I serve it up, but by now we are both starving, and it tastes much better than it sounds. I've managed to unearth an old cask bladder from the back of the sauce cupboard, with a couple of half-glasses of vinegary red left in it. Beggars can't be choosers.

To my relief, the smell of cooking rouses Gina, who sits at attention on her blanket, sniffing the air and looking hopeful. I give her a segment of my half, which she gulps before sprawling out again, content. Crisis over.

We feel better too, once we've eaten; we're smoking again, bugger the smell, I'll air the place out in the morning.

Alex has relaxed a bit, which has softened her face, lessened the etchings scraped at the edges of her eyes and mouth. She's still not entirely at ease – the nightly symphony isn't completely drowned out by the blaring TV, and it can be pretty confronting even when you're used to it.

She asks for coffee and I have just put a cup in front of her when a banshee wail fills the night. Alex cringes and her coffee slurps onto the table. 'Spending the night here is not something I would ever have added to my must-do list.'

I fetch a cloth from the sink and wipe up the spill.

'Why do you stay?' she asks.

'You're the mind-reader.'

'There must be somewhere you could go?'

'An invalid pension won't even cover rent in today's market.'

'But wouldn't the government help?'

'They don't want to know. Way out of their jurisdiction. Exceptional circumstances don't cover haunting. It's been made clear that as we don't fit into any of their categories, we don't qualify for assistance, case closed.'

'What about family?'

'No.' I don't mean it to be so abrupt, but my tone is like a slammed door. She doesn't pursue it. Outside there is a fresh burst of laughter.

'How long has it been like this?'

'Nine months or so. It started last winter, at solstice.'

She winces. 'A powerful time.'

'Yeah. Life-changing.'

'What set it off?'

'Beats me. Beats everyone. I reckon you'd know more about these things than I do.'

She shakes her head.

'Don't you communicate with the dead? Pass on messages of condolence and "By the way, where did you hide Granny's diamonds"?'

Alex looks peeved. 'I'm a psychic, not a con woman. There's no such bloody thing as communicating with the dead, everything comes from the living. All those practitioners pick the information they need from the minds of the people they're dealing with, then they claim they've made contact with "the other side" '– her fingers again – 'it's all crap. Once you're dead you're gone. Game Over.'

I think of Milly's Gavin. If only that were the case.

'Here the dead aren't gone. They're incorporated into the mist, become a part of it. We lost some people when it first started, before we realised how dangerous it was.' It still makes me angry. 'The authorities won't even declare them dead. They're "missing". No bodies, no motives, no suspicious circumstances. Too hard. They're just "gone".' Alex's finger quotation marks are addictive. Or simply appropriate. 'But they reappear. Every night. In the mist.'

Alex looks a little ill. 'So this mist is made up of the "undead"?'

'Oh no, they're definitely dead.' Again I push away thoughts of Gavin. 'I have no idea. It can transform itself into living people – visions of them, anyway, like holograms. That's why we have to keep the curtains closed. It gets at you. Liz, for instance.' I take the dishes to the sink. 'We've tried to find out what's going on – one of our number, an ex-schoolteacher, spent a fortnight in Canberra at the National Library. She couldn't find much at all – any documented "paranormal" experiences are either ancient or they've been proved hoaxes, or it was clear that even the authors had no bloody idea. The internet's too full of bullshit to be any use.' I remember Milly's exhaustion and her despair when she came back, after all that work, empty-handed.

'In the first months, when it started up, we had several teams of "experts" roll up, filling people's houses with all kinds of gadgets and machinery. They measured everything from atmospheric pressure to magnetic fields. Might as well have tested our bloody cholesterol levels, at least then we might have learned something useful. Turned out they knew bugger-all; liked to spout a lot of crap and get juicy grants. Then they'd publish incomprehensible garbage full of meaningless buzzwords, so that no one would cotton on to the fact that they had no idea what they were talking about.' Again Milly flashes to mind: she'd told the last lot, with wry dignity, where they could file their metabolic disturbance charts.

'But it just suddenly started? Like that?' Alex clicks her fingers.

*

Snap! A tiny movement, the gesture of an instant. But potency distilled needs only an instant. *Click!* and a bomb goes off: buildings collapse, people lose homes, entire families. *Snap!* and a bone is broken: a pain-free, physically easy life is over. *Click* and a door is closed, a blind pulled taut over a window.

Snap and a border is crossed, a mind shattered.

I remember when Julie was little, we used to play the card game Snap! You'd remember it – when two cards the same appear at the top of the pile, you slap your hand on them and cry 'Snap!'

Snap! *I win*. Snap! *I win*. Snap! *I win*.

I used to let her win, of course. That's what being a dad is about. Her eyes would glow and she would giggle herself into a fit of the hiccoughs – so rare as a kid to be able to get the better of an adult.

It's only when you get to the other end, become an adult yourself, that you learn the obverse of Snap! *I win*.

Which is, Snap! *You lose*. Snap! *You lose*. Snap!

You lose.

It's easy enough to pinpoint the beginning of the mist as the first night it rolled over the town: 22 June 1998, the night of the winter solstice and the day the line of grey four-wheel drives cruised into our town and then disappeared out to the cemetery. Literally.

Most of us had noted them: they cried out to be noticed, with their deliberate sameness, hulking size and tinted anonymity. Their air of menace. They'd driven in slowly, and that too was a threat in itself, denoting power, but power contained, subdued. As if awaiting release.

The five vehicles had cruised up the main street, unhurried, maintaining an arrogant, possessive pace, as if they owned both the town and time itself. They parked just out of our reach, beyond the local shops, purring to a halt one after the other, as if connected by an invisible cord. Three men emerged from each car. The engines remained running and the drivers did not appear; curiously, they were not observed by anyone, even though by now a number of people were watching the spectacle of the new arrivals, unusual in a small rural town.

Fifteen men gathered on the footpath beside the cars. They were all absolutely nondescript. When witnesses tried to recall them afterwards, there was not a single defining feature that anyone could come up with, nothing to identify or distinguish an individual. Only this uniform, suited grey mass.

Merle Goodman, who was nearby watering her garden at the time, claimed that each man carried a small black Bible, but Merle is an unreliable witness, given to embroidery. Never let the dull facts spoil a good story, is Merle's motto.

It was a Saturday afternoon, and the RSL had set up a sausage sizzle outside the pub, fundraising. The shops were all closed for the weekend, but the races were on in Perth, so there were enough punters in the front bar to keep the sizzlers busy. The smell of frying fat, burning onions, and cheap tomato sauce filled the afternoon air.

From the pub door I watched these men walk silently as far as the shops, looking around themselves dismissively

80

before turning back. Without the armour of their vehicles the sense of threat they carried dimmed, and they appeared to be little more than a group of featureless men. As they returned to the cars they clustered together, murmuring. Their words were indistinct, and the hum of their voices was like the sound of distant traffic on an otherwise peaceful day. They were utterly oblivious to us, failing to respond to the jovial offers of burnt sausages, or the Mafia taunts that pelted from the public bar. They made no acknowledgement of us at all; it was as if, even though they appeared to be looking around, they could not actually see. They moved with the contained oblivion of the blind, their eyes hidden by sunglasses, physical shields which heightened the sense of removal emanating from them.

But somehow, despite the lack of expression maintained throughout their brief survey of our home, our lives, the impression left was one of disdain. They returned to their vehicles with the same sense of defiant, unhurried purpose, and in their wake floated an evaluation of worthlessness. It was palpable and strange, but unusual rather than eerie or disturbing. The sense of menace came from the cars them-selves, their dark, monolithic, almost bestial forms. Somehow they put you in mind of jackboots, marching in formation.

Once the men returned to their cars, I jotted down some rego details on a serviette. It wasn't until the convoy started driving away, slow and snakelike, that the mood broke. Suddenly the air was full of trepidation; the intrusion had left a chill, as if the vehicles' expensive air-conditioning had permeated the atmosphere around them. The jokes stopped.

We watched the procession turn into Tucker's Lane, home of the disputed block, the four and a half acre parcel that had divided the town so bitterly. We had known, of course, that it was this piece of land that had called these men here – there was nothing else in this town to attract their like. Men like that, so removed and self-contained, alert but blind to their surroundings, had by nature to be associated with business, development. Destruction.

Although the cars were out of our sight, we remained grouped outside the pub, silently watching while sausages hissed and charred behind us. The sudden reappearance of the vehicles was a surprise, their engines were so quiet, low growl rather than roar. They'd been an unexpectedly short time; they must have only given the site the same detached once-over they'd given the main street.

Now they turned left and cruised slowly away from us, to the east. Nothing unusual in that: the road formed a loop back to the highway; they were heading out of town. The crushed serviette I'd been dutifully scribbling on suddenly seemed ridiculous. Force of habit.

I was about to turf it into the bin beside me, which was already overflowing with its grease-and sauce-stained like, when the vehicles unexpectedly signalled right, and without braking veered into McKenzie's Rise Road and passed from sight. It seemed unlikely that fifteen men in business suits would be visiting the dam on a winter's weekend afternoon. Which, of course, left only the cemetery.

'Probably want to stick a McDonald's out there,' spat Bluey Jordan, and the afternoon, which had been bright with winter sun and fragrant with food and beer, turned dim and sour. The old tension over the disputed land, the proposed supermarket, flared again and men started to jab fingers and raise voices, the start of the next race overlooked.

This moment entered the realm of folklore later on: a young mother claimed that at that precise instant (she had bet on the two-thirty trot and had just tuned in to the starting call, so she could be exact), her sleeping baby woke apoplectic with squalls for no accountable reason. It screamed nonstop for almost an hour, to the point where she was in a panic about it, before subsiding into an exhausted, whimpering sleep.

Other parents chipped in with babies suddenly crying; children happily at play inexplicably erupting into scuffles or tears.

So it goes, anyway.

And who am I discount these claims? Outside the pub the mood was tangible. Whether it had been affected by something malevolent emanating from the visitors, or whether it was just a reaction to the audacious intrusion of wealth and power, the line of luxury four-wheel drives that no man in Nebulah could ever afford, cruising through our Saturday-arvo sausage sizzle so dismissively – provocatively, some might say – I don't know. All I know is that tempers suddenly became ragged and the arguments for and against the proposed supermarket were wrestled over yet again. A gut instinct told me something here was wrong; I asked Earl if I could use the pub's phone and put in a call to Sean, saying I thought he should maybe get out here, but I was unable to give him any sounder reason than that a visiting clutch of business types seemed to be making people out of sorts.

I stayed at the pub, waiting for Sean, my eye always to the cemetery road, willing these men to reappear, with handshakes and a plausible, inoffensive explanation for their visit – preachers come to bless the graves, dignitaries visiting Anzac memorials – anything would do, as long as it shattered the bell jar of their remoteness, their presence that seemed somehow more an absence.

As I watched the road, I listened to the theories and arguments around me, while the RSL entourage bought themselves beers and scraped the charred debris from their grill. Young Markie Lamb, large and lumpy in football colours, stood beside me with a half-empty packet of bread, methodically chewing the innards out of every slice, oblivious, as he generally was, to everything going on around him. I found myself fascinated by his industry as he unselfconsciously chewed the soft middles from the border of each crust.

At one point he gazed indifferently at me. 'You waiting?' His voice was monotone, blurred through a mouth stuffed with churning dough.

'Yeah, mate – I'm waiting for my friend Sean.'

'No, waiting for the men with no shadows,' he said, in the same matter-of-fact tone.

I stared at him, but he was down to the last slice in his

bag, and was already focused on Murray's van, where the leftovers were being loaded.

When Sean arrived towards the end of the afternoon, he had Daniel Napes, his constable at the time, with him. I climbed into the back seat and apologised for dragging them all the way out for nothing more than suspicion. Sean shrugged and pulled out in the direction of the cemetery. Behind us the pub burst into activity, spilling people in our wake, and three carloads pulled out and followed us.

Sean kept an eye on the rear-view mirror. 'Sure seems to have stirred things up, all right. S'pose it's just as well we're here.' Napes looked out his window with a disgusted scowl – you could hear the thought *Waste of time and resources* tap-dancing against his shaved skull.

We'd just turned off into McKenzie's Rise Road when the radio crackled into life. The trace on the registration numbers I'd given them had come through. There was nothing. They didn't exist.

Sean turned into the cemetery car park. 'Be interesting to meet these guys.'

But the cemetery was deserted, and back at the dam we found only a carload of local teenagers with a couple of illicit slabs of beer, mortified at being sprung not only by uniformed police, but also by a few parents in our entourage. They'd been there since morning footy practice and swore there'd been no one else through that afternoon. We left Napes there to deal with them, and to placate the fathers of the unlucky girls, and returned to the cemetery.

There was nothing. No cars, no men.

No tyre tracks. No footprints. Absolute silence. The gum trees stood unruffled and vacant. Behind us the carloads of spectators, geared up for some action, stood surveying the lifeless scene, confused.

The cemetery was at the end of the road. The convoy hadn't returned to town, and there was no other road out. But they were gone. No one was game to say anything until finally Michael Tinsdale broke the confused silence. 'Jesus wept,' he spurted. 'That's a bit bloody creepy, isn't it?' His words seemed to bite through the emptiness. That was when I realised the birds had gone.

That night the mist descended on us for the first time.

*

So while it may seem easy enough to say *Snap!*, the mist started at this point, 22 June 1998, it is hard to claim with certainty that this was the start. Some would say that it began with the appearance and disappearance of the unwelcome convoy, but others would say it was merely part of a progression of events. Perhaps they *introduced* the mist, but were they really a beginning in themselves?

Could you really, when you're dealing with a situation so esoteric, as ephemeral as mist itself, snap your fingers with such a definitive *Yes!*, and aim your focus at an obvious point, and say, 'There is the beginning'? Behind every beginning is a sequence, a series of movements that leads to the climax of enforced change, labelled the beginning but actually merely the unfolding of consequences. Before each bombed building is the escalation of war, the breaking down of peace processes; before each snapped bone is the decision to follow a particular course of action, thinking, *I am invincible*, or simply, *I am safe*.

To find a beginning is like trying to identify the onset of Alzheimer's, so easy to pinpoint the diagnosis as the instant of change. But beginnings will never arrive clean and weightless, they always come encumbered with a history.

You could, legitimately, claim that the whole situation started with the proposal for the new supermarket. With the surveyors from Perth who drove into town with their maps and titles and equipment, and declined to discuss their assignment with any local who approached them, but who happily told Earl at the pub, in return for a free round, that they'd been employed by a major retail chain, which was negotiating to purchase the vacant land on Tucker's Lane for a new supermarket.

Once the news spread, opinions and alliances shattered the town's lethargic harmony. The town split, severed cleanly as if the blade of a bulldozer had torn a boundary that clearly divided loyalty and progress. Murray and Janet Monroe, the owners of the IGA that had serviced the town unchallenged for years, were suddenly forgiven for their empty, dusty shelves, inflated prices and out-of-date Twisties, and were transformed overnight into town heroes, battlers in the true Australian way: Davids facing the corporate, multinational Goliath. The loyalty camp were vehement in their support of the dusty locals, all gripes about overpriced grey meat frozen onto polyurethane pushed to one side when faced with the challenge of an alternative.

Others were thrilled with the proposition, thought with longing of uniformed sameness, fluorescent organisation, aisles of regimented variety. And, of course, the endless, clichéd carrot of jobs hanging from the end of a large corporate stick, like a cattle prod.

It was said there were deals, promises, reassurances and payouts swirling in the private background of all the above-board public negotiations, floating in whispers and handshakes over the prickly scrub that had claimed the land for years. Sometimes these rumours were recalled in the light of our current predicament, in the endless scavenge for causes.

The site remained a wasteland of discarded whiteware and thistles, but some people were never forgiven for their opinions about it.

It seems ridiculous that a few acres of dried-out scrub on the road to the local tip could really be the cause of something as diabolical as the mist, but the unknown always breeds speculation, which all too quickly hardens into certainty, the concrete weight of fact, simply from repetition or a chance collaboration.

Earl Thompson, publican of the Nebulah Tavern for over thirty years, knew the town as intimately as his own underwear, keeping the threadbare patches well hidden from any source of light. For this he was seen as the local expert;

his opinions carried the weight of proof in themselves, usually backed up by Wally Todd, the town's historian and the driving force behind its attempt at a museum. Earl's bar-room yarns, grounded by his elbow resting proprietorially on the beer taps, assumed the mantle of local fact – the real history, the only one that mattered, because it was undocumented and therefore belonged only to locals.

Earl had another beginning to offer for the mist: he reckoned the land on Tucker's Lane was marked, cursed early in the town's life by a dispute over a claim that led to the brutal and cowardly slaughter of four miners – one only sixteen – at that very spot. He talked authoritatively over his taps about spilled blood and the possibility of buried remains, while Wally, keen not to be sidelined, would nod earnestly and assert 'Yes, that's exactly right' every now and then. And so yet another *Snap!* is added to the linchpins of the proposed supermarket and the appearance of the pack of men.

But we can go back further still. It was Rolf who pointed out one day that Nebulah had no Indigenous population or known history – inconceivable in a region renowned for its climate, rainfall and fertility.

Rolf had a lifetime of association with Aboriginal people, both on the stations he worked at and on his journeys between them. 'They know,' he'd said to me once, in the early days of the mist, when we were still desperately convinced we could find a cause. He laughed at Milly travelling to Canberra, devoting weeks to fruitless research.

'Blackfellas don't come here, should tell you everything

you need to know. They read the land through the soles of their feet, have done for thousands of years. You don't have to understand it, just accept it.'

Another beginning, so far in the past it makes our present a mere fingernail, continuing to grow fruitlessly long after the corpse is cold and stiff. A present trying desperately to deny the certainty of its fate, helpless in the face of the decay ahead of it.

*

As if it can sense a stranger, the mist is ferocious tonight; it cyclones around the house in a frenzy. Even for me, conditioned by the drawn-out months that I've endured it, it's like being under siege. Alex's face is drained of colour and she has started to close her eyes for extended periods, as if gathering her wits, or suffering from acute pain. She refuses the offer of the spare room with a shudder, saying she doubts whether she could sleep in such circumstances, and I leave her barefoot on the couch, wrapped in a blanket, with Gina curled at her feet.

On the television people drenched in fake tan demonstrate exercise equipment with huge, bleached smiles, while a shrill woman delights in its 'life-changing' benefits.

It takes me a long time to get to sleep, and when I do there's no relief – I sleep shallowly, trapped in an entangled maze of dreams: long, dark stretches of bush, branches tearing at me; a dog, fangs open and reaching for my face, so vivid I can feel its breath. I swirl out of range of the jaws, but the grin follows me, like some kind of feral Cheshire cat. I stumble through doors into empty rooms, but none offers shelter because always, behind me, there is something lurking, though no matter how often I spin round, I cannot catch sight of it. My neck prickles with exposure. I am alone in the impenetrable dark, and all around me are teeth, and doors that swing open behind me or closed in front. Over it all presides the canine grin. It lights the air around it and... I break free from the image of a skeletal hand, elongated fingernails shredding a blue straw hat, and rise to wakefulness, not quite sure if it is an escape. Outside, the mist is unusually quiet, its shrieking reduced to a kind of mesmerising chant, somehow more unsettling than its howls. There will be no more sleep for me tonight.

From the front of the house floats the sound of low moaning. I pad from the bedroom in bare feet and peer into the lounge, where Alex, sitting upright, has lain her head back on the top of the couch and is gasping, her face greenish with sweat. In one hand she is clutching the bucket she used earlier to clean Gina's mess, and the room smells of vomit. Gina is awake with her ears high; she gives the slightest of whimpers when she sees me, and raises and lowers a paw as if instructing me to be quiet.

I return with water and a damp towel. Gently, I ease the bucket from Alex's grasp and wipe her face, starting from her brow. Her eyes open – she is not asleep, just exhausted, caught in the grip of something beyond my comprehension. She groans lightly at the touch of the towel and her eyes close again. I carefully wipe her mouth, then slide my hand under her hair and lift her head to wipe the back of her neck. She moans again, but it is softer this time, as if in relief. I lay her head down again, then lift her arms in turn and wipe them down, finishing by pressing both her hands between the wet towel, and squeezing her fingers through it. A part of me feels guilty at the pleasure I take from this soothing; it reminds me of Julie as a child, tiny and whimpering with the fever of measles. I would sit beside her, keeping her subdued and cool in the same way, in the time when her fevers were only physical, and damp towels and gentleness were enough.

I empty Alex's bucket and rinse it out in the laundry. When I return with strong, hot tea she is quieter, lying against the back of the couch as if drained. She looks as if she has been washed up on an ocean shore, left sprawled by the waves. She gives me a soft, very weak smile.

The worst is over. Outside the crooning is dying down, overwhelmed now by commercials for furniture outlets and soap operas. The curtains are starting to glow with early morning light – I move to the corner of the room and kill the TV.

We sit sipping our tea in the gathering silence, the time of day once full of the chorus of birds greeting the dawn.

Alex closes her eyes again and gives a long sigh. 'Thank God you found me,' she says. 'It would have shredded me out there.' I start at her choice of words, evoking the image of the blue hat torn to pieces. There is a sense that my dream was a shared vision, but this awareness comes shrouded with a disturbing sense of trespass, intrusion.

'You look like you had a rough night.' She shakes her head and raises her hand to her hair. Her pendant hangs crookedly from one collarbone. 'Is it always like that?'

'Actually, no – I have to admit that last night was worse than usual, much more intense.'

'That was me,' she says quietly, matter-of-factly. 'It got in through me – I was channelling it. I just couldn't seem to shut it out. Did you have dreams?'

My face is an admission. She lets her head fall back again. 'It can't physically get through the barriers of the house, but I was a psychic opening, it got in that way. Were your dreams bad?'

'Worst I think I've ever had.'

'Anything coherent?'

I shrug. 'Not really. More like collage, just disjointed images.'

'Write them down, remember as much of them as you can. It's very important, don't dismiss anything as random.'

I'm taken aback by her energy as she says this. 'You dreamt too.'

She winces. 'Not in the true sense.' She is draining of colour again. 'Unfortunately, I was awake the whole time.' Without warning she throws off her blanket and stumbles from the room. I watch the outside light filtering through the curtained windows and listen to the sound of her retching over the kitchen sink.

*

I'm sitting outside on the porch watching Gina shuffle around the trunks of the acacias by the front fence when Alex emerges, smelling of my shampoo. She is drowning in one of my T-shirts. I hadn't acknowledged before how small she is. As she lowers herself onto the step beside me, I'm disconcerted by the scents of the shampoo and the clean shirt – unnerving to smell yourself on another person. It's been a very long time since I experienced such an intimate sensation; it's strangely disorientating.

Alex has a bit more colour, but still looks ill. Her eyes are faded within dark pits, and when I pass her a coffee cup her hands quiver. The colour has leeched from her lips, as though it has drained into the deep lines etched around her mouth. She winces when I offer her the tobacco.

The autumn sun has reached the porch, although it is still too early for it to contain much warmth. Still, its touch is comforting, and the gentle breeze enlivens the morning's stillness. Sometimes I think I'll never get used to the absent birds.

Beside me Alex watches a clutch of clouds unravel overhead, sipping at her coffee with distraction.

'It's amazing how peaceful it seems now,' she says. 'As if last night was just some kind of awful dream. It's like waking up sober after a big night.'

'It takes a while to get used to,' I tell her, 'like seasickness, the lurch between the days and the nights. It used to be like this all the time.' I wave my hand to indicate the sunlight dappling through the dancing leaves, the dog with her nose in a small shrub – a conjuror presenting his revelation: *Behold!*

But before us is the abandoned Land Cruiser, skewed where I'd stalled it, doors still hanging open to commemorate our undignified flight the evening before.

Behind us in the house the phone rings. Three times, stops.

It's Milly, worried. Li rang her this morning and said I'd taken off without a word or my supplies. She'd waited till dark for me to return with the truck, then when she phoned I'd sounded demented and wouldn't talk. She hadn't rung Milly last night in case she'd risk going out in the dark to check on me. I tell her I had a pretty close call but I'm okay. Her voice is breathy with relief.

'Bloody men,' she says. 'You all think you're invincible.'

'Unassailable,' I say.

'Ridiculous!'

'Deluded.'

She's chuckling. She was obviously pretty frightened by Li's call. I tell her she's cooking tonight, I'll bring Li and maybe one other round later.

'One other? A visitor? You're entertaining? How decadent!'

I'm feeling better now; Milly always restores me. She is the sort of person who keeps you in perspective, with her subdued manner that belies an intoxicating vein of wryness. She's the sort of person who would have made jokes to her classes in Latin, which they would never understand, yet they would remember her with nostalgia as their funniest teacher.

I bait her now, refusing to tell her anything. She becomes dignified and crafty, trying to hook me with casual mentions of scones, perhaps a banana cake?

I hang up grinning and return to the porch. 'That was Milly.'

Alex turns to me, her face ashen like a death shroud. 'I know.'

*

I can't persuade Alex to stay on and recover, or even to come and meet Milly and Li. All the torment she endured during the night seems to have reclaimed her since Milly's call, and her movements are slight and careful, as if any motion causes her pain. She refuses to tell me anything.

When we arrive at the dam her car is undisturbed, parked under the stand of gums by the picnic table and the defunct barbie, her bags still piled in the back seat. Her battery is flat; it's a small matter to jump-start it. While it charges we wander towards the rim of the dam.

'I don't like the idea of you leaving today,' I tell her. 'You look bloody awful, truth be told.'

'Thanks very much.' Her smile doesn't reach her eyes. 'I'll only go as far as Woodford, I'll get a room there for a night or two. I couldn't spend another night here.'

'You sound like Liz.'

That pulls her up. 'I am Liz,' she says obscurely. 'I know now what she went through. She looked outside, towards it, and it got her. It got to her through her kids, through

96

what mattered to her. I lived through something similar last night.'

We have reached the picnic table by the water's edge, and she lowers herself onto its bench in the careful manner of an old woman. As always, I expect a crow to flop purposefully onto the ground from the gums, eyes greedy for an opportunity. It's funny how the absence of things so familiar that they seem inconsequential can make a whole scene wrong.

Alex's stranded look is back, as though she's spent the night at sea fighting to stay afloat, and is now sprawled on the deck of morning without the energy for anything more than recognition of her survival. But she insists on leaving. I have no choice.

I offer her my tobacco and she shakes her head. I feel like a cop about to interview a witness, which gives me pause; it's not the approach I wish to take. But Alex steps into the delay herself.

'Promise me you'll get out of here.'

'I hope so. One day.'

'Not one day. One day will be too late.' She will not look at me.

'Tell me.'

She scrapes at a bubble of old paint on the table. 'There's not much I can tell you, really. It was all very jumbled, chaotic.'

'But you said you were an opening? You actually experienced the mist?'

'To a degree. It got into the peripheral parts of my psyche – it's hard to explain. I had to keep it shut out of my essence, so to speak, or I wouldn't be here now. That's what was such a struggle, like wrestling with an octopus. God, it all sounds so flaky.' She reaches for the tobacco, then puts it down again with a wince. 'It was more like a long, disjointed dream. It's difficult to interpret straight off.'

'But did you get any idea about what it is, where it's coming from?'

'To a degree.' She shivers. 'Not really. I've never come across anything like this before. I think, though, that it's human.'

'Human?'

'In a sense. It seems to be made up of human nature. It's hard to explain because I don't really understand it myself. You know how elderly people can start behaving oddly when they lose their marbles – vicars' wives start flashing their knickers, or old men who have been perfectly harmless all their lives suddenly start getting sleazy? The part of their brain that restrained them, socially, breaks down in dementia, and they become uninhibited, uncontrollable. That's the impression I have of what's here – it's human nature unfettered, unrestrained.'

'Jesus. Like this?'

Alex shrugs. 'I'm not a philosopher. But I've seen into a lot of minds and there are always – no matter how admirable the person – closed-off areas, dark corners. The old cliché of skeletons in the closet. It's all very Freudian, but who's to say that these Pandora's boxes aren't our true selves, that our visible personalities aren't just social veneer? Look at the world at large and tell me that humans live for virtue, compassion and the common good. The old saying "It's only wrong if you get caught" pretty much sums it up.'

'So you're saying that the mist is a result of our corruption? Like a by-product?'

'Look, I don't know, I really don't. But you said the area that brought those men here was a scene of bloodshed, slaughter over a claim – greed. The men were anonymous, formal, unseeing. Removed.' Her brow is furrowed; she squints into the morning sun, which beams down on us comfort and warmth.

'Look, I'm guessing. What I went through last night was a sequence of foulness, it was like evil, pure and simple. Cruelty, and delight in cruelty. Have you ever seen that Goya print, *The Sleep of Reason Produces Monsters*? It's as though what tormented him, led him to create that powerful image, is loose here, from the same pool.'

I knew the picture well. Gina and I first met at a gallery. We'd both aspired to be creative in a previous life.

'But Goya was deaf and going mad, surely his demons were private?'

'How can you be sure? He lived through a pretty turbulent part of human history.' She bends to pick up a spray of gum leaves, then twirls it as if spinning her thoughts into some kind of order. 'You know, last night I saw what Liz had experienced, her kids devouring their brother alive. And while it seems so extreme, that type of thing can be traced back to antiquity, through our whole history, our belief systems. Mythology, religion – stories of cannibalism and torture abound. And the present, too – the things that are being done to children in parts of Africa, incomprehensible cruelty. It's all there in our daily existence, but for us it's always been at a remove.'

Beside us, the true depth of the dam is concealed by the reflections of the sky and the trees veneered onto its surface by the morning light. The surface of the water is tormented by the growing wind; the reflections career out of shape, warp and distort.

Alex kneels down and dips her spray of leaves into the dam.

'There are places where psychic energy is high, areas on certain junctions of landmasses. The Grampians in Victoria are one – there're always lots of UFO sightings there.' She catches my look. 'Don't be like that. UFOs are unidentified, that's all. "Unidentified" means unrecognised, not non-existent.' She stands and turns back towards the car. 'But there are places, too, where something terrible has happened, where the energy from the trauma has stayed on. The classic haunted-house syndrome. Am I losing you?'

She isn't. It's bewildering, none of it adequately explained, but in a strange way it all makes sense.

Her car's engine has been running smoothly for nearly ten minutes. I switch it off, then restart it: it fires instantly, the battery restored. The drive to Woodford should have it fully charged. 'I wish you'd come and talk to Milly, just for an hour. It would be a great help.'

Her reaction is surprising, her 'No!' vehement. I step away from her car door. She pauses to wind down the window. On the dashboard is a piece of paper with my address and phone number, with instructions to ring three times first. She turns back to me.

'Thank you, one last time. I owe you.'

'Just send me back my T-shirt – it's one of my favourites.' Her smile almost reaches her eyes this time.

'And if you could tell us anything at all…'

Her smile is instantly gone, and she looks at me with that unnerving stare of hers, the penetrative gaze from the night before.

'One thing I can tell you, without doubt, is that you have to get away.' She reaches and grasps my hand. 'By solstice. But promise me you won't wait till then. Please. If you're not out by then it'll be too late. It's the only thing I know for certain.'

*

At home, I regret not insisting that I escort her to Woodford. I can only hope that she will be okay. She has promised to ring as soon as she gets to the motel.

The house reeks of cigarette smoke. The first thing I do is throw open the doors and windows, before sitting outside in the fresh air to light one up. The air around me seems to hum with absence now; strange how less than ten hours of acquaintance can leave such a void. It's the isolation of my existence – any contact, however minimal, assumes importance. So that now my home suddenly seems empty, the couch pointedly uninhabited and the kitchen vacant. The cups left to drain on the sink assume a ridiculous poignancy, a sentimental still life of loss. I put them away, out of sight.

I understand now how raw the silence of Rolf's last days must have seemed. To have that sudden, unexpected intimacy, to have youth and the suggestion of family roll into the twilight of a solitary life, and then to be left behind, the empty house next door like a shrine. Only the sound of his breathing to accompany him through the long hours; the companionship of children's laughter replaced by encroaching weeds.

I hadn't realised before that I was lonely.

The pain is back in my stomach again. I massage it ineffectively with one hand and stroke Gina's ears with the other. I need to get back into shape, start looking after myself.

I need, as they say, to get a life. It's just over eight weeks till the winter solstice, now known, à la Alex, as D-day. I haven't got a hope of persuading Milly and Li to leave all that they have left within eight weeks. So if Alex knows what she's talking about – and it seemed the one thing that she was sure of – I'm effectively screwed.

One day at a time. For now I need a beer. I stir myself off the porch and go in search of my car keys, Alex's final word to me floating in my wake like the remnants of a bad dream. Four tiny letters, barely a sigh of a word, but with the same terrible essence of threat as something unknown standing behind you in the dark.

Soon.

PART
THREE

I decide to leave the car at home and jog to town to collect Li's truck, much to Gina's delight. She trots patiently alongside my stumbling gait, veering off on random scent trails with her tongue lolling.

I'm in far worse shape than I thought, and I'm wheezing, barely able to breathe, when I finally reach the truck. It's time to seriously consider giving up the fags. I flop onto the kerb, propped with my head on my knees for a minute, until my heartbeat's finally less outlandish, and then I give in and subside onto my back on the overgrown nature strip and gasp. It's a shameful spectacle. There are some advantages to an empty town.

Above me the clouds merge to form creatures both known and fantastical, and I wonder how many years – decades? – it's been since I just lay on my back and enjoyed their show. It's been so long now since I've credited anything from nature with innocence.

It doesn't take long for thoughts like these to seep into the surroundings, and under their influence the benign puffs of cloud start to seethe and transform. One that had been merely fluff, holding all the threat of a woolly poodle, suddenly tears at one end, adding to its form a gaping wound, shards of cloud along its edges jagged like teeth. The others swirl around it as if dancing in mockery.

My dream. It's time to go. I'm already thinking about a cigarette.

Li is sitting on her steps after a morning's pruning when I chug the truck in. There is a trace of anxiety in her eyes, but she looks rested now. While I load my supplies onto the back of the truck, explaining my rush of the day before, she makes egg sandwiches and we eat them on the porch steps, watching the dogs wrestle happily. Soon it will be too cold to sit outside, our confinement will be almost total.

The house doesn't seem as empty when she drops me back home, and I'm surrounded by my bags of shopping. I offer to come and collect her later, chauffeur her to Milly's, but she laughs and slaps her hand on the driver's door of the truck, saying she'll come in the piece of crap. I am not surprised or offended by this; it is part of Li's character that she will always choose independence over comfort. As she drives away, she is singing to Blackie, who runs in excited circles on the truck tray. His barks echo into the quiet afternoon.

*

Milly comes good on the promise of scones, but I don't have the appetite to do them justice. She's disappointed when I turn up unaccompanied, curious to meet my visitor. She listens without comment to my account of the night before, only raising an eyebrow when I mention Alex's claim of clairvoyance.

'You believed her?'

'I did, actually.'

'Interesting. I'd have liked to meet her. She must have been a convincing woman.'

'She was.'

I reach for another scone in an effort to avoid Milly's eyes. I don't want to tell her just how convincing Alex had been. She had rung me that afternoon, just after I'd finished unpacking my supplies, to say she was at the motel in Woodford and was feeling much stronger. She apologised for leaving so precipitously but – and here her voice had become firm, as if she'd reached some kind of resolution, a path that can't be avoided – she hadn't felt strong enough to face meeting the woman who would be the cause of my death.

The scone on my plate is still slightly warm, and the butter melts into it appealingly. Milly smiles at me. 'Great comfort food,' she says.

*

I've known Milly for twenty years or so, although for my first three years in Nebulah only on a professional basis. She and her husband Gavin had moved to the area as newlyweds in the late sixties: they bought five acres and built themselves their small house surrounded by bush and unkempt gardens. Milly taught at the local high school, and Gavin was a social worker attached to the shire. I'd met them over the Russell boys, semi-wild local kids who preferred stealing cars to sitting in classrooms. The youngest was eleven.

Milly and Gavin were idealists, but grounded too – while prepared to do their best, they were capable of recognising a lost cause when they saw one. The Russell clan moved to Perth anyway, always one step ahead of state revenue, not long after I arrived in town. It was a relief all round to see them go, even though it would be the end of the boys, who would be doomed to sink out of reach within the extended depths of the city.

I'd had a couple of late afternoon beers out at Milly and Gavin's, largely due to the Russell question, and had always been impressed by their no-nonsense manner – amused cynicism rather than airy-fairy notions. Yet they were also the type to do anything they could to genuinely help. Their house remained free of the pandemonium of children, but they were the sort of childless couple who end up surrounded by strays: cats, dogs, a one-legged crow, and for a while an imbecilic goat.

Milly was always reserved and calm, but Gavin was a more volcanic personality. He used to erupt into peals of barking laughter, the kind of surprisingly distinct laugh – always at full volume – that would set everyone around off as well. They were a self-contained couple; to be around them and see them laugh together was to feel exposed to the ideal and rare state of marriage: of minds truly delighting in each other's company.

I'd known them casually for a few years: I'd often run into Milly outside the IGA, laden with sacks of pet food, or the two of them bravely clutching plastic cups of woeful wine at community functions. Then I'd had to pay Milly the worst of official visits. A truck had lost control on a bend just south of Woodford; Gavin had been coming the other way when its trailer jackknifed and swiped him, crushing his car between it and the tree it ploughed him into.

News of the accident had electrified the town. Witnesses were kept from the scene, so speculation was rife. Milly hadn't been at all worried when she saw me turn into their drive; Gavin was attending a council meeting in Woodford, but was supposed to be staying on for a counter meal with some colleagues, so she wasn't expecting him back till later that night. She had no idea the dinner had been called off, and gave a wave from the clothes line, assuming I was looking for Gavin to help with a grieving family.

I was struck at the time by her composure, this almost gangly woman who tended to hunch into herself the way that tall girls who stand out for their height often do. She was quiet in the face of my news, and retained her calm even as the air around her reverberated with pain. I remember being awed at the time by the extremes in play – her terrible grief tornado-ing around us, and the remarkable self-control she maintained in its eye. The only physical response she gave to my news was that she appeared, noticeably, to shrink. It was as though she'd developed a leak and was slowly but visibly deflating. She thanked me when I said I'd already formally identified the body, and was dignified in the face of my clumsy condolences. She refused my offer of a lift to a friend's, saying she needed to feed the animals and would prefer some time alone at home to get her thoughts together. When I drove away she was hunched on her porch steps, distractedly stroking an ugly ginger cat that had wrestled its way onto her lap.

Much later she told me that her composure was simply the result of a lifetime of the emotional restraint necessary for survival in the classroom, and that once I'd left she pressed her bare forearm to the electric hotplate – the only way she could find to ground the emotional turmoil. Her grief was so intense it had been two days before she could breathe normally again.

In all the years I've known her, I have only seen Milly lose her balance once, when she collapsed under the strain of the horror of Gavin's reappearance, in the first nights of the mist.

*

Death is a hollowing experience. The intellectual turbulence of grief is an external assault, as every part of the life you drag yourself through reflects the isolation of your future existence. But at least Gavin's death had been natural – as tragic as it was, it had been an accident, and mercifully swift. The sort of death that can eventually be lived with, accepted, as the dripping intake of time slowly fills the void of the lost one. To have him returned, though, like some horrible monkey's paw from a moral fable, to be set upon by the mist every night, was more than the strongest mind could endure. In the face of Gavin's nightly pleas to her to come outside and help him, Milly caved in, her reserve rupturing like the crust of the earth when the pressure from below is too great to contain.

Those terrible nights were defining for us. Milly's collapse was too profound, too confronting for the remaining Nebulah inhabitants to cope with. Although most of them were sympathetic, the situation was too disturbing for them, an internal combustion that simply couldn't be endured given the external pressures we were under. Some, like Gail, simply lacked the basic human qualities of empathy and compassion, and disguised these shortcomings by attacking Milly, distorting their own callousness by insisting that what was in their own best interests was also in hers. They wanted her hospitalised.

We splintered. Milly and I had become close in the years since Gavin's death, my initially dutiful visits becoming, in the face of shared interests and stimulating conversation, frequent and founded on friendship. When I was diagnosed with cancer – which softened my daughter's hostility towards me but in no way dispersed it – it was Milly who nursed me through the treatment and my shameful moods; who kept Julie 'informed' of the situation – as she demanded – but placidly gave her to understand that her attitude was neither helpful nor endearing. I overheard one of these phone calls and I would have hated to have been on the receiving end of Milly's tone, which was perfectly calm in the way that crushing weights often are when they're in slow, gentle motion. She wasn't rude, but she made it clear that Julie's absence was far more beneficial than her presence. There was no way I would ever have considered having this intelligent, kind and incorrigibly funny woman locked away.

Li joined us. She had always been a loner of sorts, but not a hermit in the sense that Rolf had been. She was what is commonly termed in a small population a 'character', an aloof and focused woman with no time or respect for the usual female interests. Her humour therefore tended to be unexpected, which made it – and her – seem unpredictable. She and Milly were compatible by temperament, with the sort of unselfconscious nonconformity that was often labelled eccentricity. Li was a small person with an incredible backbone, which had supported her through her flight from the massacres of Cambodia, carrying nothing but a battered photo of her husband and two sons, who hadn't managed to escape the sanctioned atrocities of the Khmer Rouge.

Li never spoke of her lost family, or of the horrors she had witnessed before she managed to get out, or of the ironies of her subsequent persecution in Australia, as both an Asian and a refugee. These experiences fused into an insistence on survival that enabled her to establish and run her own farm singlehandedly, and saw her face the manifestation of the mist, so similar in many ways to what she had already lived through, with a fierce determination not to be forced to flee again.

Between the two of us we managed to get Milly through. I had some stashes of old sleeping pills left from the time of my treatment (and, I'll admit, some antidepressants – I've never been a good invalid), which I'd stockpiled for the obvious reason, and these I administered indiscriminately: getting Milly through those excruciating nights took precedent over any other consideration.

The tablets made the nights endurable, and over the course of time, as we talked and reasoned, our shared, although disparate, experiences of loss and survival forged a bond that gave Milly the fortitude to withstand Gavin's nightly entreaties. But while she recognised that the manifestation outside was only a ghoulish chimera and not really Gavin, who'd been cremated all those years ago, there was always a small but insistent doubt. As Nebulah was Gavin's final resting place, there was always the chance that he was trapped within this travesty of a peaceful afterlife, and this possibility made her determined never to forsake him, even if it meant seeing out her days in the apocalyptic wasteland of what used to be our home.

So there you go. Li refuses to leave and Milly is unable to leave, and none of us would go without the others. I could never just leave them here. I'm not flattering myself when I acknowledge how vital my contribution is to our survival.

But harder to acknowledge is the real, unavoidable difference between us. Milly and Li are determined not to be driven from this place which is entwined with their souls, whereas I, quite simply, have nowhere else to go.

*

Dinner is a surprisingly jolly affair; under the circumstances we could do with some release. Li arrives with a hibiscus flower tucked behind her ear and two bottles of John Barry's homemade feijoa wine. Milly has cooked a huge vegetable pie, with garlic bread and a trifle, and she overpowers the din of our nightly serenade with The Rolling Stones, turned up high. The wine is strong, and we shrug off the night bellowing the guitar riffs as well as the lyrics. We respond to the week's crises in a typically human way, erupting into reckless abandon once the worst is over. We may have lost Rolf, but we're alive, and I'm giddy with this after my close scrape the night before. I'm a middle-aged, scrawny Keith Richards in an Australian small-town kitchen, and I force Alex's warning into a far corner of my mind and bolt the door.

Later that night it creeps out, though, as these things do. It squirms around the corner of my barrier to drag across my mind's dream landscape: a tangle of snaking tendrils, mocking as they crawl towards me. They cluster together, entwining themselves to form a figure, human but bereft of features, just emptiness where there should be a face. As this looms before me, there is bulging movement and a sickening sound, and eyes split through the expanse of skin: Alex's green eyes, glaring from the blank mask, probing and piercing. I am frozen, riveted by the intensity of that gaze, whose intrusion into my psyche is becoming unbearable, when there is another awful tear, and the lower part of the face yawns open into Milly's mouth, hissing at me, '*Soon…*'

before raising its hands, fingernails extended like talons. My blood spatters the awful face, spilling from the gaping mouth as it shrieks with laughter.

Awake and trembling I pour glass after glass of water at Milly's sink, but I can't get rid of the foul taste in my mouth.

*

The morning is hard. We slump unenthusiastically over bowls of Weetbix, all subdued from the aftershocks of the feijoa wine. My dream clings to me like a shroud, and beneath it I feel drained and weak. In the mirror my face is haggard, unkempt, my eyes red and disturbed.

'I look like a madman,' I say to Milly.

She takes the scissors to me, longish silver tufts floating to the kitchen floor to surround us like a fairy circle. There was a time when this sort of thing would only have been done outside, but these days we're superstitious, wary of leaving any part of ourselves outdoors.

Li has not stayed to see the results of my transformation, leaving us shortly after breakfast to get to work. Tomorrow I will help her harvest apples.

My haircut is an improvement, but there is still a feral tinge to me.

At home I discover my razor is clogged and almost useless, but there's enough edge to scrape off the worst of my neglect. I have a long, hot shower, and cram every item of clothing I possess into the washing machine.

It's when I'm on my knees in the laundry, trying to

117

locate the long-lost iron in the back of the cupboard, that I begin to wonder what I'm trying to achieve. Some kind of resistance – denial? An attempt at control and order, as if this can keep Alex's threat at bay? It will take far more than a shiny surface, shaving cream and scissors to ward off the legacy of my dreams.

I change into tracksuit pants and runners, and Gina and I hit the road.

It's good. I'm quickly winded, but fighting against my unfitness gives me a sense of determination that makes me feel strong even while my legs are buckling and my breathing ragged. I concentrate on the rhythm of my feet, try to tune my breath in to it, but in my chest my heart betrays the truth, pounding a wild, desperate staccato. I turn back sooner than I'd intended, recognising the reality of my physical condition and accepting the long, slow process that I'm facing.

*

The next morning I'm shamefully stiff. I don't even make yesterday's distance. At home I shower briefly and change into work clothes. When I leave for Li's I take only the lunch I have made us, carefully leaving my tobacco on the kitchen mantle.

Li is already towing a full crate in from the orchard when I arrive. We eat my unimaginative sandwiches and Milly's leftover scones, and crunch into some of the freshly picked Braeburns.

'They're good,' I say through a mouthful, 'sweet.'

Li nods. Unlike me she has quartered her apple, neatly coring it and chewing it thoughtfully and methodically. 'Good crop this year,' she answers. 'Didn't even have to net.'

'Every cloud has a silver lining.'

'It does. By the way, you look very spruce.'

'Milly should go into business.'

'You should have female visitors more often. Good effect on you.'

'Certainly an effect.' I've told Li only the bones of Alex's stay.

'A shame she left so soon.'

'It's not a very welcoming environment. Hardly a holiday destination.'

'True.' Li is gently herding her crumbs into a pile, which she brushes onto her plate. 'True,' she says again.

'Do you think you'll ever change your mind about getting out?' I ask.

She looks up. 'No, not really.' She shrugs. 'Maybe.'

'Would you?'

She sighs, looks away from me toward her shadehouses, the grape's leaves just starting to turn with the cooler weather. 'No,' she says. 'Everything I have is here. If I have to walk away it'll be with nothing.'

'You'd be alive.'

'I'm alive now. Strange as this may sound, at least I know I'm safe here. I lock my doors and it can't touch me. I'm not going to be driven away when it's possible to survive. To give up everything I've worked for means my life will have been wasted.'

Twined with the fine crow's feet around her eyes is the unsaid, inescapable: *Again.*

A sudden glare of sun breaks through the drifting cloud. 'What if you won lotto?'

She laughs, incredulously. 'Then, again, all my work will have been wasted.'

She flings the crumbs from her plate onto the ground. We pull on our caps and head over to the tractor. Li turns to me as she fires it up.

'And I suppose I'd need a ticket.'

*

Once we've filled three more crates, Li wants to stop, reluctant to pick more till the co-op gets in touch with an order for the following week. She doesn't think they'll want more than three crates. We've just manoeuvred the tractor into the shed when her mobile rings.

'Yes, he's here,' she says, 'hang on.'

It's Stick. There is an edge of irritation in his voice and sounds of a commotion.

'Do you reckon you could come over to Tom's?' he says. 'Gail's had a bit of a fall.'

'Bad?'

'Hard to say with her. She's carrying on. Could be a broken hip, though.'

It's after four o'clock and they got their supplies the day

before yesterday. Tom will be more than half sloshed by now. There is no way St John's would dispatch to Nebulah this close to dark unless it was a real emergency. 'Can't you drive her to Woodford?' I ask Stick.

'Been here since lunch. Over the limit.'

'Shit.'

'Sorry, mate.' He's not. He's only too pleased to handball it to me, concluding his contribution with a phone call. There's only a couple of hours of daylight left. I think with longing of the beer I was about to open and reach for my car keys instead.

*

When I get to Tom's I'm greeted by a fiasco. Gail had lost her balance carrying a load of washing from the line, straining her ankle and landing on her hip on the edge of a concrete step. Tom is bleary and useless, incapable of doing anything more than doling out a couple of Panadol. Gail is still lying on the path where she fell, disheveled and streaked with tears, and obviously in considerable pain. At least Stick had the sense to take her some cushions.

When she sees me she starts crying anew, but refuses to let me lift her skirt to examine her hip. Her ankle is swollen and already a violent purple.

There is no way we can leave her in that state till morning, and no way we'll be able to lift her into the Land Cruiser. I manoeuvre their Honda as close to her as possible, and Stick and I lift her, as gently and as swiftly as we can, into the back seat. She screams and gasps, punctuating her sobs with such phrases as 'You have no idea'. It is going to be a long drive.

And it's nearly five o'clock. We don't have much time. I tell Tom to get a blanket and some overnight things for Gail. He'll need some too. He blanches.

'Don't think for a minute you're not coming,' I tell him. He stumbles towards the house. I leave Stick with Gail and go after him. Sure enough, he is at the sink, pouring bourbon.

'You've got two minutes,' I say, 'or I'll leave her here.'

He looks sheepish, but downs the drink in one swallow before staggering in the direction of the bedroom. I stand at the door barking at him: bag, nightdress, toothbrush. He is hopeless. As we head for the door he veers away to the kitchen, cramming the half-empty bottle into the overnight bag.

At the car Gail is a little more subdued through lack of an audience. Stick is leaning against the bonnet, surly, his eyes hooded and red. He is unshaven and looks as if he hasn't seen soap for a few days. He's obviously going to wait till I'm off the scene before he drives home. Not that drink-driving is of much consequence in Nebulah these days.

Gail is a woman of no resilience. She whimpers and cries out with every bend of the road, every touch of the brake. When I point out to her the darkening sky and the need to clear Nebulah as soon as possible, she starts to keen. By the time we're safely out of town my nerves are shot. Beside me Tom is a useless blob, slumped and remote. When we pull up at the small emergency department of Woodford Hospital, just over three hours later, I'm wrung out and exhausted.

When Gail has been manoeuvred onto a stretcher and wheeled away, I park the car and then pocket the keys. I wouldn't put it past Tom to bugger off the next morning and leave me in Woodford. There's a phone by the hospital entrance. I ring the motel, but Alex has already left and there is some kind of car club meet passing through town – they're fully booked. I ring Sean. He says he'll meet me in a pub nearby sometime after nine.

I put one last call through to Milly, tell her what's happened and say I'll ring her in the morning to see if there's anything they want picked up in Woodford. She's concerned about Gail, but more sympathetic towards me. In the background I can hear Neil Young crooning. I wish I was there.

It's only a ten-minute walk to the pub and I find myself wishing it were longer, it's such a novelty being out after dark. But it's getting chilly and I'm still in my old work clothes, and I don't want to risk being too late for a feed. And I am, just: the kitchen closed ten minutes ago. Luckily a table of late orders means they're still cooking, and the barmaid is Sally, a plump and jolly woman whose ample bust adorned the front bar of the Nebulah Tavern for many years, till the mist moved her to Woodford. She winks and says they'll rustle me up a chicken schnitzel no worries, before pulling me a much-needed pint of Guinness. Earl is doing a stint as publican out at Meekatharra, she tells me. His hair has never grown back, though.

The pool players call for another round and she

sashays off to pour shots of Jim Beam and refill jugs. I try to remember the last time I ate out at night, or was even out for a drink. It's disorienting, being suddenly launched into a normal, public life again. I'm glad of my sudden decision to groom yesterday morning, but I mourn the whim that made me leave my tobacco at home. I try briefly to persuade myself that this is a good opportunity, but quickly descend into self-serving congratulation about how virtuous I've been, rushing Gail to hospital – I've soon convinced myself that I have both earned and deserve the reward of a cigarette. The cigarette machine beckons the way I imagine a poker machine calls to a gambler.

The tailor-made cigarettes are putrid; they crackle with chemicals like party sparklers and burn up within a few puffs. But my schnitzel comes piled with chips and salad – there is something to be said for ordering at the close of service. I have a second Guinness, then a third and a fourth with Sean when he arrives. Again I am glad of my haircut and shave, he looks relieved when he sees me and offers no further lectures on my health.

When we get to his place he produces a single malt left from his birthday, and the night wears on as we discuss the ridiculous amount of annual leave he is owed, and his need for a holiday. Rachael is fretting, talking about refitting bathrooms and installing a new kitchen, so he's planning a trip to Queensland to see some family, to distract her.

'God,' he grunts as he tops our glasses, again. 'I hate renovating.'

The next morning Sean is on a later shift, which is just as well, with both of us more than a little bleary at the breakfast table. Rachael has already left for an early meeting. Next to the depleted whiskey bottle there's an amused and sardonic note about the tidal effects of my company. I'm glad to have missed her, though: still in my work clothes of the day before, I feel grotty and on the nose.

Still, at least I'd had a bed, unlike Tom, who was forced to try and doze on the uncomfortable-looking chair next to Gail's bed, deprived of his bourbon, which a nurse sternly confiscated. When I arrive, late morning, they'd had the X-ray results and Gail's hip is indeed badly broken. They'll be keeping her in for several days. She has taken to the role of invalid with great enthusiasm and natural talent. Tom's keen to get away. I arrange to pick him up in an hour and leave him to receive instructions about visiting hours and lists of toiletry and wardrobe requirements.

I ring Milly again from the public phone. She is grim – the Barrys called Li that morning with their final order. The bank has refused to refinance them, even for the short term, and they'll be closing the co-op at the end of the month. They'll take one more delivery next week, but it will be the last. Li is okay; the Barrys recommended a possible outlet in Mandurah, but it all depends on the cost of freight. Milly has to come to Woodford on Friday for a doctor's appointment, and will do the weekly supply and post run then, but asks for some milk.

I buy the extra milk and some bread, and add a box of

the particular Swiss chocolates that are Li's guilty pleasure. A bleak future is a pretty good excuse for an indulgent present.

While I'm at the shops I decide to swing by the co-op and offer condolences. Already it seems dusty, the stands of fresh produce peculiarly altered by the imposition of a deadline. The cheery murals appear frozen, as if aware they are soon to be shut away.

The Barrys are reeling. John is convinced there is a secret agenda working against them; he keeps his back resolutely turned away from his shelves of stock, transformed by a single phone call from a business to a failed dream.

'We only needed to hold on till the new subdivision was established – another year, tops, would have been enough. We'd have more than recovered.'

'We'd been planning to add a nursery section out the back, with a little cafe,' adds Evelyn. Her eyes are red, she looks as if she hasn't slept for a week.

'We've been nutting it out with Suzanne O'Neil for months. Her kids are at school now and she was going to take on the cafe. Nothing major, just cakes and coffee. She was really keen, she's been experimenting with gluten-free brownies for weeks.' I shudder. 'We'd have been able to employ someone as well.'

'Local employment only matters if you want to destroy something,' I say, probably not helping.

John's face is bitter. 'Yeah, you're not wrong.'

'Did they offer any hope? Advice?'

'Come off it. Apparently our "rationalisations" aren't

cost-effective enough. As if a friggin bank knows anything about sourcing organic produce, edible food. But there you go. Computer says no and we're down the gurgler.'

'Will you stay in town?'

'Nah, doubt it. What would we do, get jobs at the IGA? Nup, time to regroup. Evelyn's brother has a banana plantation in northern Queensland, biodynamics. We might think about setting up something along those lines, somewhere new. It'll take time to get back on our feet, though.'

I compliment John on his winemaking, and suggest it as a potential new direction. He chuckles, rallying briefly. 'Yeah, that batch turned out okay. Reckon we're gonna be needing it over the next few weeks.'

'After two bottles I thought I was Keith Richards.'

'Christ! That's a scary thought. I'll give you another bottle before you go – might be enough for an Eric Clapton.'

I'm the driver on the trip back to Nebulah; Tom's eyes are too red and his hands too unsteady. He'd demanded his bourbon back from the nursing staff, and swigs openly from it on the journey, abandoning all pretence. With bad grace I invite him to join us that night, and with obvious relief he accepts. I pray Gail doesn't draw out her convalescence.

*

I've often been struck by the cruel indifference of nature, how it casually refuses to correspond to our moods and circumstances. Bad news can be accompanied by the most stunning weather, like being thumped with a perfumed glove. And then, if you manage to convince yourself that the glorious sunshine is a gift, a reminder of all that life still has to offer, the next setback is accompanied by the most oppressive of skies, clouds of disapproval and ill-will, to disperse any breath of optimism. Sometimes it's hard not to believe that it's intentional rather than random. Or is that just me?

I can still remember leaving the doctor's surgery all those years ago, reeling from his grimly professional prognosis. I stumbled out of the clinically sterile reception area with what seemed like the dead weight of my own corpse on my back, only to stagger outside into brilliant spring sunshine. Even the trees seemed to hum with the joy of being alive. There were tiny honeyeaters flitting between a grevillea laden with delicate flowers and a birdbath on the lawn, and their speed and their song, the energy and life they embodied seemed, in the face of my diagnosis, some kind of malicious joke.

The days following the Barrys' news are of a similar hue. The sun bursts through the morning dew: nature's equivalent of unbridled laughter. As evening falls the air fills with scent, the bush responding to the unseasonal warmth. The fragrance floats through the dusk to dissipate at our closed doors, locked with even more resentment than usual.

I had lent Li the Land Cruiser and she, wasting no time, filled it with boxes of sample potatoes and apples and drove off on missions to Mandurah – fruitlessly, to risk a pun. The only possible distribution outfit refused to cover freight costs for what seemed to them insignificant consignments, and offered such small returns for her produce she would actually lose money. The supermarkets were contracted to suppliers already. A cafe was interested, but the quantities involved were so limited it wouldn't be worth Li's time or petrol. Not to mention the unavoidable expense of replacing the truck.

In the unseasonal weather her trees shine with health, already laden with a record yield of glowing, unwanted apples. I sometimes think that if there is a God, then she is a sour bitch.

*

Li's crop isn't the only one thriving in the generous weather. I stumble across Stick's as I'm foraging for firewood in the bush down behind Evans's old place. It's less than 200 metres from the old farm's crumbling back fence.

This crop is much, much bigger than the one I was already aware of. Evidently our lethargic Stick has a work ethic after all. I estimate there's easily several hundred plants nestled into a scrubby boundary, a nicely hidden copse. I would judge it to be dangerously close to the main road out of town – which is a shrewd bluff – and a considered distance from Stick's own place. Due to the overgrown surroundings, despite its vicinity to the road, it's quite a remote spot; it is only by chance that I come across it.

The plants reach towards the mottled sunshine, their pruned branches eloquent in the morning silence.

At first I keep Gina back, keen not to leave any trace of disturbance that would alert Stick to our intrusion. But I soon relinquish these worries – what the hell. In my pocket is the remains of the packet of Winfields from the pub. I light one up and keep exploring.

It's a huge crop, way beyond the menial challenge of keeping the Woodford back bar deadbeats in pot. The plants have been pruned rather than harvested – evidently his technique is to concentrate on the valuable heads alone, rather than risk trying to transport entire plants when he's confined to daylight hours.

The cuts are still green, recent. It's unlikely that he'll have had time to dry and dispose of the yield. A light breeze stirs the surrounding bush and the sunlight starts to dance. The whole scene is utterly peaceful, Eden-like, fertile and forbidden. I think of Li's apples withering on her trees. Stick will have no trouble selling his produce.

This is a God-forsaken place.

*

I don't think I've been out to Stick's more than a handful of times. He lives just beyond the town's sealed roads, down one of those long dirt driveways that look as though they lead only to an archetypal Australian bush clearing, strewn with the remains of long-cold fires, littered with half-burned debris and faded aluminium cans. His small fibro house is hidden from the road, on the opposite side of town to his gardening efforts.

It's an uninviting place, even without the demented Elvis's blood-curdling greeting. The house doesn't nestle, in the way that bush-enclosed dwellings usually tend to do; instead it echoes Stick's presence, hunched and hooded, unremarkable yet vaguely disturbing. While not unkempt or neglected, it epitomises disengagement – a small vegie garden is purely utilitarian and somehow unappetising, and the uneven strands of clothes line sag with age, the framework rotting from lack of paint. His trips to the tip are obviously sporadic.

There's no sign of Stick or his Patrol when I pull in. I make no attempt to conceal Li's truck and take a perfunctory stroll around the house. Its vacancy is somehow malevolent; it's as though the house has its own gaze, its emptiness seems to seethe with scheming. Even though I'm sure Stick isn't here, I find myself unwilling to turn my back on it.

By the clothes line round the back is a faded timber shed, the kind legendary for hoards of dried-up old paint tins, rats' nests of shredded paper and huge cocoons of dusty cobwebs. It looks disused, its windows blockaded with junk, but beneath the rusty bolt on its door hangs an expensive, new bronze padlock.

I turn back to the house. Every window is closed and every curtain drawn; I imagine the stale air trapped inside, the time-layered stench of unwashed clothes, smoke and dog. It would smell like Stick himself.

The windows are all locked, and the back door is padlocked with the twin of the lock on the shed. The front door is an outdated commission-house special, its four horizontal panels of ridged glass opaque with dust. There is only a standard circular Yale lock. It is an open invitation; he might as well have left the door open. I reach for my wallet.

But I've already changed my mind and put away my ATM card when I hear the approaching grind of Stick's gearbox. It's not that I'm worried about being caught, it's more that I'm suddenly overwhelmed with inertia, a sense of pointlessness that sees me turn my back on the house with all its dull sordidness. I retreat down the porch steps and slump against its concrete edge. There is no sense in breaking into Stick's, he's way too cluey to have the haul in there, and I find the thought of entering his house vaguely abhorrent. I've been in so many houses like this, closed and stale, with the threads of corruption concealed but still so evident that they cling to you like cobwebs. The effect of their crawling touch coats you for days. You become steeped in them, in a cynicism that congeals into disgust, and eventually taints your very humanity. I've seen people who live in this atmosphere, faces sallow from years of contact with the webs, as if mummified, their only visible emotion a predictable mix of animal cunning and fear.

Plain and simple, I just don't want to go in there. The old copper urge I succumbed to at Rolf's is conspicuously absent here. I can't face being exposed to it all again. I've digested and accepted my reluctance when Stick pulls in beside the truck. Gina sits bolt upright in the cab.

Elvis starts going berserk in Stick's back seat. Stick closes the car door on the dog, keeping its frenzy contained. He is nonchalant as he approaches me, but his eyes are sharp and alert. I see him immediately note the Winfield packet in my shirt pocket.

'Pete,' he says with a nod. 'You're a long way from home.'

'Sure am,' I agree mildly. 'Firewood mission.' Stick's eyes flash to Li's truck, with the chainsaw and a motley pile of branches.

'Yeah, should be thinking bout that meself. Getting on to that time.'

His eyes keep darting back to the cigarette packet. I pull it from my pocket and offer him one.

We use our own lighters, his old black Bic struggling to achieve more than a spark. When he manages a dull flare he draws deeply. His eyes are hooded. 'I see you found me farm,' he says. His eyes glance at Gina still at attention in the truck and he flicks his ash. 'Dog turd. Winnie butt. Didn't know you smoked tailors, couldn't think whose it was.'

'Cigarette machine at the pub in Woodford. No choice.'

He nods, understanding. We smoke. After a minute's silence he straightens and grinds his butt. 'So, you here for a friendly cup of tea?'

I shrug. 'Where's the harvest?'

He guffaws. 'Not here. Fuck!'

'I want it.'

'Bet you do.'

'I destroy it, I keep my mouth closed.'

Stick scratches his stubble. I try not to notice the flakes of skin. His expression is closed.

'It's the best I can offer you,' I tell him.

When he laughs he sounds disturbingly like his dog. 'Okay,' he says, 'here's the deal.'

'I don't deal.'

'That's your word. Me, I tell your bluebottle mates you've been in on it for months, keepin quiet for a cut. Only you get too greedy and when I won't give, you suddenly up and shop me, like a good ex-cop. Everyone knows you're always prowlin round, keepin tabs. You can plead innocence till your arse is raw, but Joe Public loves a bent cop.'

'Baby talk, mate. Telly crap.'

'Yeah, well, it's easy, in't it? Keep your mouth shut and we're both safe.'

'We could've been. But you're a dickhead, Stick, if you think you can stand over me. You've just issued your own arrest warrant.'

I leave him leaning against his dingy porch. He's still slumped as before, a cowboy, seemingly unperturbed, but his shoulders are set in a way that belies the tension in them.

'Drop round any time, mate!' he calls as I walk to the truck. 'Door's always open.'

I look back over the bonnet. 'See you soon,' I tell him.

Thankfully the truck starts first go. I keep my fingers loose on the steering wheel and the gear stick, but I cannot unclench my teeth. It's as if I've got them clamped around Stick's scrawny bloody throat.

At home I sink a beer in two swigs. I ring Milly, ask to ride with her into Woodford the next day.

*

Milly picks me up early. I swing an esky into the back of her ute. Gina leaps up beside Felix, and the two dogs immediately cram their noses into each other's bums, tails wagging with delight. On the floor in the cab are a spill of library books, a thermos and a packet of Tim Tams. I hadn't joined Milly and Li the night before, saying I'd had a shit of a day and was going to turn in early. Milly's used to my moods, and she greets my battered morning-after face as if it's all she expected.

'Sleep well?'

'Need to restock the liquor cabinet,' I tell her. 'Already.'

'Thought that might be the case.'

'I'm on a health kick, you know.'

'It's obviously doing you the world of good.'

I burrow my head into my jacket collar, trying to keep it as immobile as possible.

'Anything up?' says Milly. 'You've seemed distracted lately. Since your visitor.'

'Gloomy,' I tell her, keeping my eyes closed. Alex's *Soon* wafts in my head in time with its throbbing. A tiny word but immensely weighty when pondered at length. Was it advice, warning, threat, instruction? I badly want to talk it over with Milly, but I couldn't give her such an undeserved burden. I have to be responsible for my own decisions; she does not ask me to stay here with her. She owes me nothing.

I've decided not to tell her about Stick's little enterprise, either. He's proving to be a vindictive little sod; it's safer if she's not involved in any way. I realise, though, how much I rely on talking things over with her, how sane it keeps me. Without her I feel closed in and closed up. Aside from all its other possibilities, *Soon* is also a very effective barrier.

Milly's looking at me sideways. 'Well, you've already found the primary cure for gloom. Next step's in the glove box.'

I open one eye. 'Shotgun?'

'Panadol.' She pauses. 'Shotgun's under the seat if you'd prefer it.' She doesn't meet my gaze. 'I borrowed Li's. I don't know why, really. Just… I don't know.'

She shrugs as if it's nothing, but it isn't. Milly is the only one of us who refuses to keep a gun with her. Li keeps hers in a locked built-in case behind the seats of the truck, and mine lives in one concealed under the spare wheel in my boot. Even Tom and Gail have a handgun, although Tom at the trigger would be more dangerous than anything they could possibly face. What we could ever need these guns for is unacknowledged, and Milly's refusal to consider owning one steadfast. For her to have taken the step of borrowing Li's is worryingly out of character.

I cough. 'It's only a doctor's appointment. I'm sure he'll renew your prescription without persuasion.'

She sniffs. 'Bloody quack that he is. It's not loaded, anyway.'

*

The Panadol does the trick. By the time we've been on the road an hour I'm feeling vaguely human again. As we

136

approach the rest area eighty kilometres along the highway – our usual stop when we venture to town – Milly asks if I'm ready for coffee.

I'm ravenous. I hold up the Tim Tam packet as she digs out cups. 'No scones?' I say, feigning outrage.

She grimaces. 'Joints've been bad.' I notice that her skin is pallid, her eyes tired, and curse my self-absorption.

The rest area is strewn with rubbish from torn bags. Crows wail from branches above the overflowing bins. The dogs are off into the debris before we even have our doors closed.

Caffeine and sugar complete my restoration, but the weak early sunshine makes me lethargic. I light a cigarette and close my eyes. Milly flings the dregs of her coffee on the ground and stretches like a cat. 'That's better,' she murmurs for us both.

I open my eyes. There is colour in her face again.

'Want me to drive from now?'

'How's your blood alcohol level?'

'Reduced.'

'Legal?'

'Acceptable.'

'Accepted.'

With an effort she hoists herself from the concrete picnic bench. Her movements are small and careful, and she is stooped, limping slightly. But once she's completed the slow manoeuvre of getting upright she raises her fingers to her mouth, and with a consummate skill that would have any schoolboy in awe, emits a piercing whistle. There is crashing in the scrub nearby and Felix appears at a run, Gina close behind him. They launch themselves onto the back of the ute, excited and panting.

Milly turns back to me. 'With gratitude,' she adds regally.

*

We're in Woodford in good time, and manage to get most things done before Milly's eleven o'clock appointment. It's much easier when there's two of you, and the shopping's been reduced by almost half, with Tom and Gail out of the loop. (The carers' unit at the hospital found temporary accommodation for Tom in a hostel nearby.) And Stick was out of the equation; I was buggered if I was going to be running errands for him.

I drop Milly at the surgery and arrange to pick her up in an hour, calculating a forty-five-minute wait and a ten-minute consultation. At Woodford police station I don't allow myself to pause or reconsider. Stick's time is up. When I peer over the counter without ringing the buzzer I disturb Denham, who is reading a *Men's Health* magazine with his feet on the desk. I've just missed Sean. Denham doesn't expect him back before lunch. He's put out at being caught skiving.

'Is it important?' His hostile emphasis on the word gets my back up.

'Yes,' I tell him, 'so I guess it'll have to wait till Sean gets back. Tell him I'll be back later.' I let my gaze fall to his magazine, its headline *The Metrosexual Issue!*, before pointedly turning my back.

Milly's already filled her prescription when I meet her, and is ready for lunch. At the pub we curl over soup and garlic bread, then toss a coin and share cheesecake instead of sticky date pudding. There aren't many diners, and the room is cosy with subdued chat, bursts of laughter. The normality of it makes me ache. I could stay all afternoon, every day. We both know our unavoidable curfew though, inescapable, like a mental tattoo. We need to be on the road by two.

With reluctant sighs we leave this comfort zone and head to the hospital; we still have time to do the right thing and visit Gail. At least, needing to catch Sean, I'll be able to escape quickly, much to Milly's annoyance.

But when we arrive at Gail's bed a dour Greek woman is propped in front of a grating American sitcom. A nurse tells us Gail has been moved to another ward, adds that we won't be able to see her unless we're immediate family, but won't tell us anything further. In the foyer we run into Tom, who is hurrying from the opposite direction looking distracted – at first not even recognising us. He tells us Gail has picked up some kind of infection, the kind that hospitals specialise in for culling their elderly patients, and she is about to be transferred to Royal Perth. Support services have arranged accommodation in Perth for Tom for the duration, and are canvassing for a nursing home unit for them both once she's recovered. It's unlikely she will ever regain her former mobility, and it's still unknown how badly the infection will affect her nervous system. Tom perks up visibly as he fills us in. He's just heading home to collect what they will need for the immediate future; their things will be sent on later. He's leaving for Perth tomorrow.

'I have to say, it's a pretty good outcome really,' he says of his wife's grave condition. 'I can't see how else we would ever have gotten out of the bloody place. You just can't live like that.' He thrusts out his hand to me, insists on giving Milly an affectionate peck on the cheek. 'I guess it's up to you and Stick to look after the girls now,' he says to me, and never have I wanted to punch that smug red face as much as I do that moment.

'What an arsehole,' says Milly, out in the car park. 'If he'd known an accident would get them out he'd have thrown Gail down the stairs himself.' She frowns at her car keys. 'I suppose, when you think about it, they were just burdens really. At least Stick's vaguely useful and he can look after himself.'

My headache's coming back, with a piercing jackhammer thump. Milly checks her watch. 'You going to see Sean?' she asks.

'No.' I let the dogs out of the car for a stretch. 'Not now. Let's just get back.'

Before we leave town I jog across to the newsagent's. And even though I know it's naff, I rub the Buddha's belly as I buy Li a lotto ticket.

*

At the Caltex on the outskirts of Woodford we refuel and decide to shout ourselves ice-creams, even after our cheesecake. I personally need all the sugar I can get. We sit at the plastic tables outside, where trails of ants are colonising pools of spilt soft drink. Milly seems thoughtful as she bites into her Golden Gaytime. She sighs.

'And?' I ask.

'I was just thinking that we're going to be in for an even rougher time now. We're dwindling. Four seems such a vulnerable number.'

'Most likely three. I wouldn't count on Stick.'

'Oh,' says Milly. 'Crap.'

'I need to do some weighing up.'

'Do I want to know?'

'No.'

A small child on a bike has stopped by the ute and is trying to get the dogs' attention. They glance down their snouts, aloof, pretending they can't see him. If he'd been holding a packet of chips he'd have been their god.

'If we're down to three,' I say to Milly, 'it'll be impossible for us to stay. You know that. Even four's a huge risk. I think we really need to start making plans to get out.'

'To where?'

I screw my ice-cream wrapper round the stick. 'Anywhere. We could get a caravan, become Grey Nomads. Join the throng.'

'I'm too old and you're not grey enough.'

'Balls.'

'I could be your mother. And I'm practically a cripple.'

'You're not and you're not.'

'What about the dogs?'

'They'd love it. Chasing roos.'

'And Li?'

'Caravans are big these days.'

Milly looks at me, her eyes glittering. 'You'd have to give up smoking.'

'Harsh.'

'Essential.'

'Unnecessary.'

'Mandatory.'

'Then if that's all it takes, consider it done,' I say. 'Too easy.'

'Come off it! All those retirees with their Happy Hours and CV radios.'

'CBs.'

'I'd hate it. So would you.'

'All right, drop that one then. We could get a place, though – with the three of us we'd manage.'

Milly is still smiling, but when she sees that I'm not she subsides, the ground suddenly unsteady beneath her. I keep my eyes on her face; she keeps hers lowered.

The breeze is starting to get up. I reach out for her hand. We never touch.

'Consider it?' I ask.

Milly's lips barely move. 'I couldn't. I'd never cope with leaving, knowing he's still trapped there.' Her voice is like crumbled ashes. 'I mean it when I say I'll be dying there.'

That's it, then. Standing, I aim my ice-cream wrapper at the bin and resist the urge to answer her: in that case, it seems I will be too.

*

I had thoughts of leaving once. This was when there were more of us still trying to hang in there, hoping it would blow over.

My ex-wife, Gina's namesake, had decided to drop her All-Men-Are-Bastards facade, largely because she'd met one who was keen. But Julie, my daughter, wasn't. At all. Terry was a house painter with artistic leanings. Gina had met him at her CAE watercolour class. He wore big gold rings and shiny shirts, and had an unattractive inflated chin, like a comic book superhero. He liked to play it camp, in a seventies sitcom kind of way, which like the chin and the bad shirts was not endearing. Julie didn't like the way he joked with the boys, and his habit of raising his unfortunate chin and grinning at people over it put you in mind of Luna Park. Leering, she called it.

Suddenly, it was important for me to have a role in my grandsons' lives. This realisation coincided with Gina's announcement that Terry was taking her to Tasmania for Christmas, to meet his family and paint.

I must admit I was reluctant. I hadn't seen Julie since she'd visited me in hospital after the tumour was removed. It had been an uncomfortable reunion, for both of us. I was in a fair amount of discomfort after the surgery, which embarrassed me, and she, defensive and brisk in a manner that warned not to expect any kind of reconciliation, took my winces and occasional groans as deliberate attempts to disconcert her and extract pity. She hardened every time I closed my eyes or fumbled for my water glass, her gaze like concrete towards the end. She'd been suckled for so long on Gina's determined bitterness, her spirit was as sour as her mother's.

At least her mother had the excuse of mental imbalance.

Julie had expected me to be overjoyed at the offer of spending Christmas in Sydney with family. She took my hesitation as financial, and impatiently offered to pay for half my fuel. I felt cornered. I came close to saying no (resentment, after all, works both ways), but hope is such a distorting aspect of human nature. This was an opportunity – the first *real* one, I told myself – to reconnect with my daughter and establish a relationship with her family. What twenty years' estrangement, a cancer diagnosis, and my high-risk living conditions had failed to do, Christmas in Sydney would be sure to achieve. As I said, hope is malicious. Blinding.

I don't think I can pinpoint with any clarity exactly when I realised that the trip was a terrible mistake; it seemed to go wrong from the very start. If I'm honest, I can admit that I knew I was wasting my time before I'd even left home: I remember how heavy my bags seemed as I carried them to the car, and the temptation to just lug them back inside and pull the curtains till the new year was almost overwhelming.

But misgivings, no matter how well grounded in fact, are easily dispelled (or ignored, at any rate) by the temptations of hope. In my mind's eye there was a ridiculous *Brady Bunch* scene of happy families: Julie realising that whatever had happened between her parents shouldn't poison her, and that she wanted her father, who wasn't a bad bloke after all, to be a part of her life. I had images of playing cards with the boys, who were overjoyed at their grandfather's company, welcoming me as the antithesis of their unctuous merchant banker father. Grandad would never, of course, stoop to encouraging them to criticise their father, just allow a small, loaded chuckle whenever they used my pet nickname for him. The Toad.

Of course they came up with that name themselves.

Ridiculous scenarios, shameful in hindsight, and even though I recognised this at the time, somehow they persisted until I was across the Nullarbor and it was too late to consider turning back.

Of course it was the mist that put these ideas into my head. The thought of being rescued, of *deserving* to be rescued, as if the same force that created such mayhem must also be responsible for justice. As if some presiding entity would recognise that it had to uphold a balance and would point a long, divine finger my way and say, 'Well, there is a flawed but fundamentally good man who has suffered enough. Deliver him.' And with three taps of the little red shoes on my size 9 feet and the chant of an appropriate platitude (*There's no place like home!*) I would be transported from the cyclonic hell that had been foisted on my life, into a family scenario of love and comfort, laughter and kindness in the mist-free, sophisticated suburbs of Sydney.

So great is our egotism. As if *I* should be any different to someone trapped in a war zone or caught in the impersonal brutality of a natural disaster. Only fairytales offer us justice (and you'd think as an ex-cop I'd know that intrinsically): good people restored and the villains dying a foul and excruciating death. So unsatisfying when the baddies simply repent and are forgiven, getting off scot-free. Better that Cinderella's stepmother is forced to dance to her death in iron shoes heated with burning coals – red shoes always the instrument of deliverance.

'Deserve' is an interesting word, really, the seven-letter equivalent of a grasping hand. As if all of us Good People who haven't *deserved* the calamities that have befallen us wouldn't snatch at those little red shoes we're convinced are ours by divine right, whether it be by driving across the Nullarbor at Christmas or, in more desperate situations, pulling ourselves to safety using the bodies of others.

*

Things went wrong from the word go, of course. I knew as soon as I saw the house – a large boxlike concrete thing, with pebbles for a front yard and rose bushes mangled into balls on sticks like leafy confectionary – that this wasn't going to work.

I'd swagged it on the long drive over, nights on the side of the road with camp fires and limited water. I should have thought to go somewhere first to clean up, shower and shave. It was stupid of me to think that they'd welcome my arrival, after all this time, in any dishevelled state. That they'd laughingly point me in the direction of the shower and the washing machine, just glad to see me. I'd been free of the city too long.

The contempt on their faces was mortifying. James, the youngest, actually held his nose when I shook his hand. They didn't reprimand him. I don't know what Julie was mortified by most – my state after a week of roadside camping, or the discovery that I had Gina with me.

'I can't believe you brought your dog!' She tried to establish an unconvincing air of amused exasperation, yanking vertical blinds aside and flinging open an enormous ranch sliding door. Beyond it, a manicured shoebox masqueraded as a yard. 'She'll have to stay tied up, we can't have her destroying the garden.' The 'garden' comprised concrete borders and uniform shrubs in wincingly straight lines. Julie began to gather up the cushions from an enormous, uncomfortable-looking outdoor setting.

'She'll be all right, she's a good dog.' Gina didn't look like a good dog, though: her ears were flat and she was clearly distressed by the unaccustomed walls around the yard.

'Mum,' intoned Lachlan (the boys were hovering at the back door, alert to their mother's precariously heightened mood), 'why is the dog named after Grandma?'

Needless to say, dinner was strained.

Christmas Day was marginally better, with everyone more settled and making an effort, and Julie determined to be the perfect hostess. She frowned when I declined to accompany them to church, saying I'd take The Dog (I was forbidden to call her Gina) for a walk, but didn't press the issue beyond pointing out that I should be concerned with being a good role model to the boys.

I loitered outside in the 'garden', having a smoke and waiting for them to go. Julie's heels clattered round the house like artillery and the boys squabbled and whined.

'No,' I heard her say to them, 'Grandad doesn't have to come to church, but you do.'

'Is that because he's dirty?' asked Lachlan, all innocence. There weren't going to be any card games.

There were no pubs open on Christmas Day. I swiped a couple of Todd's expensive imported beers and took Gina to the park. Large family groups picnicked around me, mainly Europeans, laughing and playing. I watched them enjoying each other, their harmoniousness, each person a part of the whole, and wondered for the hundredth time what I thought I was trying to achieve. For their part, they kept a wary eye on me, this scruffy solitary man loitering in the park with his dog and his beer, carefully monitoring my proximity to their kids. I wished them a merry Christmas and the greeting was returned, but it was clear I made them uncomfortable. I decided to call it a day.

Things were more relaxed when they got home from church, duty done, appearances maintained. Their shiny surfaces could be allowed to dull from the showroom polish, a bit of grime allowed back into the crevices. The boys raced for the TV and Todd strayed off to doze over the *Financial Times*. Julie kicked off her heels and unclasped the string of pearls around her neck.

'Phew,' she sighed. 'Tea?'

I was about to accept when she reeled suddenly. 'Actually, stuff tea. It's Christmas, bugger the yardarm. I'm going to have a glass of wine. Do you want one?'

'Yeah, I'll join you,' I said carefully.

And so it came that instead of announcing my intention to shoot through ('It's been nice and all that, but…'), I ended up perched in Julie's kitchen, peeling spuds and listening, while she crammed a sun-dried tomato concoction into a turkey's orifices and told me about her life. Or what accounted for a life: the boys' school fees (Todd insisted on sending them to the most expensive of the private boys' schools, feeling the social contacts they would make there would ultimately justify the expense); how Lachlan didn't like rugby, which was a shame as the school was very big on it, but at least he didn't mind cricket, and both boys enjoyed golf. Etcetera.

She'd opened a second bottle of wine by the time she got round to Terry, his sleaziness and distressing chin.

I didn't know what she wanted from me. Julie had clothed herself in Gina's grievances, real and fabricated, and withheld herself from me for nearly twenty years. After all the blame and recrimination I'd had dumped on me over the course of those decades, I was buggered if I was going to sit and chat about my ex-wife's love life over a glass of riesling. I was not accountable for Terry.

I refused to be drawn.

The turkey was ready, small bright parcels of tinfoil wrapped around the knuckles of the drumsticks where its feet would have been.

'You know,' said Julie, as she turned from the oven.

But the boys' DVD had finished and they burst into the kitchen demanding to know when the presents would be opened. The flint look that had been in Julie's eye when she'd turned from the trussed turkey was chased away by the reminder that it was Christmas. And, as in all good fairytales, Christmas is a time for Happy Families.

'Yes, okay, let's open presents.' She topped up our glasses. 'Go and wake Daddy.'

But I felt like I'd already had my present: the stone that had been about to be flung had been dropped. For now it could stay on the ground.

I stuffed up the gifts too, of course. I barely knew the boys; had only, in fact, met them once, when they were very small children, barely more than infants. Woodford's retail opportunities are pretty limited, and I hadn't had time to chase anything up on the way over. The $20 notes I'd shoved into Christmas cards for the boys were woefully inadequate; turned out their pocket money was $50 a week. They recited their thankyous with eyes cast down; Grandpa's stocks were declining rapidly. Todd exclaimed with an amused smirk over the bottle of Johnnie Walker Black Label I'd forked out for, and pointedly added it to the expensively overstocked shelves of his bar, which had the Christmas tree erected beside it for maximum effect.

But Julie looked startled at the perfume when she unwrapped it. For once, Gail's inflated tastes had been useful.

And, I will admit, I was taken aback at my own present. A bread machine. Whether they realised it or not, it was perfect, about the most useful thing I could have been given. No more buying bread in bulk on weekly town trips and doling it out from the freezer. I was touched by the thoughtfulness of it. I hate frozen bread. For the first time since my arrival, I felt like maybe, after all, there was a chance.

Dinner was late – Todd had to make the Christmas call to his parents on the Gold Coast. They had declined the invitation to join the family, preferring their annual ritual of dinner at their club. I took Gina for a walk; when I got back everything was ready: a ceremonious masterpiece, with crackers at each place, and two bottles of very impressive champagne, of which the boys were allowed to partake. Candles glowed at intervals along the table, their flames reflected off the polished surfaces around us.

Julie had the glass doors open; the evening breeze was light and refreshing, making the candle flames dance a little drunkenly. I remarked how pleasant it was to have doors open to the evening, to a twilight breeze.

James looked at me. 'Grandpa, is it true you live in a haunted house?'

'James, behave,' warned his father.

Behave? I thought. *He's asking me about my life.* 'Yes, it's true. Only it's the town that's haunted, not my house.'

'Shall we say grace?' interrupted Julie.

'Yes.' Todd manoeuvred his napkin below his belly. 'I think that would be more appropriate. We don't want to be giving the boys nightmares.' He gave me what he obviously considered to be a pointed look. Even his eyelids were bloated.

When the family raised their eyes from the amens, Todd held the carving knife aloft while Julie whipped off the turkey's tiny tinfoil shoes and crushed them deftly. I found myself clinging to the stem of my wineglass as if it were a life raft.

*

Boxing Day was D-day, as I tend to think of it now. No, I should be more exact: D-day is how I think of it when I can't avoid it, otherwise I do my best to forget it completely. If only I'd stuck to my original intention of heading off early, instead of being lulled by chatter over bottles of wine.

The day began badly, with champagne and port heads all round – we'd all crammed ourselves with rich food and then drunk too much over Christmas dinner. Boxing Day should traditionally be spent in bed, or at the cricket nursing gentle beers. But Julie and Todd were of the social set that like to think of themselves as 'hosts' and are into making 'occasions' – the year before they'd had people over for a Boxing Day barbecue, and now felt it had been a significant enough event to establish as an annual institution. They were obligated, Julie's cross preparations in the kitchen asserted; people expected it from them, as if they were some kind of social royalty. Look how they suffered for their generosity. All these *guests*. The dishwasher clanged shut.

I tried to take myself off for the day, but it seemed my presence was required, no doubt as some kind of public show of Julie's magnanimity: Exhibit 1: Errant father, unforgivable husband, neglectful grandfather, freeloading on his daughter's good graces. *Ah, she's a saint, that one. And he even brought his bloody dog! Would you believe the old bugger's cheek?*

Maybe it was just me, a dose of paranoia in unfamiliar surroundings. But I don't think so, I've been a cop for too long – you learn to read just about everything you need to know from someone's face when they greet you. People often don't realise that thought processes are tangible. From the involuntary shift of the eyes, it's instantly apparent who has something to hide, who will be studied with their use of the truth. When each of Julie's guests chanted graciously 'Nice to meet you', their eyes told me that they already knew all there was to know about me, and what was nice about meeting me was having their curiosity sated. They could now elucidate opinions on me, justified because based on first-hand knowledge: *I came, I critiqued. I decided.* I would be hung, drawn and quartered with delight over many a mid-morning latte.

You can probably tell I don't get out much anymore.

There were six guests in all. The first to arrive were two middle-aged couples; the men were associates of Todd's, already soft and nondescript. They feigned jolliness under their receding hairlines and teeth squared from grinding, their fattening necks in polo collars. All belied the realities of life in the commercial sector. Their wives wore bright, barbecue-appropriate colours, and veneered their viciousness with lipsticks in pink and amber.

The last couple was younger, and obviously new to the proceedings. They sported gym-buffed physiques, and wore their fitness like an expensive brand; it was evident from the envious faces of the others that they judged this to be ostentatious and crude. The older women tried to dismiss the younger one's slimness, averting their eyes from her toned arms, and casually splaying fingers encased with expensive rings, pushing hair aside to expose bland but expensive gold earrings.

The younger couple were too inexperienced and pleased with themselves to recognise their social gaffes – they lost points for leaving their young children with family instead of bringing them to mingle with the boys, and they evidently didn't appreciate just how grateful they should be for their invitation. They were too casual, too accepting of their inclusion; it was obvious that this would cost them dearly.

Just another friendly barbecue in the right suburb.

I began to long for the enforced solitude of Nebulah. I wanted a cigarette, but felt this would mark me out further. I was fairly certain that only the lower classes smoked these days; the rich clogged the roads with bicycles and ate expensive, low-GI food like blueberries and Asian greens.

I glanced at Gina, who echoed my feelings physically:

flattened forlornly on the lawn, where she'd been chained as far as possible from the 'patio' area. A compromise – I'd refused to lock her in the car for the day.

Bottles of wine were being conjured from cooler bags and eskies with great ceremony. There was an unacknowledged but strict etiquette to this – the wine had to be impressive but only quietly expensive. A flagrantly pricey bottle was a faux pas, a sign of trying too hard. The correct form was something expensive but unusual, preferentially purchased directly from the cellar door, with connotations of picturesque valleys, sunsets and, naturally, limited production.

My own contribution, two New Zealand whites in the $15 to $20 range from the drive-in, screamed inadequacy. Julie hid them away in the fridge 'to keep cool'. When Todd asked me what I'd like to drink I asked for beer, something I could gulp. But I was handed a tall thin stubby, with a slice of lemon wedged in its neck.

I decided to have a smoke after all, and took Gina out the front to desecrate the nature strip. The Land Cruiser, muddy and battered, was like a sore thumb, surrounded by spotless bus-sized 4WDs, showroom shiny.

It was the sight of these vehicles, oversized, expensive and pointless, dwarfing the street, that made me face reality at last. While I'd known all along that any hopes of escaping to here were ludicrous, it was these people, with their pecking orders and their ridiculous cars, that made me accept that coming here, even simply as a way out, would not be an escape.

So in hindsight, a lot of what followed was down to me.

The surrender of my delusions made me cynical and socially reckless. I felt I had nothing to prove to these people – they could take me as I was or not at all. No games. No effort. Not the best of attitudes.

When I got back to the kitchen, the gathering had moved outside; the cushions had been restored to the over-sized outdoor setting, the kind whose chairs are so heavy it is impossible to manoeuvre them, and women usually end up perched at their uncomfortable edges, trying to eat from plates three feet away.

I took another beer (sans lemon) and settled on a concrete garden edge nearby. The conversation was, predictably enough, about property values. One of the polo shirts – Colin, I think his name was – had already refilled his glass. He turned to me.

'So, Peter,' he began, evidently thinking himself a social pioneer for his efforts, 'I understand you're from the famous Nebulah.'

'Famous for all the right reasons.'

There was a general stir: curiosity, but reluctance to initiate a conversation on a subject where someone else could be an authority. But then these days, everyone who watches TV is an authority on everything.

'You actually *live* there?' said the younger woman.

'Some people do,' I answered.

'But isn't it dangerous? Haven't people gone missing?'

'Yes.'

A bowl of Asian rice snacks was passed down the table.

'But aren't you… worried?' She couldn't bring herself to say 'frightened'.

'Worried?' I resisted the urge to tell her that worry was for people whose lives depended on interest rates. 'It's terrifying. But as long as we stay inside after dark, and keep the doors locked, we seem to be safe.'

There was an incredulous silence. 'I hear it's bikies,' announced another wife, digging her glossy nails into the snack bowl.

I scoffed. Feathers ruffled.

The woman's husband was a natural authority. 'Danni's brother,' he asserted, nodding towards his wife, 'is a reporter with the *Herald Sun*. He has close connections with the CID, and I mean top shelf. He says that rival gangs are trying to clear the area for a drug war.'

'What a load of bollocks.' I say it quietly, but the effect is the same.

'Dad,' muttered Julie.

'I live there!'

'What's your explanation, then?' asked the younger woman.

And then I felt stupid, knowing how bad it would sound. 'I don't know exactly,' I hedged. 'I guess traditionally you'd call it ghosts.'

There was indulgent laughter from the couple with the well-connected brother.

'Oh, right,' he burst. 'Far more credible!'

'I believe *Four Corners* did a story on the place to

that effect,' chipped in Colin. 'But there was no proof, no footage or anything. Just some frankly unconvincing locals screaming for compensation.' He coloured, coughed. 'Pardon me, Peter.'

The younger man, Michael, was enjoying this conversation. 'So have you seen them?' he asked me over the expanse of the table.

'Of course I have. Do you think I'd sit here and claim I live among ghosts if I hadn't seen them?'

'What do they look like?' started the unpleasant woman, with a smirk, but she was cut off by Colin.

'But could what you've seen be faked? Someone playing funny buggers, trying to scare you out? It's odd that they haven't managed to film anything. I remember the journalist who covered the story sounded a bit dubious.'

I remembered the journalist who did the story too. Not one of the bravest souls to visit us. Dubious is always a better front than cowardly.

I cleared my throat. 'I've seen people killed. I saw a living person torn limb from limb. Someone I knew. You can't fake that.'

I knew they would not like this. There was a shocked silence, tremendously awkward. It was obvious, though, that it was due to embarrassment; a comment on my sanity rather than acceptance of what I'd just said.

'Dad, that's enough,' started Julie.

'But apparently,' interrupted Danni's husband, and the others pricked up their ears, keen to see how this would be dealt with. 'They said on *Sixty Minutes* that there haven't been any bodies.'

'There aren't.' I suddenly felt worn out; I knew I could never convince these people, it was too far beyond what they were capable of coping with. They judged everything by what they were told by the media, unable to think beyond the interpretations they were served up, cooked into facts. Digestible; much more credible than an eyewitness. 'They become part of the mist. That's why they're defined as missing rather than dead.'

There were subdued mutterings about the authorities, along the lines of 'as if…'

Todd was getting irritated. This was his social event, and it wasn't the conversation he wanted at his table. 'More wine?' he boomed, gesturing at Julie, who went to fetch new bottles from the kitchen.

'It's all very *X-Files*,' said Colin's wife, who up till then had been occupied with picking the green crackers from the Asian nibblies. 'If it's as hellish as all that, why would you stay there?'

It was a staggeringly insensitive question. They waited. 'Because,' I told them, 'I have nowhere else to go.'

There was a terrible, loaded pause, then everyone leapt into an awkwardly energetic reprise of the property value conversation. The only person who didn't join the general clamour was Julie, who stood rigidly beside the table with two newly opened bottles. I did not have to look at her, I knew she was staring at me, mortified by what I had just made public knowledge. I knew she would never forgive me for it.

By the time lunch was served, I was so jagged it was hard to eat. No burnt sausages and coleslaw, but fatless marinated butterfly cuts, cooked in machines like portable kitchens, the barbecue equivalent of the cars parked outside. Large, expensive and fundamentally pointless. I looked at the flawless cut of meat on my plate and longed for something charred over a heat bead.

Julie also had little on her plate. She was clearly livid, a condition exacerbated by the fact that she had to contain herself until her guests had departed. My candidness had earned me no allies, either; my assertions about ghosts were too far out to be socially acceptable. Instead, logic dictated that I was clearly a bit of a fruitcake. If I was acknowledged at all, I was patronised, as if I were a child or some dotty old aunt out for the day. Whenever I left the room the hostile polo shirt, Doug – whose name suited him perfectly – reasserted his privileged insider knowledge, and announced with confidential gravity ('not to go further than this table') that in fact ASIO would be rounding up the culprits very shortly.

'I rather like the idea of ghosts,' said the younger woman, to general merriment.

But Julie wasn't the only one incensed at my hijack of the Boxing Day soiree. I could feel Todd's hostility pulsating around the emptying bottles. I was an embarrassment, with my cheap wine and inappropriate conversation; I'd wrecked his ambience, strained the atmosphere and insulted his generosity of spirit. He was itching to put me in my place. And unlike Julie, who was far more terrifying, he would rather dish out his comeuppance publicly.

Which didn't worry me in the slightest. My son-in-law is an idiot, the son of bingo-obsessed morons who happened to strike it lucky on the stock market. He is one of those stupid men who think that a bank account is a sign of intellect, and mistake their wealth for proof of superior intelligence. I'd never had any respect for this painfully dull man, and I was drunk and feeling unfriendly – aggressive might be a more accurate description – and I couldn't help goading him, raising him a provocative toast every time I opened another of his expensive beers.

The conversation, since my home town had become a contentious topic, revolved around money. Politics briefly reared its ugly head, but only because all these people were in agreement, and their political values were confined to purely economic policies. Inevitably the subject turned to tax.

This was Todd's specialty; his eyes gleamed. Full of largess, he casually boasted of exploited loopholes and misdirected shareholders, openly advising the others on methods for concealing assets in offshore funds. His posture changed as he recounted his own shonky dealings, as if they were entertainment, anecdotes suitable for the dinner table. He leaned back in his chair.

'But I should be more circumspect.' He swished the wine in his glass, studiously distracted as if its colour were of more significance than anything to do with money. 'My father-in-law, after all, is an ex-policeman. He might not approve of my creative accounting.'

His statement didn't have the intended effect. It had been an unsuccessful lunch all up, discordant, with Julie's self-conscious civility failing to overpower the palpable tension. They'd had enough confrontation for one day, and Todd's deliberate effort to provoke more was badly judged and inappropriate. But he is inept, and he thought he had a topic which would ostracise me further.

Even so, I was drunk and the man was a toad. 'Creative accounting,' I said to my beer, 'is the spin name for it. The correct term is stealing.'

'*Stealing?* That's a bit heavy-handed! I don't believe I'm doing anything actually outside the law – just making use of some convenient grey areas. In corporate circles it's known as enterprising.'

'In human circles it's known as immoral.'

The women started gathering up the dirty dessert dishes. Todd flushed.

'Morality and legality are separate issues. What is it they say? "It's only illegal if you get caught."'

'I must have missed that commandment. But you're the churchgoer, so you should know.'

There was a general, unspoken consensus among the guests that it was time to call it a day. They began to search for cooler bags.

I didn't bother joining the farewells out the front. While shrill thankyous were volleyed around the row of SUVs, I crammed my clothes into my bag.

The debriefing was predictably bitter. The boys, ignoring their father's orders to vacate, hung around the kitchen door with delight.

'How dare you?' bulged Todd. 'This is *my* table.'

'Christ, it certainly isn't mine.'

'Don't you dare judge us!' shrieked Julie. 'Don't you dare! Pronouncing your judgements on us in front of our guests, as though you're some kind of visiting Messiah.'

'Jesus, Julie, bugger your guests, what about your children?'

'Don't you drag my children into this!'

'Drag them in? They live here, they're exposed to everything you do. All this wank about it being all right to lie and steal because it's not technically illegal. Why don't you care about looking bad to them?'

'This has got nothing to do with them. This is about you, your behaviour.'

'My behaviour? It was your husband who proudly pronounced himself a crook and a hypocrite.'

'Oo-ooh!' chorused the boys.

'I demand you retract that!' sputtered Todd.

'Retract what? That you're instilling your family with the values of a leech? Bringing your children up to have no respect…'

Julie, in her fury at this, was divine, a Greek goddess whipped up to war.

'You, of all people, dare to criticise the way we bring up our children.' She launched a plate across the kitchen, where it shattered two wineglasses. 'We invite you to share Christmas with us and you sulk about, looking as though you're above us all, disapproving of everything. Who made you so God-given superior?'

I was taken aback at this. 'Julie…'

'And *then* you start telling us we're bad parents! The gall of you, after what I had to cope with, what you did to Mum.'

It had to come, it always did. 'Julie, that's not fair. I did my best with your mother, you know she has a mental illness. You can hardly hold me responsible for that.'

'I can and I do. You were always cruel.'

'I was never cruel!'

'You've named your bloody dog after her!'

I had to concede that point. I tried for lightheartedness. 'A little bit of misplaced irony?'

It wasn't the right tack. Another plate was launched, this one losing strength and crashing to the floor before the sink. Even Todd was looking worried by then. 'You're a pig!' she shouted at me.

I can't stand violence. It's too easy. I've seen too much of it and I hate seeing it used for effect. Julie had learnt this behaviour from her mother.

'Your mother found it easier to be a victim than to face up to her own flaws. And you've always encouraged her, the two of you conniving to make me a tyrant because it was easier than the truth.'

'The truth? She was sick, she was suffering and you were

164

never there. You just left her to cope. She needed you and you just turned your back.'

'That's not…'

'You only ever thought about yourself.'

'That is not true…'

'Then you come here and look down your nose, ignore my children and insult my husband.'

There was nothing constructive to be gained by this. I picked up my bag. 'Enjoy Terry,' I said. 'I hope he makes your mother happy.'

Another thing about these modern houses is that there's no sound insulation. As I led Gina to the car, neighbours were clustered nearby.

'She didn't like her Christmas present,' I told them with a wave.

I shouldn't have been driving but I didn't care, I needed to put as much distance between me and that suburb as I could. At Katoomba I stopped for coffee and a sandwich. Its edges were dry and unappetising, as if it had been frozen. It was only then that I realised I'd left the bread machine, that most thoughtful and appreciated of gifts, in their lounge room, among the wrapping and general Christmas debris. As if it didn't matter.

*

I drove pretty much straight through, only stopping to sleep when my head got too heavy. By the 29th I was back on my porch, swigging on a stubby. I was surprised at my sense of relief at being home again.

When I first moved here I planted a row of grevilleas along the fence by the road, and they quickly became established as home to butcherbirds. Dreadful birds, I know, killing other birds and destroying their eggs. But I'd always loved their song, their challenging eyes, telling you they own the place.

Todd had shuffled my grandsons from the room when Julie started throwing things. They'd been nowhere to be seen as I drove away. I wondered if I'd ever see them again, and was surprised at the lack of grief this thought aroused. The absence of emotion was distinct.

But even so, I still reeled from the shambles. I wondered whether I should try writing to Julie, but would have to work out first if there would really be any point, and if I cared enough to bother.

Milly had rung about four. She'd seen my car.

'How was Christmas?' I asked her.

'Pretty diabolical, Gail on a soggy dive. Yours?'

'Monumental.'

'Colossal?'

'Let's just say that worlds collided.'

'Oh. Did anyone fall off?'

'Just me. A true tumble.'

'Will you be able to remount?'

'I don't think so. Moved out of orbit now.'

Milly gave a tsk. 'Come for tea?'

My pause was only for show. 'Yes. I'd like that.'

I went inside to clean up and get ready. I was relieved

at the invitation. I hadn't wanted to sit at home with Julie's final words, hurled with as much contempt as her crockery.

'I just pity the next woman who enters your life. I hope for her sake she never needs you, because I'd stake my life that you won't be there for her!'

*

In our lives, it's words that really have the power to wound us. Everything physical, all those highly emotional or unutterably painful experiences retreat from memory, their visceral substance unable to be retained in any other way than by their translation into language. We condense their intensity into tiny capsules, the essence of existence contained within the shell of words. Hardened slugs with the potency of bullets.

And there are words that threaten the future, rather than conjure the past. Words like Alex's *Soon*, a virtual labyrinth of possibility. Or the words of Stick's casual threat – words that may prove to be powerless, or may have enough edge to them to slice through the remaining tethers to any life I still have. There was no proof behind his claims of my involvement, but sometimes that can hardly matter, the words themselves can be enough on their own. Platitudes like 'where there's smoke…' swirl around accusations, especially unsubstantiated ones. You can volley the assertion of innocence all you like, but it will never be enough to completely extinguish the smouldering coals. I could tap-dance my innocence along the main street of Woodford but, as I learnt with Julie, once words are spilled, guilt is the public domain, and innocence only a private quality.

I just don't know if I have the energy to go through with it. And on top of that, the thought that we would be reduced to just three makes my very bones ache with exhaustion. I need to think things through.

So when Sean rings that evening to follow up on my unexplained visit, I hedge, saying only that Stick was acting furtive and I thought he might be up to something. I say of course I'll keep an eye on him.

'Don't take too long,' he warns. 'As of the twelfth of May I won't give a toss. I'll be winding my way east for two beautiful months of the simple life. Fishing, swimming, Happy Hours. Rachael lazing on the beach, all thoughts of new kitchens washed away with the tide.'

'You got your leave!'

'Eight whole weeks. My brother's jacked up a place at Tin Can Bay for us all, just south of Hervey Bay. Man oh man, my bags have been packed for two days. You ever used those rubber baits?'

'Not with any joy. Who's holding the fort while you're away?'

'They're trying to get Joey Holmes from Kalgoorlie to cover. If not it'll be Denham, would you believe?'

'What about Kath? Or Davies?'

'Kath's pregnant. Her last check-up her blood pressure was way up, so she's looking at cutting back. Davies is past it, doesn't want the bother, just wants his pension.'

'Christ, Denham's barely out of nappies.'

'He's okay.' Sean is defensive; in his mind he's already reeling in barramundi and sinking beers. 'He's a bit green but he's not a fool. Well, not completely. And it's only a few weeks, for Christ's sake. I'm owed three times that. I hear you got up his nose today.'

'Both nostrils.'

'Let me guess. *Men's Health*?'

'In one. Hey, did you hear Tom and Gail are leaving us?'

'Yeah, I saw Ivy from the hospital in the Arms earlier on. Gail's pretty crook, apparently.'

'Tom's over the moon.'

'Cretin. Born for a ditch. You coming over for a drink before I head off into the sunset?'

'Should be able to make it. It's Li's last delivery on Tuesday.'

'Yeah, the Barrys reckon their doors'll be shut by the end of May. John's gutted.'

'So are we.'

Outside a distant howl rises, coyote-style. 'Gotta go, mate. Time to batten down the hatches.'

'Stay safe. I'll see you next week?'

'You will,' I reply, not realising how much weight these words would carry.

*

The weekend is largely uneventful. I try to keep a quiet eye on Stick, but he is sticking to home, aware he is in my firing line. He drove past me once when I was staggering along Pearson Street, doing my laughable imitation of a fit person, and gave me a honk, a cheeky wave.

I already know that my decision to stay quiet is wrong. I just haven't brought myself to face up to it yet.

Gina and I spend the nights at Milly's, with Li and Blackie. Milly's house is the largest, the most comfortable, set up originally as a home, shared, not a solo space. Milly and I play Scrabble quietly, while Li wrestles her BAS return for the quarter, although the receipts involved are hardly overwhelming. She is distant while we eat, remote. I realise I can't remember when I last saw her smile.

At one point Milly and I leave her with her head down over her invoices, to clear up the dishes together. Milly is thoughtful, she closes the door gently and asks if I have plans to go into Woodford any time soon.

'Probably Thursday week. Said I'd catch up with Sean. What's up?'

'It's Li's birthday the following Saturday. I was thinking we should do something special, celebrate.'

'A party?'

'The works. She needs it.'

'Party hats for three.'

She's quick. 'Not Stick?'

'Not Stick.'

She shrugs. 'Three can be a party. Exclusive.'

'Elite.'

'Refined.'

'Elegant.'

She chuckles. 'Hardly.'

I spend nearly all of Monday with Li, picking apples and loading spuds. The Barrys will take everything she can bring them, in the hope they will have enough trading days left to shift it all.

We work hard, till my back is aching. Sometimes it's just as well we have the mist to beat us inside – Li would work all night, I reckon. At four-thirty we stop for a beer. Already the days are finishing early, we have to be careful not to be caught unexpectedly.

The truck is loaded up. I've checked the oil and water, and made sure there's plenty more on board. It'll be a slow old trip, but for now at least it's the last one. So far Li's efforts in Mandurah have been pointless.

I nod towards Blackie, snuffling round the truck's wheels. 'Blackie'll miss the heap of shit.'

'Yes. I'll have to take him for drives round the farm. Otherwise he'll fret. I won't miss it, though. That constant overheating, having to sit all the time. I've been close to torching it.'

Torching it. She is such an Aussie. 'We'll have a bonfire when you get back,' I say.

She gasps. 'Blackie'd never forgive me. It's his truck.'

'Shame he can't drive.'

'He would if he could. You've seen him on the tractor.'

I grin. Blackie loves any kind of machinery, anything he can ride on. He sits in the driver's seat of the tractor as if he's a king. If he ever worked out how to turn on the ignition we'd never see him again.

It's time to go. I stretch.

'You sure there's nothing you need from town?'

'Nah, I picked up everything with Milly the other day. Actually – would you mind grabbing me some papers? I'm low.' So much for giving up the smokes. I reach for my wallet. Wedged at the front is the lotto ticket I bought her the Friday before. 'Hey, I forgot to give you this. It was for Saturday.' I am about to say, 'All your hard work might have been for nothing after all,' but under the circumstance I change it to, 'You might already be a millionaire.'

'Woo hoo!' she sings, taking the ticket. 'This is the one, for sure. What do you say we buy a huge property in Tasmania and commandeer the local apple industry?'

'Sounds bloody good to me. You can give the heap of shit to Blackie and buy yourself something flash. An Isuzu.'

She nods, kisses the ticket. 'Done!'

I'm worn out when I get home, narrowly again. I have to get used to the earlier dusks; winter is almost upon us. I don't want to think about it. I rustle up an uninspiring feed: chops and mashed potato, broccoli I overcook to mush. I hit the sack early, thinking the day I'd had would see me sleep like a newborn, but, like the hands of a drowned man reaching up to drag me into the twining reeds of a river, my dreams are ghastly and inescapable.

In the sky above the turnaround outside Li's place I desperately balance on the tray of the truck, which careens through the air while Gina and Blackie howl at me in terror from inside the cab. Below me I can see a clutch of figures; as the truck dips towards the ground I make out Milly and Li, sitting on the steps of Li's porch. But they are not human, they are grotesque carnival clowns, swivelling their heads from side to side with their mouths gaping, shelves of gaudy prizes lined behind them. Their eyes are staring and their faces blank; their hands rest on their knees, and fingernails like claws drape down their shins. In Li's left hand is a shredded lotto ticket.

As their heads swivel in unison, their mouths spew huge quantities of money, which is caught in the slipstream from the truck and whirls overhead, while the other figures, who emerge to me now as Julie and Todd, and Gail and Tom, dance screaming around the steps, grabbing at the notes. Each time one gets close, either Milly or Li, without so much as focusing her eyes, raises a hand and swipes, so they all wear curtains of blood from deep slashes, but still they dance and chase the notes. Through the cab's back window I can see the temperature gauge rising, and the hissing from the truck's bonnet echoes the hissing from the clowns' mouths. Just before the truck bursts into flames I see that Milly's eyes have focused and are riveted on me.

Laughter flies out of her mouth with the money.

*

It's a relief the next morning to throw open the doors and take my tea outside into the day's chill. The heat of the shut-up

173

house is uncomfortable, prickly instead of cosy, and I need the crisp autumn air to disperse the cloying remains of my dream.

The early morning is deliciously fresh, one of those clear cold days that attain a sense of purity, everything stripped back, clean and calm. It's funny how the cold can seem purging; heat can be hobbling with its languor, inertia, but the cold is exhilarating. It sharpens edges that heat blurs.

I feel better than I have done for weeks, despite my terrible night. The sun shines through the cobwebs that have been clustering in my brain; I feel them dissolve and fall away, taking my awful dream with them and leaving me with the mental clarity I've so needed. By the time I hear Li's truck rumbling off along the Woodford Highway, I've made my decision.

I give Gina the vegemite crusts she is drooling for, and go in search of my camera. Today I'll take my run out by Evans's old place and take some holiday snaps of Stick's enterprise for Sean.

But mental clarity can be an elusive state; while it may seem attainable in the unsullied light of a new day, once the sun has risen enough to illuminate the surrounding landscape, strewn with half-finished and half-remembered tasks and plans, the clearness can start to fug. When Gina and I set out, in my zealousness I think that I'll pace myself there easily, forgetting it is almost fifteen kilometres away and I've been jogging again for less than a week.

It doesn't take long for my fervour to dissipate – by the time I've reached that side of town my breath is burning my throat and my legs are wobblier than a DIY bookshelf. I have to slow to walking pace. Which doesn't change the fact that I'm only just over halfway. At this rate I might get there by lunchtime. But I've come too far to backtrack, and I don't want to alert Stick by driving there. Jogging wouldn't concern him – he wouldn't think for a minute I'd be stupid enough to go that distance on foot. How's that for irony? Bit of mental clarity?

When it no longer feels as if my lungs are being flayed, I accelerate to a power walk, feeling more than a little ridiculous. Gina gives me a sideways look, but seems content with the new pace. When I've taken my photos I'll cut through the bush behind Stick's crop and get Milly to pick me up along Mackie Road. That would make the entire distance only twenty k's, perfectly doable. The last week should count for something.

A length of shadow stretches across the road ahead of me, elongated, twisted gum trees, and I realise I don't have my phone with me. I have a water bottle and the camera, but my phone is on the kitchen bench, with my car keys. And my house keys.

It is going to be a very, very long day.

*

It's lucky I didn't know in advance quite how long, but it would have been bloody useful to know how pointless. I'd been careful, checking the camera for film before I left – it's been ages since I last used the thing. When I realise that

175

I've taken off without my phone and keys I have a clutch of panic and recheck. Yes, a new film, only a couple of shots used, God only knows what for.

At least something's going right. I keep on with my shameful combination of jogging, marching and stumbling.

It takes me almost four hours to get out to Evans's, and by then the sun is well overhead and my morning toast is long gone. I have nothing with me except the small water bottle, which I share with my poor dog, who by now is looking as pissed off as her namesake used to. I am absolutely starving, so much so that I worry I might blur the shots.

But there's no need to worry. Because to take photos your camera needs a battery with some life in it. The one in mine is as flat as roadkill. I have just run (in a manner of speaking) fifteen kilometres, and achieved nothing except confirmation of my physical and mental decline. I am, unavoidably, a complete and utter dickhead.

Milly's place, which is closest, is nine kilometres away – probably a three-hour walk. The sooner I start the better. My mind fills with images of cheese Twisties, which I don't even like. I think at that moment I would have been prepared to kill for a packet. In front of me Stick's crop beams calm and safe.

'I can't believe I'm standing in a dope crop with the munchies,' I say to Gina. She looks at me as though it's all she could have expected. So much for crisp mornings.

*

It's after four by the time I stagger up Milly's drive, and I've given up all pretence of being even remotely fit. I've decided to swear off health completely, it's just too bloody painful. From now on I'll drive to my own letterbox.

'Anything,' I mumble at Milly, 'cooked, raw or still frozen, I will eat anything you put in front of me.' She slots bread into the toaster and opens a tin of baked beans, while I try not to make myself sick gulping orange juice too fast.

'What on earth made you think you could cover thirty kilometres on foot?'

The cold juice has made my head spin; bright lights are flashing in my eyes. Gina is gulping from Felix's water bowl for the third time.

'Delusions of grandeur? I think my dog hates me.'

'With good cause. You're a clever girl, aren't you, Gina?' Milly bends to rub the panting dog's ears. 'Smarter than your owner, aren't you? You wouldn't go all that way without testing the camera first, now would you? No. That's something a stupid person would do.' Gina is lapping it up. When Milly serves my beans she pointedly spoons some onto half a piece of toast and puts the plate on the floor. Gina looks at her with utter devotion. 'Poor thing,' croons Milly.

I try not to guzzle, but I barely chew the food I'm so ravenous. Milly watches with amusement. 'I've never seen anyone inhale solids before,' she comments.

'All athletes eat like this.'

'Good grief,' she says to the wall.

I start to feel human again once I've downed a cup of

tea and nicked an apple. I wish it was Wednesday night, the night we cook up a feast for Li's return – I could really go a roast meal, lashings of Gravox. I decide to make an apple pie again in the morning, to hell with repetition. And I'm certainly not going to go for a bloody run. I'll probably be lucky if I can stand. With thoughts of hot, sugary pastry in my head, I wander out onto the deck for a smoke.

Milly joins me, tea in hand. She's enjoying herself. 'You mean to tell me you left your keys and phone at home, but didn't forget your tobacco? Where are your priorities?'

'You've just laid them bare.'

She's looking at the sky. The sun is already falling towards the trees. Such a peaceful time of day, so calm; an empty room awaiting the arrival of its guests.

'There's more tea in the pot,' says Milly, gathering our cups. 'Or would you rather I ran you home? Figuratively speaking, of course. There's still time.'

The sun seems to be sapping the remaining dregs of my energy as it sinks languidly towards the horizon. I'm absolutely beat. 'Would you mind if I just crashed here? Even the thought of getting in the car exhausts me.'

'Vegetable curry for tea.'

'Fine. Beautiful.'

She returns with our cups refilled. 'So what will you do about Stick?'

'I'll ring Sean when we go in. Stop dicking around. I should have just done it on day one, instead of going round there, thinking he'd cooperate. Stupid.'

'Just desperate. We're losing everyone. It's going to make things so much harder.'

'It has to be done, though, it's too much. In my position I can't just turn a blind eye. I'd be crucified. And I owe it to Sean.'

In the house the phone starts to ring. Milly looks reluctantly at the last of the day and goes inside. The air is starting to cool. I stink, I need a shower. But there's probably another twenty minutes, half an hour, of outside time left. I start to roll a last smoke when Milly calls out to me.

It's Liz on the phone. At last.

*

It's a long, emotional call. So much has happened since she left. Milly deflects her questions about us at first, diverting her with queries about the boys, their whereabouts. They are okay, Liz says, they're in Denmark, west of Albany on the south coast. A friend lives in some kind of collective community there, and she's staying in a caravan they use for accommodation, working about the place as rent in kind. It's freezing and not ideal, but the people are great and have been really supportive. There are other kids there, and it's been made clear she's not to feel pressured, she can stay as long as she needs to. She's applied to Social Services for a place, which will take forever, and thinks she might be able to pick up some work in Albany for now, even though it means a hefty commute.

She's good, she says. She still has traumatic dreams, but

179

she's settling. But what about us? Are we looking after Rolf for her?

I can hear Liz's grief from where I am standing. I leave Milly murmuring comfort into the phone and check that the house is closed up, then I indulge in a disgracefully hot shower that leaves me feeling broiled. I return to the kitchen where Milly is still on the phone, but now chuckling. The worst is over.

'Hang on,' she says, 'he's back now, and he's all pink. I'll put him on.' She holds out the receiver. Her eyes are still smiling.

'G'day, gorgeous.'

'Hey, old man!'

'Bout time you remembered us.'

'I know, I'm sorry. I wanted to have my head straight – hey, not to mention my *life* – before I got in touch. I know what you guys are like, you'd just worry like a pair of old chooks if I hadn't.'

'I'll have you know I'm nothing if not pure goose. And anyway, you're a very worrying person.'

'Me?' she squeals. 'What's this I hear about your Iron Man delusions, trying to jog thirty kilometres and nearly killing yourself? Talk about a bloody goose!'

'That's just Milly's version. I happen to be in fine form. Thirty kilometres is a mere stroll.'

'You dag!' Liz, always an excitable person, is practically screeching. 'Thank God you've got Milly and Li to supervise you, keep that ego in check.'

'They certainly do that.'

'Milly said Li's lost the co-op.' Skirting other news.

'Yeah, today's the last delivery. It's going to be hard on her.'

'She should get out while she can.' Liz's voice has taken on a tremor. 'You all should. Before there's no one…' She breaks off. I can hear her breathing, working to stay in control.

'I'm really sorry about Rolf, Liz.'

'Oh God!' She breaks, then calms herself again. 'It's awful. Awful. But I had no choice, I couldn't have stayed, I couldn't.'

'You would have sacrificed your children if you had.'

'That's what Milly said too. And it's true, I know that.'

'He had that time with them, it was worth everything.'

'I know. And he's safe now. I guess that's something.' She gulps. 'Where is he, um?'

'He's been cremated. His ashes are still at the crematorium, they're having trouble locating a cousin.'

There is a sizzle behind me and the smell of curry paste warms the kitchen.

'Anyway,' I say. 'How are the brats?'

'A bloody handful, I can tell you! As always. But coping well now, they think living in a caravan is being on holiday. It's full-on.'

'No aftershocks?'

'A few, mostly Dylan. Stevie and Tyler are okay-ish. Quite a large ish. It'll take a while for them to settle.'

Settled is hardly a state I could imagine ever applying to those kids.

'Hey, I'm sorry I missed Li, I forgot it was Tuesday.'

'Ring again tomorrow, she'll be thrilled.'

'Milly says it's her birthday on… shit, I've run out of credit. Hang on, I might have another phone card, or some change.'

'Saturday week. Call then, we're having a shindig…'

But she's gone, too busy fumbling for coins to get in a goodbye.

Milly's stirring vegetables in the wok. 'Lost her, she ran out of money,' I tell her. The room is cosy with spice. It's like a haven. 'It must have cost her a fortune – look at the time.'

'I'm so glad she rang, though. I've been so worried about her.'

'She sounds like she's on her feet.'

'In a Liz, drunken two-step kind of way. Can you imagine those kids in a caravan? It would be a shambles.'

'Chaos.'

'Diabolical.'

'Unbearable!'

Milly's turning from the stove with the next word when the phone rings again.

'She's back!' I grab it. 'Nebulah Health Resort.'

There's a pause. 'Hello?' says a man's voice. 'Pete? Is that you?'

'Sorry, yes.'

'Pete, it's John Barry.'

'John! Sorry, I thought it was someone else.' Talking to Liz always makes me perky. 'What's up?'

'Look, I'm sorry to bother you, but I can't get any answer at Li's and I just wanted to make sure she got back okay. I thought she might be there.'

I feel the warmth of the kitchen start to seep away through my feet. 'What?'

'She wouldn't stay, said she had no shopping to do cos you guys were in town the other day and were all stocked up. She wanted to head straight back.'

I can hear his words, but my skull is closing up. I don't want them.

'She said she'd phone to let us know she got back okay, but we haven't… I was worried, I know she's been having problems with the truck. I've been trying to get on to you since five, but there was no answer at your place, and Milly's phone's been engaged.'

Yes, it had been engaged. We'd been keeping it busy, laughing with Liz. My bones feel like they've been doused with ice water.

'Have you tried her mobile?'

'I don't have the number.'

'I'll try it now.' I put the phone down.

My hands are shaking. Milly has turned from the stove and is watching me, eyes wide and worried, spoon suspended. I keep my face turned away. I know all the blood has left it.

'The person you are calling,' chirps a happy automaton, 'has their phone switched off, or is out of range.' My arm drops but I can't get my hand to release the receiver. I cannot bring myself to hang up. 'To leave a free text message…'

And then I realise. Even with the phone hanging at my side I can still hear the recorded voice clearly.

It's been dark for nearly an hour but it's silent outside the house. The mist is somewhere else.

PART
FOUR

I aged a great deal after that night. We all did. Listen to me – 'all', as if two people could constitute such a state. Milly and I, the only two left, aged a great deal. Li's death was like a series of body blows, each impact just that touch more bruising, making it that bit harder to breathe. A slow, one-sided assault. We crumpled in the face of it, the stuffing knocked out of us. Like a pair of old scarecrows.

That first night marked the beginning of our decline. John Barry's phone call was the first, the most winding, punch. Then the seemingly endless hours of waiting, and the terrible mocking silence outside – the silence we'd longed for all these months. A shrieking silence, void of life, like sitting in a morgue. We kept the curtains closed, terrified that the mist might come to find us, and dreading what it might bring with it.

And knowing, through all this, that Li was out there. Praying that the piece of crap had shit itself before she reached Nebulah, that she was safely stranded somewhere on the side of the Woodford Highway. But getting only, over and over and over, that automated torment: 'The person you are calling is not available…'

We endured the night at the kitchen table, slumped and uncomfortable but unable to consider bed or the cosier lounge room. The vegetable curry congealed, untouched, in the pot; every now and then one of us would respond to a growling stomach by shoving a piece of bread into the toaster, and eating it standing, leaning against the sink. As if we weren't really eating. I made pot after pot of tea, just to mark time.

We didn't speak. There wasn't anything we wanted to say or hear. We could only have talked of hope, which was pointless, or reality, which we weren't ready to face. We simply sat, waiting out the night, with our eyes and minds closed.

Sean and Neil Davies were in town just after daybreak, and had found the truck abandoned on the side of McMahons Road before I'd even reached the rendezvous point. The engine had seized. The cab was unlocked, but the keys were gone. When I checked beneath the seat the gun cabinet was open and empty.

She would have headed to the nearest house to try to find sanctuary. About three kilometres away, Evans's old place. She wouldn't have known what I did: that the back corner window had been smashed by a branch. There would have been no shelter from the mist there.

A spasm of pain in my abdomen, like a bruising jab, almost doubled me up. I reached out to the front of the truck for support, and something on the dashboard caught my eye, pulling me in like a vacuum. The lotto ticket. She'd taken the time to check it. And she'd been right, it had been a winning ticket. On top of it was a payout slip. Division 5. $17.55.

The house looked like a whirlwind had been through it. Every window hung open, and the doors gaped like mouths open in shock.

I couldn't bring myself to go inside, and waited, stooped and cowardly, in the faint morning sun at the side of the porch. At the door Sean called out and waited – both a formality and an excuse to pause, prepare himself. The house remained silent.

They weren't inside for long, but they were a decade older when they returned to the sunlight. Davies, grey-faced, moved quickly around the side of the house, out of sight.

Li was in there. But she'd managed to escape before the mist had reached her. She'd shot Blackie first.

*

I stay with Milly until the sleeping pills take effect, then take her keys and drive home in the ute, to shower and get clean clothes. I feel like a sleepwalker, a ghost, numb from shock and my sleepless night. I have a strange sensation of weightlessness, as if my steps aren't connecting with the ground, instead I'm floating just above it. Drifting.

I let myself in round the back with Milly's spare key (in Nebulah you leave spare keys with each other, not hidden outside). My keys lie in a lifeless pile on the kitchen bench, with my phone.

I do not want to pick it up; my mind is in recoil, but it's as though its shutdown is complete and my body is acting of its own accord. I watch my fingers flip the phone open, and the screen bursts into blue life.

The missed calls are like a flurry of blows. Fourteen of them, in the space of half an hour. The last one was at 5.28. Dusk. It's like looking at a record of her screams.

I am back at Milly's table and already halfway through a bottle of Famous Grouse when Sean arrives a couple of hours later. I still haven't managed to feel its effects. Sean shakes his head when I hold up the bottle.

'Murder a cup of tea, though.'

I go through the motions while he douses his face at the sink. He slumps into a chair with the water running down his neck and wipes his hands on the knees of his pants.

'Where's Milly?'

'Pills. She'll be out for hours.'

Sean nods sadly, then reaches over for my glass. 'I hope,' he says, 'I never have to live through another day like this one. Christ!' He starts rubbing at his dripping face, his neatly trimmed hair awry.

'It could have been worse.'

He grimaces. He'd seen what the mist had left. Thank God she'd had the gun.

'There's more.' He sighs. 'Know what we found tucked away in the bush out the back, less than fifty metres from the scene?'

'A bloody enormous crop.'

He frowns. 'You knew?'

'I only found it the other day. It was new to me.'

'And you were planning to tell me?'

'Last night. I was about to ring you when things… went pear-shaped.' I still can't bring myself to let my mind open.

'It's Stick's?'

'Yep.'

'Are you sure?'

'He admitted it.'

'To you?' Sean's incredulous.

'He wasn't bothered about me knowing at all. I went to see him after I found it. He said if I shopped him he'd claim I was a silent partner.'

'When was that?'

'This is embarrassing. Thursday.'

Sean's gaze is level. 'I spoke to you on Friday night.'

'It's what I came to see you about that day. Before I found out Tom and Gail were leaving. I'm sorry.'

He takes the mug of tea in silence. The only sound is the tapping of the dogs' claws as they mooch about on the verandah.

'I have to say, bad call. Withholding information. Makes you an accessory.'

'I know.'

He sighs. 'The drug squad are coming from Perth. We might stick with you only just found it.'

I shrug. 'If you like.'

'Any idea where Stick might be?'

'He's not at home?'

'Car, dog and clothes gone. Looks like he shot through first thing this morning.'

'This morning? But how could he know?'

Sean looks grim. 'Li's call registry.' He waits for me to catch up, speaking gently. 'When she couldn't get hold of you or Milly, she called him. At seven minutes past five.'

My eyeballs feel as though they are crackling. 'She got through to him?'

'There's a four-minute call to his number logged on her mobile. He doesn't have an answering machine.'

5.07. There would still have been time. If he'd hurried, there would have been time. What had he said to her, with his crocodile mouth and hooded eyes? Did he tell her to hang in there, that he was coming? Did she wait, thinking he was on his way? When would she have realised that he was leaving her there?

Or did he just say: Forget it. You're on your own.

There'd been time. He'd known. And he'd left her there.

I've never been a violent person, never. But the urge that comes over me at that moment is overwhelming, and for the first time I understand violence at its very foundation, instinctively rather than intellectually. I understand it because for the first time in my life I want to cause someone pain. I want to hurt someone, and I know I'd relish their screams.

The sense of power that comes with this desire is immense. If Stick had been within reach at that instant I would have killed him with my bare hands. Easily. And slowly.

Instead I wait for Sean to leave and then I put my head down on Milly's kitchen table and weep.

After the build-up of jabs over the last twenty-four hours, this is my knockout blow.

It's a funny thing about loss of control. Whether you're succumbing to violence or to grief (or both), you have no idea, before the gates swing open, how much is being contained by them. Ten months of living in captivity, in fear; the bewildering deaths; the awful failure of my attempt at Christmas. The loss of everything: our town, our freedom, our lives. The single finger that flicks the gate's latch can be so small – missed calls on a mobile, or the tragic mystery of a four-minute conversation.

When I give in, when everything crashes around that short, unknown phone call which could have changed everything, I find I can't stop, can't hold back. I weep until I retch, heaving up whiskey, followed by the bile of emptiness.

*

The week that follows is played in slow motion. My main memory is of silence, a sort of insulated detachment, the distortion of being underwater.

Which we are. I move my things out to Milly's, and together we float through the days. I start drinking just after lunch, and Milly chases sleeping pills with a hefty whiskey around dusk. Neither of us can face the nights.

It doesn't take them long to catch up with Stick: he's picked up only a couple of days later. A family having a picnic in Geraldton called his numberplate in after Elvis attacked their dog. He was pulled up shortly afterwards heading north out of town.

The huge haul was gone, but there was plenty of residue in the boot, not to mention his personal stash of several ounces, clumsily secreted in homemade compartments in the dashboard, easily enough on its own for a trafficking charge. There was also close to $35,000 crammed into the tyre of his spare wheel, which he tried to dismiss as a repaid debt, from someone who might as well have been called Joe Bloggs, of no fixed address. Things weren't looking too good for Stick. He swore he had no connection with the crop by Evans's, and tried to bargain on the trafficking charge by claiming that he'd bought the stash off Li; that it was common knowledge she stayed in Nebulah for the express purpose of cultivating cannabis. He claimed that Li had phoned him that night threatening to pin the crop on him if he didn't risk his life to come and get her. Of course he would have saved her if he could, but his car wouldn't start, and then it was too late. In the morning he panicked about what might be pinned on him, and took off. They were working to hit him with as many charges as they could make stick, even an added extra of social security fraud, but to prove manslaughter on the basis of an unknown phone call was beyond their expectations.

For now we have to be content with him being on remand, with no one to make bail. Apparently he's having a bit of a rough time of it: had run into a few old associates, who were more than pleased to have the opportunity of following up on past dealings. Even a crocodile can be a small fish if the pond is heavily populated.

We hear all this from Sean, who is now having to patrol Nebulah fairly regularly in the face of the media frenzy since Li's death. Over cups of tea on Milly's porch he keeps us filled in, while Denham glowers by the car and keeps his distance. The forensic team has finished out at Evans's, and the autopsy is scheduled for the next few days. The cogs have already creaked into action, and the outcome of the autopsy is a foregone conclusion: Li's death would be found, correctly, to be suicide, a single fatal gunshot to the head. The mutilation of the corpses had occurred after death, and looked to have been caused by the claws of animals. It would be attributed to the nocturnal activities of marauding wild dogs, known to be common in the area. The local member – a straight-shooting civil servant with the community's welfare at heart – would be outraged, and demand that resources be provided for a cull.

The media, naturally, are having a field day – drugs and a gory death, what more could they ask for? 'Victim Shredded in Drug Crop Massacre', screamed the *Herald Sun*, which insinuated that the crop had been Li's, and that she'd been viciously murdered by territorial drug barons. They repeatedly stressed her Asian origins, as if this were proof enough in itself, and the supposed drug barons had, of course, the obligatory bikie connections.

It made me think of the pugnacious couple at Julie's Boxing Day barbecue, how pleased they'd be at this piece of masterly 'exclusive' reporting. The dinner parties they'd enthrall with accounts of their argument with a loony Nebulah local, who'd claimed the town's problems were due to ghouls. How they'd cut him to size.

We never answer the phone anymore. And word soon gets round to the ones who would intrude in person that if they venture within our fenceline, they are likely to encounter the local police when they arrive back at Woodford, who would, on an entirely routine vehicle check, find their tyres bald and their brakes dodgy, or their mufflers dubious. It could be costly.

I am beyond caring. It's all so predictable. I just nod, slumped on the porch steps. The others drink tea and carefully avoid noticing the receding bottle beside me, the way people's eyes rove around a physical disfigurement.

'Li's body will probably be due for release next week,' Sean tells us.

Milly clears her throat. 'We'll need to make arrangements.'

'If there's anything we can do,' Sean begins. Constable Denham, leaning by the patrol car, shifts his weight impatiently and crosses his arms. He fixes his eyes on the almost empty glass in my hand and then raises them to my face with open contempt. The arm bearing his watch gives an eloquent twitch.

'I've postponed my leave,' Sean is saying. 'We'll be here for the funeral.' He squeezes my arm and stands up. 'So, seriously, mate, if we can do anything.' I know what he's getting at; he had practically ordered me to bring Milly to their place, an open invitation. But Milly won't budge and I'm living in a drunken fog, counting the days till solstice.

I stand up with him, but I'm rumpled and bleary, squinting in the sun. Milly pulls herself to her feet with the help of a cane and shuffles to the top of the steps, but doesn't attempt to descend. Denham gives her a brief nod, scowls towards me and gets into the car. Sean reaches through the back window and pulls out a shopping bag and a small bundle.

'I pulled rank at the post office,' he says, 'brought your mail.' As he hands Milly the bundle he briefly holds her hand and she gives him a watery smile. To me he passes the shopping bag: eggs, milk, bread and a bottle of Grant's. 'Go easy,' he says. I nod, but I look away. In the car Denham sits rigid, staring straight ahead.

Li, being the sort of person she was, had organised and paid for her funeral long in advance. Her solicitors in Woodford are the executors of her will. The bundle of mail contains a letter from them asking us to contact them, as they haven't been able to reach us by phone. Our details, according to Li's instructions, have been passed on to the funeral directors, to confirm arrangements for the ceremony. There is a letter from them as well, also requesting contact.

And there is a further letter, enclosed in the package from the solicitor. It is addressed to Li's executors, but after reading the contents they decided it was more appropriate to forward it to us. It is our first introduction to Alice.

*

Outside the funeral parlour's small chapel, a small knot of people circle nervously in the weak sunlight after a wet dawn. Sean and Rachael are there, and poor Neil Davies, who still looks haggard after the events of that morning. Sean had told me he'd insisted upon bringing his retirement forward, effective almost immediately. John and Evelyn Barry are pale; John, rigid beside his wife, looking haunted.

It is too soon for Liz to be able to cope with this; she is being looked after by her friends in Denmark. There is a small clutch of old Nebulah residents, those who were able to stay on in Woodford. They mingle unhappily, with carefully solemn countenances, like returned veterans. But it's the young Asian girl standing on her own who catches my eye. She is a small and slender woman in her early twenties, striking in a slim-fitting dress of subdued green. She looks like a river reed. Her enormous almond eyes are candid, obviously relieved at our arrival, but her accent, when she shakes our hands, is as Australian as most of the barflys in the Woodford Arms.

Xi Dong – 'but please call me Alice, everybody does' – has been studying at uni in Perth for the last two years, she'd told me when I rang the number on her letter, but was born in Sydney. Her parents had followed her uncle and aunt there from Cambodia after they were granted permanent residency. It was this now elderly uncle who'd begged her to write, to ask permission for her to attend the funeral on his behalf. He was infirm, in a nursing home in Sydney, and was incapable of travelling. But he had known Li, remembered her with great emotion, and was keen for his niece to pay his respects in his absence.

He was devastated when he read in the papers of her death, she'd written. *During the long, arduous journey to Australia she had shown much kindness to his wife, who suffered intensely from seasickness and a prolonged miscarriage. For many years after their safe arrival they exchanged cards and occasional meals, but when Li moved west they lost touch. He does not often speak of those years – my aunt never fully regained her health, and died not long after my parents arrived in Australia, so I never knew her, or experienced his grief at her death. But the news of Li's death has affected him profoundly. I would not have ventured such an intrusion had it not meant so much to my uncle in his distress.*

Her uncle requested that we permit his niece to read a poem at the funeral, by a revered Cambodian writer who had been swept away in the first tides of the Khmer Rouge.

Alice apologises repeatedly to us now, for what she calls 'gatecrashing' the private ceremony, but her uncle, normally a subdued and placid man, had been adamant that the family owed Li their respects. She says this with a small, tense squeeze of her shoulders and an embarrassed smile, as if to suggest that the young have no choice when faced with the whims of the elderly.

She is evidently uncomfortable about attending the private funeral of a stranger, one that is guaranteed to attract unwanted attention and the most morbid kind of sightseers. We introduce her to people as a special friend of

Li's and she relaxes gratefully, greeting everyone with a shy, beautiful smile, so natural it doesn't seem at all out of place at a funeral. Over her head Milly and I catch each other's eye and smile sheepishly: we are both entranced, convinced Alice is the image of Li at a young age. We keep her close, like an honoured guest.

The service is short and painfully routine, as these things tend to be. The celebrant, who'd never even met Li, relates what little he knows of her from his sketchy notes, his words the consistency of ashes.

Alice is introduced by her Cambodian name. She stands at the side of the podium and faces the small group that has washed up on the shore at the end of Li's life. Her address is brief; she says the piece she is to recite gave great consolation to the terrified and grief-stricken refugees who'd clustered on the ramshackle boat that would see them either saved or killed. 'It is,' she explains, 'difficult to translate adequately into English.' She recites it first in Khmer, then English.

> 'Like the breeze
> bearing the mountain's song
> so death is movement.
> Our souls entwine
> with bursting seed
> and bloom towards the waiting sky.
> Thus, the heels that crush
> The tender growth
> are defeated
> by the mountain's endless tune.'

She adds a few words in Khmer and gives a small bow before slipping back to her seat. I close my eyes. I feel like I'm listening to Li, alive in the vibration of these words. It is a small oasis of peace, the first I've felt in all the days since her death.

*

Li has already been cremated. After the long drive back we gather in a small group beside her apple orchard, and spread her ashes among the trees. To the left of the site, Blackie's grave is marked with the tyre lever from the truck. A cold breeze lifts the dust we scatter and carries it to the edges of the west field, where winter growth is already tingeing it a deep green.

It is 17 May. Ten days ago we should have been an exclusive party of three, celebrating Li's fifty-sixth birthday with cake and stupid party hats, and delusions of Keith Richards.

I've had nothing but cups of tea all day, and a quick Guinness at the informal wake in the Woodford Arms with those who couldn't face a six-hour return journey for the scattering of Li's ashes. Now, as dusk begins to close in, and the Barrys and Sean and Rachael take their leave, Alice produces a bottle of rice wine from her overnight bag. We'd been reluctant to allow her to stay, had refused outright at first, but she'd pointed out that returning to Woodford would have meant an additional two hours on her journey back to Perth the next day. And, to be honest, our rebuttal wasn't heartfelt anyway: the idea of company, especially today, when loneliness hovers at the side of every conversation, is more than a little intoxicating. And this small woman seems to have the calm strength of a mountain; she is both lively and soothing. Now, with the others gone, we change into comfortable clothes, trackpants and thick socks, and put the first of the huge condolences casseroles in the oven to heat. As the light fades the gathering murmurs outside don't seem quite so threatening.

Alice, in her mauve pyjamas, is bashful, but raises a rice wine toast to Li, in Khmer for her uncle and in English for us. In the orchard, as the wind had lifted the dust that was all that remained of our kind, funny friend, she'd pressed her hands together in front of her chest and bowed, deeply and solemnly.

But despite her dignity, her eyes are candid, and every now and then she forgets herself and erupts into a delighted laugh. At one stage, when she answers a call and murmurs happily into her mobile to someone called Rob, I realise I am more than a little in love. She is everything that Julie has never been, I think with a pang as I watch her stroke Gina's ears with rhythmic gentleness.

*

The noise builds slowly that night. As we fill our plates a hissing starts at the window, vicious and barely audible. Alice looks up from her plate, her face draining.

'I'm sorry,' Milly tells her. 'We should never have agreed

to you staying.' She darts a glance at me and I look down. I know it was irresponsible, but the company is such a tremendous comfort. I don't regret it a bit.

The hissing starts to grow, becoming whispers, a gathering mass of strange words. Gradually it becomes uniform, the voices fall together, forming a lilting chant that is somehow even more disturbing than the usual wailing. Each voice remains distinct; although their chant is like a chorus, they approach it in different tones, and each takes a turn in rising above the others: one mocking, one threatening, one howling, one as if it is in a trance. Even though the words are incomprehensible, the effect is chilling. As it continues to increase in volume I get up to put the television on.

'No, wait!' It's Alice, her head raised, listening intently. 'That's amazing,' she tells us. 'Do you recognise it?' We stare at her, faces blank. 'It's Khmer, Pan Yu's poem, the one I recited at the service.' Her face is still pale, but bright with enchantment. 'It's unbelievable.'

The voices reach a crescendo, then subside in tempo back to the whispered hissing, a sinister croon. Alice gets up and moves to the window.

It's such an unexpected movement we are slow to react. 'No!' calls Milly and I am half out of my chair, the dogs up and alert at Milly's tone, but already Alice has drawn back a couple of inches of curtain and peered outside.

'Alice,' Milly says quietly, 'it's not safe.'

The noise outside is dying down, the chanting subsiding, until the last whisper floats into silence. Slowly, the night descends to stillness. Alice pulls back from the window, letting the curtain drop over the dark again. 'Wow,' she says. Her face is tranquil rather than horror-struck; she looks almost mesmerised. She remains standing by the window entranced.

'Are you okay?' I ask, more to break the mood and bring her back to us. She glances up.

'I'm fine,' she says, shaking her head. 'That was amazing.' She drifts back to the table. Milly is looking at her intently, worried rather than relieved. Alice hasn't quite come back to us yet, she remains dreamy, lost elsewhere. 'I saw the mist,' she tells us. 'It was out there.'

'You were very lucky,' Milly says. 'Extremely lucky.'

Alice looks at her, confused. 'But it was beautiful.'

We are silent in the face of this. 'Of course,' Milly answers eventually. 'It can be anything it wants to be.'

'It was a sea,' says Alice, dreamy again. 'But there were people in it. My uncle was there, and I think the woman must have been Li. They were dancing, reciting as they moved. And then they just dissipated, drifted away. It was immensely peaceful.'

She looks up at us again, and her expression is almost an accusation. 'I can't believe it sang the poem. It was lovely.'

It is the most frightening thing she could have said to us. Outside it is utterly silent. I get up and put the television on.

*

We spend the rest of the night slumped through a terrible movie, Bruce Willis leaping off buildings and sprinting down labyrinthine corridors, blasting people away with an enormous semiautomatic. Piles of corpses line his wake. But that's fine, there are always hordes more people round the next corner, waiting to be shot. I find myself going back to the poem Alice recited at the ceremony, its simple dignity. It seems a world away from this, the noise and the mayhem, the casual massacre. Another realm.

I glance over at Alice, where she is curled into one of the armchairs. Her eyes are on the TV, but she is not really watching. Her expression is distant, she is worlds away too.

It's then that I realise with a sickening lurch what the mist had been doing.

It had been calling. The dance, the chant, the poem. It was a seduction.

*

The night passes in eerie silence; the mist doesn't return or resume its usual night-time serenade. It's unnerving, and I'm sober for the first time in weeks. I sleep badly, tensed against the stillness. I throw the blankets off, then ferret around retrieving them. Ears strained to the night, I hear the dogs moving around the kitchen, their claws scraping on the lino. They are restless too. I think of Alice in the next room, and listen carefully for movement. I'm worried about her expression. The expression of someone enthralled.

In the kitchen the next morning Alice looks tired. She says she didn't sleep well either, she was too 'wired'. From her position by the toaster Milly's eyes meet mine, they are an echo of my own thoughts. Neither of us likes this choice of word. We bounce words soundlessly across the kitchen at each other, while Alice yawns and pours juice.

It's chilly out on the porch, but we never waste the opportunity to be outside. Our toast and eggs are cold almost immediately; we gulp our coffee quickly. In spite of her bad night, Alice is alert and talkative during breakfast. She questions Milly, asking her about the research she did into the mist. Milly doesn't have many answers to her questions; she ends up sounding evasive. Alice keeps using the word 'fascinating'.

When we've washed up and showered I take Alice back to Li's. We load a crate onto the tractor trailer and head to the orchard. When I start the tractor I automatically pause, waiting for Blackie to come bounding, leap onto the seat. I avoid looking over to the house, to the porch steps where Li and I would sit, sharing our lunches of egg sandwiches.

The morning is crisp; Alice eats apple after apple and glows. She laughs and chokes on the fruit flesh, and alternates between giggling and coughing until she has hiccoughs and laughs even more. In her jeans and grey T-shirt she looks far younger than the elegant young woman she was yesterday. Her energy is infectious. I am smitten. I smile at her giggling hiccoughs, the purity of her delight, and can't help wishing again that this was my daughter.

As we sit over a last cup of tea and Milly's special coconut cake, we are prepared for what we suspected might happen.

'You know,' says Alice, keeping her eyes on the cup that she's twisting in her hands, 'I don't have to rush away.'

'Yes you do,' I say.

'Really, I could stay longer. It seems a shame to have come all this way for such a short time. And I've only just met you guys.'

Milly has her best schoolmistress voice on. 'Sorry, Alice. It's not possible. You shouldn't even have stayed last night.'

'But it wasn't that bad, it was fine.'

'That's what's worrying.'

'Could it be petering out?'

I stand up. 'Get your things together. I'll escort you to the highway.'

'Ouch! An eviction.'

'You bet. You have most definitely overstayed your welcome.'

'Just cause the rice wine's finished. I know your type.'

'Too right.'

At the kitchen door she turns back with a laugh. 'I'll do your ironing.'

'Out!'

She starts gathering her things together while I lean in the doorway. 'Anyway, ironing'd ruin my naturally crumpled demeanour.'

Milly nods. 'Like human puff pastry. Very appealing.'

'Apple pie,' I say. 'I haven't made one for… weeks.'

'Definitely overdue. You might lose your touch.'

We smile, and I feel for the first time as if we might be

coming back. From the bedroom Alice is singing at Gina, about thigh bones connected to knee bones, dem bones dem bones dem bones.

It's as good as birdsong.

*

I escort her to the town's boundary and part from her at the highway, her Daihatsu crammed with apples and potatoes and containers of funeral casseroles. Though we tried our best to make it seem less like an expulsion, it clearly is.

'I'm sorry,' I say to her through her car's open window. 'If we lived anywhere remotely normal I'd say stay as long as you like, move in. Believe me, you'd be more than welcome.'

'That's okay,' she says. 'I can't really afford to miss class tomorrow anyway. Exams start in two weeks.' She scrapes her hair into a ponytail, securing it for the long drive. 'Maybe I can come again?' She peers at me, questioning. 'After exams?'

'When'll that be?'

'Mid-June. The twentieth.'

'We'll be gone by then. I'll ring you, let you know where we are.'

She's eyeing me. 'Seriously?'

'Seriously.'

'Milly?'

'Milly.'

'I'd be surprised. She doesn't seem to be planning to leave.'

'She will.'

'I would say she seems determined to stay.'

'And I'm determined to go.'

'Ooh!' She shudders. 'Stalemate.'

'I'm getting her out of here if I have to drag her.'

'Reckon you might. Have to. But my money's on her.' She sticks out her tongue, raises her sunglasses. 'You know, it wasn't nearly as bad as I expected it to be. It was almost, peaceful.'

I reach over, gently brush some fluff from the edge of the car door. 'So peaceful it disembowelled Li.'

She flinches. 'It could have been dogs,' she says, tentative.

'It wasn't dogs.'

Her eyes are defiant but uncertain. 'Are you sure?' she asks.

I straighten up. I feel as though she's hit me. 'You need to go now.'

'Hey, please don't be angry, I just meant…'

'You need to go now.' I'm walking away, back towards the Land Cruiser, but she's out of the car and has run up behind me. She grabs hold of me around my waist and hugs me hard.

'Pete, I'm sorry, I didn't mean it to sound like that. Please, I didn't mean it, I'm sorry.' Her embrace makes my skin tingle, my scalp crawls across my head with delight, bristling with sensation. I could swoon with it; I think how long it's been since anybody hugged me.

And then I realise. At Li's funeral everybody hugged me, men and women. Yesterday. Either I am coming back to life, or it's simply Alice. I could stand with her wrapped round me for days.

*

After she's gone I linger at the side of the road, having a smoke and watching Gina, who's bored and impatient. When I'm sure that Alice is really gone I look at the empty sky and head for home. I feel as though I've already been missing her for hours.

When I get back Milly has started spring cleaning, cupboards awry. I put the kettle on and she joins me. I notice her noting that I'm having tea, even though it's well into the afternoon.

'Once I've got this place sorted out a bit and you've finished moving your stuff, we should start cleaning out Li's, really,' she says.

I grunt. The solicitors had informed us before the funeral that we are Li's sole beneficiaries. A few thousand dollars in superannuation and savings and the farm. A generous bequest on paper that is a major headache in reality. Li was younger than us, and as much as we both love the farm, we aren't up to it, and we'd never be able to off-load the produce. Selling the place is an impossibility, and giving it away? To who – Liz? Alice? Trapping someone else within the borders of Nebulah? There was nothing for me at the farm without Li and Blackie.

'The food, anyway,' Milly continues.

I nod. 'Once all the legalities are finalised we can sell the equipment. Shifting the farm won't be an option, though. We'll just have to leave it.'

Milly looks surprised. 'I thought you'd want to keep it on.'

'What on earth for?'

'Well, you always seemed to enjoy working out there, keeping busy.' There is a pause. 'It did you good.' She means that it gave me something to do besides drinking.

'Milly,' I say, gently, gently. 'We can't stay here anymore.'

Her hands are clasped around her cup. She doesn't raise her eyes. '"Can't" is an ugly word,' she says. 'It implies lack of choice.'

'That's right. We have no choice.'

'We do.'

'We don't. We. Can't. Stay. Here.'

'Everything I have is here.'

'Everything I have is here too.'

'But. I. Cannot. Leave.'

'Li is dead,' I say. She recoils. 'Li is gone,' I repeat, 'because she thought she could stay here, that if she was careful she'd be safe. Then she wasn't careful and now she's dead. Do you think if she'd known what was going to happen she'd have stayed?'

Milly is shaking her head. 'I don't know.'

'It will get us,' I push. 'There's only two of us now, there's only us to stalk.' I think of crocodiles watching campers, lying in wait near their fishing spots, the places they'd take their rubbish. Waiting, learning. 'It doesn't matter how careful we are, it will get us.'

She looks up at me, slowly, sadly. 'You don't have to stay.'

'I can't leave without you.'

'Yes you can.'

'I can't.'

'I don't ask you to stay, I've never asked that.'

'I know that.'

'Then leave.'

'Not without you.'

'Then that,' she says, hobbling from her seat over to the cupboard, then limping back with the whiskey bottle in her hand. 'Is your choice.'

*

For two more weeks we circle each other, together but separate. The mist is subdued too; instead of the torrent we expected to have unleashed upon us, the nights remain peaceful; only the peculiar chanting accompanies the darkness. We find ourselves getting used to it. It's almost seductive. Lulling.

Some nights I think I prefer it to the repetitious circus of American action heroes, pumped up with steroids and clutching weapons the size of small cars, pulverising anything that comes between them and their goal, which is always altruistic, of course. The television isn't the distraction it used to be.

Nearly every morning we drive over to Li's; Milly sorts through the kitchen and store cupboards while I finish harvesting apples from the far row of trees. It's ages since I last made a pie. I hate to think how long it's been. I try not to pay attention to the date. The thought of the days that are passing scares me.

*

At my abandoned house I dig in the cupboard for my pie dish. Milly has one, of course, but mine is part of my specialty, a territory thing. The pie wouldn't be the same in another one. As I rinse it at the sink the phone rings three times and stops.

When it starts ringing again I answer it.

'Where have you been?' It's Alex, sounding almost in tears. She's been ringing for weeks, she says, was on the verge of getting into the car and tracing her steps back over the Nullarbor again.

I try to defuse her. 'Always looking for old men, aren't you?'

But she's in no mood for this. Li's death was in the papers and she's been worried sick.

I'm shamed. I should have called her to let her know I was at Milly's, that I'm all right. But to be honest, the truth is that I didn't want to. I already knew I didn't need to hear what she had to say, would say – is now, sure enough, saying.

'For God's sake, what are you still doing there? You must know how close it is to solstice.'

'It's been quiet,' I tell her. 'Things have really calmed down here.'

She is sceptical, then exasperated. I am brisk with her as she pleads with me; I think of her fluid green eyes, lined with concern, and it puts me in mind of Alice, small and poised in her watery green dress. I think of all the wonderful, strong, admirable women I have met since my disastrous choice of a wife. I think that in the weeks before winter solstice, I'm unlikely to meet any more.

I give Alex the phone number at Milly's place. And she gives me, in return, that word, four letters to burn into my psyche, to carry with me over my remaining days.

Soon.

*

Milly's finished stowing the last of the supplies from Li's and the kitchen is spotless; surfaces gleam in the afternoon sun. It makes my old chipped pie dish look disreputably scruffy. There is a vase of yellow grevillea on the benchtop by a bowl of apples, like a Margaret Preston still life. From the other room come the strings of a Debussy concerto.

It is a simple, beautiful scene. Peaceful. It is everything a home should be. It is my home.

I suddenly lose the urge to make my pie. Instead I pour the first drink I've had in weeks.

*

When Gina and I first married we had a Margaret Preston reproduction in pride of place in our kitchen, a profusion of wattle by a dish that was a burst of colour. We were both keen but amateur painters – we actually met in the Australian collection of the Art Gallery of NSW. We'd started chatting in front of this Margaret Preston, the stunning original. When Gina had found the print and brought it home, flushed and happy, we'd made a ceremony of hanging it in the heart of our home, where we'd see it every time we ate or cooked together. It used to always make me smile, at first with happiness, and then ironically. But then, eventually, not at all.

That print watched over our deterioration. Late at night after a double shift (Julie was quite right – as Gina got sicker and more difficult, I stayed away as much as I could), I would look at the picture over the edge of my glass and speculate with bitterness that in nature the spray of colourful blossom would long ago have wasted and rotted away.

Shortly after this we went to a gathering together, a barbecue for a friend's birthday or something like that, and Gina made a shocking scene, publicly accusing me of drunkenness and abuse, which no one believed but everyone listened to, including our thirteen-year-old daughter, who stood shocked and teary until someone noticed her and had the presence of mind to hustle her inside.

I'm not proud of my subsequent behaviour. Gina wasn't diagnosed or adequately medicated until long after we'd played out our own version of a Shakespearean tragedy, so I didn't understand that she was sick and delusional, I just saw the lies and the corruption she subjected our life to, and I responded with fury. I remember going home and looking at the beautiful print and thinking that everything around it had withered now, its time was long past. And I took it round to the house of a colleague whose wife had always said how much she liked it, and even though she was clearly reluctant to accept such an unexpected and bewildering gift,

I refused her hesitation and insisted. In actual fact, I bullied her into taking it.

At home Gina cried in front the dusty space on the blank wall, but I was so far gone in bitterness by then I couldn't have cared less.

*

In Milly's kitchen I finger the delicate grevillea and think how I've always associated Australian native flowers with comfort and happiness, with their unruly aestheticism. I've never seemed to be much good at sharing this appreciation with women, though.

The phone bursts into its three-ring code beside me, and I answer warily, thinking it might be Alex with another four-letter shroud for me.

It's not. It's Sean. The media presence since Li's death has now dwindled to pretty much nothing and he's exhausted. They're off on the weekend. We agree to meet for a drink on Thursday. He wants to make sure I have his house keys before he leaves. I only hesitate for an instant, and then I think: *Soon. The sooner the better.*

Two days later I'm up at sparrow's fart and loading the Land Cruiser with farewell presents – apples and a fresh pie. Milly opts to stay home; a mild forecast and a good book have won out over the prospect of the long drive. Or so she says. I suspect she's giving me 'space'.

She hands me a thermos of coffee and double-checks I have the shopping list – one of my specialties is leaving things behind. When I go to check the glove box, Gina leaps into the passenger seat and sits upright with a half-pleading, half-cheeky look in her eyes. She shoots a glance sideways at me and thumps the upholstery with her tail. I give in, as she knew I would.

'Do you want me to take Felix too?' I ask Milly. He is sitting at attention by Milly's side, watching proceedings with keenness, alert to any possibility of a drive. Milly scratches his ears and he stretches his mouth into a toothy grin.

'No, he can stay here with me. I'll let him snooze in the ute.' As if he understands, Felix puts a paw into Milly's hand, licks his lips and grins even wider. Like all Milly's animals, he started life as a stray, and is devoted to her. Far from the vehicle-mad Blackie, who would have crammed himself into the back seat by now and refused to budge, even for Li, Felix would always choose Milly's company over anything. And if there's a sleep in the sun-filled cab of the ute thrown in – well, no contest.

If only people were so easy.

Or tyres. I stop at our usual rubbish-strewn rest stop for the coffee and linger over a smoke, watching Gina and enjoying, like her, the sense of freedom that always comes with being on the road and out of Nebulah. If it wasn't such a long trip, and diesel wasn't so expensive, I think I'd make the drive to Woodford every day. I wonder if I'd feel the same way about it if I lived there. I have a strong suspicion that, under the circumstances, I might.

But freedom inevitably seems to have a price, and when

I've stashed away the thermos and circled back to the driver's side, I discover the back tyre on that side is dead flat. I must have punctured it when I pulled in; the ground all around this stop is littered with debris. There's even an old tyre and a dusty car battery in the patch of bush beside the unemptied bin. You can't blame the crows for everything.

It's as well I'm in good time: either the prick at the garage was channelling Superman last time he did the wheel nuts up, or I'm in far worse shape than I'd imagined. It's a long, drawn-out battle to get the last two off, so prolonged I have to stop for a couple of breathers. At one stage I think I'm not going to manage, that I'll have to call Milly and get her to come and tow me back, but finally, sweating and swearing and arms trembling like buggery from the effort, I get the final nut to shift. I'm going to kick that apprentice's arse when I get to Tommo's.

Out the front of his workshop, Tommo wipes his greasy hands on an even greasier rag and rolls his eyes. 'That'd be right,' he growls. 'Useless sack of shit.' From inside comes the clatter of a thrown tool and a burst of shouts. 'He's Paul's best mate, got into a bit of trouble. Paul got up me to take him on, give him a bit of a break, but he's just a feral dickhead, and a bludger to boot. I'll rark him up. Again.'

Tommo had brought Paul, his only son, into the business as a partner a year ago, hoping he'd settle down and eventually take it over. Personally, I reckon he'd be better off selling up. As a local ex-cop, I had good reason to be familiar with Paul Thompson's character traits. He isn't someone who likes being told no, either in business or in his personal life. He's a thug; I wouldn't trust him within half a kilometre of an innocent like Alice.

The head of the nail protruding from the tyre would be obvious even to a blind man, but Tommo's kneeling and running his thumb round the edge of the spare, shaking his head.

'Don't like the look of this bastard,' he says. 'How old's it?'

'Bout as old as me. Good as gold.'

'I reckon you're lucky you got here in one piece mate, it's rooted. Accident waiting to happen.'

I hesitate, torn. 'Next time,' I say, 'I've got the dog, a hundred things to do.'

He shrugs. 'Your call. Personally, in your situation, I'd be seeing it as a risk.' Another four-letter word. They're crowding in on me.

'Let me grab the shopping first, I can't do it without the car.' Everything else I could manage on foot.

'How soon can you get it back?'

I calculate. 'Twelve?'

'When do you need it by?'

'Gotta be on my way by two.'

Tommo winces. 'Get 'er back as soon as you can. We're flat out today, already backlogged.'

'Sorry, mate. I don't live in a world of convenience.'

'Yeah, I know. Don't worry, we'll have her ready.' From the workshop comes another volley of swearing. Tommo's eyes narrow and he cusses under his breath. As he stalks away he pulls his shoulders back and seems to start inflating; by the time he strides through the workshop door he looks to be twice his original size.

I pull the shopping list out of the glove box and gaze with dismay at the boxes of apples on the back seat. I'll have to dump them round at Sean's now, before I can do anything. I look at my watch. I think of another four-letter word.

*

I get the car back to Tommo's by twenty to twelve, free of apples but laden with groceries. He's grim and businesslike as he takes my keys; the atmosphere in the workshop is heavy and sullen. I double-check that the gun cabinet under the seat is securely locked.

I just have time, Gina on a lead, to collect the mail while Milly's prescription's being filled. There's a letter from Li's solicitors updating us on the probate, but I won't have time to see them; I'll have to call them tomorrow.

I'm only just late when I get to the Woodford Arms, but Sean isn't there yet. I buy a pint and roll a smoke in the front bar. There aren't many in yet. The barmaid is young and bored, already overweight and not given to conversation. She flicks back hair dyed in two equally drab tones, and plonks my change on the counter in a manner that makes it clear that all transactions are now terminated until I need a refill. One function only.

It puts me in mind of Rhonda, a seasoned pro in Mildura, who'd had a reasonable brain and a fairly good heart beneath a pretty worn exterior. She was known to the cops, but operated discreetly and without trouble, and at over fifty was still managing to earn a fairly decent living. She'd told me in the pub once, when we were the only two there and we'd shared a late afternoon beer, that experienced men tended to prefer the older whores to the young girls, no matter how much better looking they were. The young ones give no comfort, she said, to them it's just money, lie back and serve your time, but that's it, they're cold. The older ones know the score, will give a bit of companionship, a chat and a laugh beyond the menu items, and often it's this warmth, a bit of female friendliness, that a lonely man craves, that will keep him coming back.

I could imagine her raising her brows with disapproval at the skinful of unfriendliness who's taken up position on the back wall of the bar, her arms crossed and her mouth working round the piercing in her tongue as if she's chewing cud. She won't be in the job long.

I take my change and head for the table by the window, where I can keep an eye on Gina, tied up outside.

Sean's late – by the time he arrives there's only an inch in my glass, even though I've been trying to take it slowly. At the bar he gets even shorter shrift than I did; I watch with amusement as he's served with downcast eyes and palpable fury.

'Cheers,' I say, as he plonks a Guinness in front of me. 'You survived Miss Personality 1998?' I nod towards the glaring barmaid. He glances back towards the bar;

from her vantage point the girl straightens and attempts to resolutely hold our gaze, but her defiance is shaky and already regretted – it's obvious that there's no admiration in our expressions.

Sean turns away with complete disinterest and she sags with relief. 'Stacey?' he says, lifting his drink. 'Her dad's been unemployed since we did him for DIC. Again. She's got a chip.' He takes a deep swig of the stout. 'And not much of a brain. I'm surprised Wal's employed her.'

The door opens and a mob of tradies enter. The distraction of the sudden noise and activity diffuses the tension in the air and we settle to our drinks. Sean's not in a good mood. A gang of kids have been out at the bus depot and the neighbouring truck rest with air rifles. Three of the town's four school buses are out of action and Sean's had to placate a clutch of large and livid truckies, one of whom has five flats on a rig full of cattle and is determined to lynch someone before he clears town.

'How many days left?'

'Of work, one. We're off first thing Sunday morning, I don't care what happens.' He grimaces, remembering what held them up last time. 'Figure of speech,' he murmurs, 'you know what I mean.'

'You'll be right. Milly and I'll make sure we're not slaughtered between now and Sunday.'

'If you are, you'll be in Denham's hands. Remember that if you feel inclined to take risks.'

I check my watch. 'Risks are off my agenda. I plan a long

and utterly sedate old age.' *Soon* croons into my conscience. I push it back, reach for my drink.

Sean's digging in his pockets; he reaches over and puts two keys in front of me. 'House keys,' he says, 'and I didn't get them cut for nothing. I want you to use them.' There's a hesitation. 'Please.'

I pick the keys up. 'Mate, I'm not brave and I'm no action hero. I'd be out of there like a shot.' Bad choice of words; both our eyes flicker away briefly. 'I'm doing my best to talk her round.'

Sean rubs his eyes. 'Even after Li?'

'I don't know what it will take.' Alex's fury on the phone the other week comes back, her insistence that Milly will be the death of me if I don't get away. But there's no way I can just leave her there. Instead I steer the subject to safer ground: Sean's trip, the ridiculous number of books Rachael's packed and the far more reasonable – though larger – stash of his fishing gear. The barramundi he intends to land and the open fires he will grill them over, with just a knob of butter and some lemon.

It sets off an urge in me that is almost an ache. Fresh fish, a barbecue. There's nothing to stop us during the daylight hours. My desire becomes need; I'm almost through my second pint and I haven't had time for lunch and I'm determined. Tomorrow, at home, I want to build a bloody great fire and grill some fresh fish.

It's ten to two when we finally separate, and I need to see to my vehicle. He offers me a lift, but I know that officially he's not allowed to take animals in the squad car, so I tell him Gina needs the walk. And I'm feeling furtive – I want to duck back down to Harry's Meats, where he has slabs of local(ish) fish in the freezer. I'm besotted.

It's already quarter past two when I swagger into Tommo's, pleased as punch, swinging my plastic bags, the last one containing a hunk of jewfish and another larger piece of snapper. I'm in great spirits: I'm full of Guinness and now I'm heading home with a car full of booty.

The workshop is empty. My vehicle is over to one side, one wheel off. The defunct spare is lying on the ground nearby, the wheel rim of my flat next to it.

I find Paul and his deadbeat mate sprawled in the tearoom, beers in front of them, listening to the races.

'Don't give me a fucken hard time, Tommo was meant to do it. He got called away to the bus depot. An emergency, had to get the school buses back on the road.'

'Got to get them schoolgirls off the street, safely tucked up,' leers his mate, who affects a signet ring; his hairline is already receding.

'Yeah, and I'll bet he never told you to finish up for him. I'll bet, you useless shit of a son, that nothing's been done here since he left.'

Paul flashes up. 'You want your car, you better show some fucking respect.'

I pull out my mobile. 'Tommo's number,' I bark. He shrugs. I pluck the business magnet off the fridge door. An orange-toned woman with an unnaturally arched back and a pair of self-supporting basketballs supposed to be boobs falls to the floor. I start punching in the mobile number.

Paul gets up. 'Jesus. Fuck. I'll do your fucking car now. Leave the old man out of it.' He heads for the door.

'Leave the spare, just fix the puncture. You've got ten minutes or I'll take the ute.' Paul's hotted-up, bright yellow ute was his reason for living.

'Over my dead body.'

'If need be. Got a twenty-two in the gun cabinet under the seat agrees with you. I'm already fucking tempted to use it. Nine minutes.'

While he grumbles over the tyre I help myself to the phone in the office. Milly answers quickly, she must be in the kitchen. 'I've been on the phone,' she says. 'Liz rang.'

'She okay?'

'Yes, fine. Sounds a lot more settled. I got nervous talking to her, though, as if I shouldn't be tying up the phone line. In case.'

'There's not too many "in cases" left.'

'Only you. Where are you?'

'Woodford.'

'Still?'

'Long story. Just threatened Paul Thompson with the twenty-two, so hopefully I should be on my way shortly.'

'Hmm.' Milly's calm is unwavering. 'I taught Paul Thompson briefly. A twenty-two would have been most helpful. Will you stay in Woodford?'

225

'No, I'm heading back.'

'Will you have time? You'll be cutting it very fine.' From the workshop I hear the pneumatic gun rattle – my tyre will be back on.

'I'm on my way. If I grand prix it, I'll be fine. I'll need a drink, though.'

'Ice cubes and all, will be waiting.'

In the workshop I jam the spare home and toss ten bucks at Paul's feet. 'I'll get the wheel balance done next time. At Beaurepaires, where I'll be taking all my business from now on. Tell Tommo that from me. He'll understand.'

Paul flushes and gives me the finger. As I pull out, his toadlike mouth forms a single syllable.

I seem to be collecting four-letter words.

It's almost three o'clock. My Guinness euphoria has completely dissipated and I'm grim and pissed off. This constant watching the clock, the sky, racing against time. I'm sick of it. At this rate a heart attack will get me long before the mist has a chance.

I sit on 130 the whole way, the engine wailing. I keep the radio on, to keep track of the time through the news updates, not wanting to risk taking my eyes off the road for a second, not even to glance at my watch. Gina has caught my sense of urgency and she fidgets, looking first out of the windscreen, then turning to the passenger window, as if continually gauging our progress. As we fly past our usual rest stop she throws me a puzzled expression.

When we reach the Nebulah turn-off I still have the

headlights off, but the light is starting to fade. We have about ten minutes to spare.

At Milly's I screech into the long driveway and pull up right at the front door, don't bother going round the back, there's no time. I grab the esky and whatever shopping bags I can reach and sprint up the front steps just as the sun drops completely behind the trees, which start to writhe with sunset murmurings.

None of the curtains are shut and the house is open. I dump the esky in the hall and slam the door behind Gina. I check the back door and pull the curtains on that side of the house, then see to the ones in the lounge before heading into the light of the kitchen.

Milly is on the phone. I try to catch her eye, mouth 'Liz?', but she keeps her eyes down and won't look at me. Outside the mist has already built to a howl. I pull the kitchen curtains as Milly says into the phone, 'Yes, he's here now. Would you like to speak to him? No, actually, I think I'd like to speak to him first.' She sounds unusual, there is a touch of strain to her; she is conclusive, almost harsh. 'Well, I can't really thank you for calling or say that I've enjoyed talking to you. But it's been most interesting.'

By now I'm intrigued. I'm pulling a beer from the fridge, still hyped from the rush, when Milly puts the phone down. Only then does she meet my eye. 'You made it,' she says flatly.

'Just. Who was that?'

'Your friend. The "mind-reader". The one you find so convincing.' She entwines her fingers and places her hands

227

firmly on the benchtop. It is through the preciseness of this gesture that I can tell how angry she is.

'We had a most charming conversation. She said that I will be responsible for killing you.'

I take a long pull on the beer. I say, carefully neutral, 'Yes, she's told me that too.'

'And you believe her?'

Outside there are fingernails scraping at the window and a frenzied scratching at the back door. Laughter rises. Neither of us moves to turn the radio on. It is the background noise we need for this conversation.

I clear my throat. 'Yes,' I say. 'I think I do.'

'You've met her once, when she almost got you killed, and you're willing to believe any unfounded, malicious thing she says. Sorry – predicts.'

'She's not like that. She's… normal.' I'm struggling. Outside there's a shriek.

'Normal,' repeats Milly. 'Ordinary.'

'Sane.'

She won't play. I have never seen her like this, her face is grey and stretched tight. 'I wouldn't have believed you could be so underhanded, keeping this sort of thing from me.' She delivers each word with deliberation. 'I have never asked you to stay here with me and I have certainly never asked you to martyr yourself for me. How many other people have you discussed your noble sacrifice with, going valiantly to your doom because of a stubborn, selfish old woman who doesn't know what's good for her?'

'You're overreacting.'

'No, I'm reacting. I'm furious and disgusted, and tomorrow you're packing your bags.'

'I won't go without you.'

'I don't care what you do. Move back to your own place if you're too stupid to leave town, but you're not sacrificing yourself for me any longer.'

Outside there's another howl and a thump that shakes the house. The laughter starts anew, shrieking and gleeful. Gina starts to pace and whimper.

I look down at her. My stomach lurches. 'Milly…'

'I won't be accused. I won't be seen as a death warrant. If you stay here, it has nothing to do with me.'

I turn on the radio to drown out the noise and Milly raises her voice. 'More than capable of looking after myself,' she's saying, and then she suddenly stops as I kneel beside Gina, who's trembling and whimpering, her ears flat. And the radio isn't quite loud enough to drown out the noises from outside, as she realises that the phone call that upset her so much had distracted her from Felix, who was outside, asleep in the ute, when darkness fell.

PART
FIVE

I don't mind the cold of the winter nights, even the streetlights are still a novelty. I get a kick out of the biting air, being out in the darkness, with the humid warmth from a steaming parcel of fish and chips, deliciously vinegary. I've taken to finding excuses to go out for something just on dark: a newspaper, milk, rollie papers. It's not a long walk from Sean's to the shop, but it's not exercise I'm after. It's the sense of freedom, still so new, and such a celebration.

Once I get back to Sean's, Milly and I will wrap ourselves in blankets and sit outside to eat, even though it means our food is instantly tepid from the cooling evening air. There aren't many stars to see so close to the centre of town, but we silently acknowledge the need to get ourselves out into the dark, recondition ourselves to living normal lives. Otherwise we'd continue as before, holed up like moles, nervous and, in hindsight, probably stir-crazy.

Milly is already in position on the back deck when I get there, wrapped in her doona with a beanie pulled down over her ears, a glass of wine in front of her and a beer ready for me. Sauce, lemon wedges, salt and pepper. Even a candle. Little things. For us, fish and chips is a special meal, a treat to be savoured. We frequently assert how bad it is for us, swear off it, and still succumb to it every second night. The salty taste of civilisation.

We left Nebulah the same morning I buried the little that remained of Felix, Milly too limp with grief and guilt to resist. Strike while the iron's hot, was my thinking, grim but determined. Poor old Felix. But he'd been the linchpin I'd needed and I wasn't averse to making sure his death wasn't in vain. *You see,* I was geared up to say, *see how easy it is to be careless, and it only has to happen once. No second chances.* But I'd spare her the details of how he died; I couldn't be that callous.

But after all these months of resistance, I didn't even have to say anything. The instant she realised she'd left Felix outside in the mist, she knew she was lost. She had no chance of asserting safety or survival after that. Felix had been her responsibility, her devoted pet. And I was getting desperate: I wasn't prepared to offer placations, or say that his death wasn't her fault.

She'd spent that night sitting rigid on the couch, her hands clasped like claws in her lap. No tears, no pills. I tried to sit up with her at first, but the day had been too much for me and I staggered off to bed around midnight, to spend a hellish night filled with hunks of rotting fish, writhing between the jaws of a dirt-encrusted dog. I woke up feeling demented, worn to the point of collapse; much more and

I'd be joining Rolf. That was when I determined that Felix wasn't going to have died for nothing.

But my carefully rehearsed speeches were never given. When I shuffled out into the kitchen I found the cupboard doors open, and most of the food already sorted for packing. A suitcase and a box of books waited by the door.

Milly's face was grey, her eyes huge dark pits. 'There's coffee on the stove,' she said.

I poured myself a cup, strong and black. 'Did you sleep at all?'

She shrugged, shook her head tensely. 'Don't think I'll be sleeping for a while,' she said softly.

'Milly, I don't know what to say.'

'Yes you do. Only you know you don't need to. That would just be cruel.' She bent and peered into the cupboard by the stove. 'I guess we won't be needing the saucepans for now. Come back for them when we're settled somewhere.' She trailed off. There was a patch of weak winter light which had peeped around the corner of the unopened curtains, gleaming faintly on the benchtop beside her.

'Are you okay?' I asked.

She turned to me, her face utterly bereft. 'No,' she said. 'My dog. I'm a coward. I haven't even been outside to check.'

'I'll go.'

'I have no right to ask you to.'

'Forget it.' I cleared my throat, awkward. 'Can you keep Gina in here?'

'God, of course.' She beckoned Gina over and hooked

235

her fingers through her collar, scratching her neck, then she straightened up again. 'I'm so sorry I'm asking you to do this.'

'Just keep packing. As long as you keep packing, that's all you need to worry about.'

*

I buried what remained of Felix under a tall, stately gum, the kind of tree that would be an interesting conversationalist if it had the power of speech. I had to use the hose and the outside broom to clean off the back door, the coffee sour in my gullet. I was glad of my empty stomach.

We didn't take very much: the food, some clothes and bedding, papers and books. By lunchtime we were loaded up, Gina already in position, although subdued, in the passenger seat. We left in convoy, me tailing Milly's ute. As we turned from the driveway she didn't slow or look back.

At our rest stop she watched Gina sniff around the scrub and her hands shook.

'Well,' she said, raising her coffee cup. 'That's that, then.'

'A beginning as well as an end.'

She flung the dregs from her cup. 'Oh, it's an end, all right. It's over.'

*

That was over three weeks ago, and things are okay. We've avoided the question of where we will live, or how. The chances of finding a rental affordable for two pensioners, even in Woodford, are pretty slim. Our two homes, looked after and loved, worth nothing at all. I have no idea what we will do. But we have Sean's for nearly another month, plenty of time to worry. For now, we are revelling in fish and chips, and suburban evenings spent sitting outside, Gina still unsure and alert to every movement. The noise of people; distant laughter that doesn't make your blood run cold.

I ring Alex. Solstice is three days away. Her relief is palpable.

'Couldn't have you lose another old man,' I tell her.

'Thank God,' she repeats over and over. I couldn't really have asked for more.

I ring Alice too, but only get her answering machine. I remember she'll be well into exams, is probably snowed under. I leave a brief message, just asking her to call when she can.

Liz cries for Felix in the same way she grieved over Li. Always extremes. She's been advised by social services it could take over a year to provide her with state housing. I have plenty of time to worry about that sort of thing. It's a grim thought, and one that makes me feel extremely lucky.

*

Saturday 20 June dawns cold and wet. We sit by the open front door, watching the rain through the steam from our coffee, our picnic packed and ready and now forlorn on the kitchen bench. Not long after our arrival we'd wandered past the nearby school at lunchtime, and the noise of children playing was intoxicating. We breathed it in, filling our souls in the way that people rescued from drowning gulp to fill their lungs. The sounds of children, snatches of music from passing car stereos. People jogging, people with noisy leaf blowers, with prams and bags of shopping and screaming toddlers, anything. We started to feel drunk with the unaccustomed movement, the energy and the noise, realising with a start just how vacant our lives had been, confinement notwithstanding. The lack of company we've suffered, that basic human contact, however brief or fleeting, hits us with a force obvious in hindsight, but unexpectedly affecting.

We discovered the urge to get out, to be around company, and had taken to spending time at the riverside barbecues and picnic benches, lolling close to groups and bathing in the sounds of families at play together. We spent our first weekend at the local park, with sandwiches and a thermos of tea like a pair of displaced grandparents, watching parents cheer junior football matches, clustered in groups to laugh and barrack. Couples wandered past, and women with kids who chased the seagulls unendingly. It was all magic.

Birds.

Milly's book lay unheeded in her lap as we soaked up our surroundings like the sun's rays. It went without saying that Saturday's picnic lunch was already prepared and packed before we turned in on Friday night.

But now the rain, driving and insistent. There would be no family outings, no barbecues.

'Bugger,' Milly curses, the prospect of a day cosily confined unappealing now that our world has expanded.

We regard each other with shamefaced disappointment. By lunchtime the rain still isn't letting up, and we've accepted defeat. Milly has settled with *David Copperfield* for probably the hundredth time, and I've rummaged through Sean's hall cupboard and found a 1500-piece jigsaw, a tiny distant villa surrounded by acres of autumn leaves. I've spread it over the dining table and am halfway through sorting it into edgy bits and middle bits, thinking about the egg sandwiches wrapped in the fridge, and perhaps a beer, when my mobile shrills. I'm not in the mood, but when I check it the display says it's Alice. The day brightens.

'Hey,' she sings to my greeting. 'Where are you?'

'I'm in Paradise. Where are you?'

'I'm at your place.'

I feel a chill like a hand with long cold fingers. 'What?'

'In Nebulah. Where are you?'

'In Woodford. With Milly.'

'You're joking! That explains why the place is all shut up. I was panicking a bit there.'

'What are you doing there? Why didn't you call?'

'Well, it was a whim thing, really. As soon as I finished exams we decided to take off, left last night in a rush, stayed with friends in Mandurah, and now here we are!'

'You should have rung first. We're at Sean's for the time being, but there's probably enough room for you.'

There's a short, uncomfortable pause. 'Um, there's five of us.'

'What?'

'There's a group of us. I thought maybe we could stay at Li's place.'

'What the hell for?'

'Well,' she starts to hedge, 'when I got back to Perth I was talking about what I experienced here, you know, the figures and the poem. And a few people were really interested. My friend Alan is Cambodian as well, so he was pretty taken with what happened, and Xandrea is an expert at supernatural phenomena.'

'An expert?'

'She's a medium. Don't laugh.'

'It's not funny.'

'Don't be all cynical. There are people around who are tuned in to these things, like a special frequency. Xandrea's a really powerful witch, and she thinks she can translate what's happening with the mist, she was totally unfazed by what I told her. I know you probably won't believe me.'

I feel like a complete hypocrite, but I'm also angry. 'Who are the others? Witch's apprentices?'

She ignores this. 'Rob's my… friend, and Polly is studying the occult with Xandrea.'

'The occult. With Xandrea.'

'Don't be like that. I'd have thought you of all people would be open-minded. She thinks she'll be able to help.'

'I am open-minded, but I'm also familiar with Nebulah. Believe me when I tell you she won't be helping.'

Her voice is small. 'You sound angry.'

I take a breath. 'I won't be when you're safe in Woodford.

I'll book you some rooms at the motel. Two? Three?'

There's an awkward pause. I can hear muttering. A woman's voice says, 'I haven't driven all this way to stay in a friggin motel in Woodford'. Alice covers the phone, then returns a moment later. 'Um,' she says, 'everyone really wants to stay on here.'

'Alice, you can't be serious. Nebulah isn't a holiday destination.'

'Well, it's just. You know. It didn't seem that bad to me when I was here.'

'That's because it wanted you to come back.'

She takes this the wrong way. 'Really? Well, I wanted to come back too. I guess I felt that connection.'

'Alice, for God's sake, it was seducing you.'

'It was like that. But it was magical, a really affecting experience. To be honest, quite lovely. I feel like it's unfinished, like there's more it wants to tell me. And Xandrea's pretty sure she'll be able to communicate with it.'

I think I hate this Xandrea. 'Alice, this isn't some gentle northern breeze whispering sweet nothings. It's deadly. It kills people.'

'Xandrea thinks we'll be all right as long as we don't intrude on it. She's pretty experienced.'

'Experienced? She's seen people torn apart before?'

She's getting miffed. 'We're not stupid. We'll be careful, stay safe.'

'Where will you do that?'

'I'd thought Li's. Or maybe Milly's?'

'No way,' I say to Alice. 'Be prepared to leave. I'll be there in less than three hours.'

I hang up, aware of my blood thumping in my ears. I'm so angry I feel like putting my fist through the window. So much for hating violence. Milly is standing by the couch watching me, her book hanging at her side. 'What's happening?'

'Alice is at your place with an action team led by some flake who calls herself Xandrea. They're expecting a spiritual evening, a bit of om shanti and a nice chat with the mist.'

'Alice? Surely she's too bright for that?'

'Remember the night she was with us? It hooked her, reeled her in. Singing Cambodian poetry, all that chanting. It was after her. Hook, line and sinker.' I can't believe how stupid we were to let her stay.

'Where are my keys?' I still haven't got any better at them.

Milly limps to the stereo and picks up my keys but doesn't hand them to me. 'Are you sure?'

'There's still time. I can't leave her in the hands of some moron who claims to be psychic.'

There's an uncomfortable pause while Milly stands holding my keys. 'I thought psychics could be trusted?' she says. Then she sees my face and pulls back, holding up her hands in submission. 'Sorry.'

'Milly, I've got to get going.'

'At least call the station. Don't go alone.'

I'm impatient, about to dismiss this, but it's probably

a good idea. I'd been planning to threaten them with trespassing charges – if I've got the local constabulatory with me it'll save arguments. And time.

Thankfully it's Kathy on duty when I call. She's a good cop, brisk, efficient. When I tell her there's a group of intruders at our place in Nebulah with a view to spending the night, she asks what time it is, calculates quickly, and says she'll be over to pick me up in ten minutes. As I leave I ask Milly to book rooms at the motel. At the Land Cruiser I unlock the gun cabinet.

Kath notes the coat slung over my arm when she pulls up, and she frowns. She knows the .22 is under it. 'If that comes at all, it stays locked in the boot.'

'Your call.'

She drives fast, skilfully, her seat pushed far back to accommodate her belly. She must be seven months by now, she's getting large.

'How come you got Saturday?' I ask her.

'Denham hasn't had a day off since Sean went on leave. I'm only part-time now.' She pats her stomach. 'I offered.'

'Ah.' I can't help smirking. 'Dedicated Denham.'

She shoots me a look, half measures of amusement and disapproval. 'He's a hard worker.'

I acknowledge the rebuff and let it drop. 'When's bub due?'

'Two more months. The sooner the better, according to my blood pressure. And my back.'

'Otherwise okay?'

'Not taking any chances.' She gives me a hard look. 'None. We're getting this over quick smart. You'd better fill me in on your little mates.' I start to feel more relaxed. I know Kath when she's on a mission. I'd hate to be in Xandrea's shoes when we get there.

*

It's over mercifully quickly. They're at my place, and are shamefaced and cowed when they see the squad car. They're still outside, exploring the locked house, trying to find a way in; they drift to an uncomfortable group at the sound of the approaching car, crestfallen when they see the insignia. When the owner turns up with the cops, you can't really argue that you've been invited. Excitement is quickly defused in the face of stark reality. The rain has slowed to a fine drizzle.

Alice moves to the side of the man who has been trying the front door, a stocky, unkempt youth with sandy hair. He reaches an arm around her. The others examine their feet as we pull up. The sharp slam of the car doors ricochets around us. Kath hoists up her belt and adjusts the rim of her hat. 'Afternoon,' she greets them, her voice deadpan. 'I'm assuming you guys are well aware you're on private property?'

The woman called Xandrea, an unimaginative goth with overdyed hair and too much jewellery, begins some bravado, claiming that as free citizens they can go where they like, but Kath doesn't even bother with her. The look she directs into Xandrea's heavily kohled eyes is withering, and she isn't even angry.

She turns to address the others, effectively writing Xandrea off. 'It's your choice. You can get back in your car and leave this minute as "free citizens", or I can arrest you for trespass and attempted break and enter and escort you to Woodford police station for charging.'

They look uneasy, recognising that they have no choice, but they're reluctant to bow to such heavy-handedness. Alice stands with her eyes lowered, looking bereft. Kath glances at her watch. 'That wasn't a question. In the car now or I start reading rights.'

The Cambodian boy, a serious-looking beanpole with trendy geometrical glasses, breaks from the group and stalks over to the station wagon, folding himself into the back seat. A young, overweight girl with pigtailed hair trails awkwardly after him. The boy next to Alice – Rob, I assume – takes Alice's arm, stroking it gently. 'Come on,' he whispers to her. As they pass she looks at me, half-beseeching.

'Milly's booked rooms at the motel in Woodford. But you two can stay with us if you'd rather.'

Alice looks torn. As yet she hasn't said a word to me. The boy puts his hand on her back. 'We'll talk it over,' he says. 'Thanks.' At the car he gets into the driver's seat and fires the engine.

'We'll be tailing you into town,' Kath calls to them, then turns with a no-nonsense expression to the remaining woman. 'Coming, love?' There is more than a faint trace of sarcasm in her voice.

The woman crosses her arms, uncomfortably defiant.

Rings laden with gaudy stones in Celtic settings weigh down her fingers.

'Maybe she should stay,' I suggest, quietly.

Kath appears to ruminate. 'Well, she is a free citizen, and if she has your permission, then legally there's nothing I can do. Right, well, let's get these others back to safety, then.'

Xandrea's flush is so deep it almost overwhelms her henna. She's not convinced we're bluffing. Which is as well for her – we're not. She manages to hold her ground till we reach the patrol car and Kath calls to the others to get a move on, then she stalks over to the station wagon. I note that although it's Alice's Rob driving, Alice herself is crammed into the back seat with the other two. Xandrea rides in the front.

I'd very much like to leave that one here after all.

*

Back in town we steer them to the motel. As Kath drops me off she shifts uncomfortably in her seat, then hauls herself out to stretch. It isn't till then that I notice the strain around her eyes.

'Too much?'

She's pressing her fists against her lower back, leaning back against them. She nods. 'Long drive,' she says. 'Don't think I'll be doing much more of that for a while.'

'Bath,' I say.

She checks her watch. 'Very shortly.' She lowers herself back into the car, groaning. 'Good luck with this lot. Happy to lay charges against the Moon Goddess there.' She gestures towards Xandrea, who is regarding the motel office with obvious disgust.

'I'll get Milly over,' I tell her, 'she'll sort her out.'

Kath laughs. 'Too right she will.' She gestures towards the boot of the car. 'I'll drop your accessory off on my way past.'

Alice and Rob approach as she drives away. Alice is grey and looks close to tears.

'I'm so sorry,' she begins immediately. 'I should never have come without asking you first.'

'No,' I say. 'You shouldn't.'

'It just seemed such a great opportunity. I got overexcited.'

'It's dangerous to be overexcited in Nebulah.' I look at the man standing beside her and nod.

'God, I'm hopeless today.' Alice jumps. 'Pete, this is Rob.'

We shake hands. He doesn't try to impress with his grip and his gaze seems steady, through messy hair.

'Will you stay with us?' I ask.

Alice looks awkward. It's Rob who answers. 'It might be more diplomatic if we stay with the others. Under the circumstances.'

'Fair enough. I can recommend the Arms for a good feed.'

'Sounds good. Will you join us?' He adds, almost coyly, 'Alice talks about you guys all the time.'

'Please,' Alice chimes in. 'I owe you a drink. Several.'

'Line em up, then. Bout six? Give you time to get sorted out.'

Rob looks towards the numbered rooms lining the car park and checks his watch.

'I could eat a bloody horse,' he says. 'Six sounds awesome.'

As they move away he puts his arm around Alice's waist, and next to his solid presence she seems tiny, almost fluid in her frailness. Perhaps it wasn't just the green dress that gave the impression of a river. They pass reception just as the others emerge, and stop to confer. Xandrea looks over towards me. I haven't seen a scowl like that since Christmas at Julie's.

*

Milly's enthusiasm for dinner with Alice is thwarted by a steady day's rain on arthritic joints; the thought of sitting up is too much. She scrawls a note for Alice, and curls up in blankets on the couch.

I'm a bit late, and they're there when I arrive, huddled at a table near the fire. Rob goes for drinks while Alice introduces me to the others. They all look a bit awkward, except for Xandrea, who has clearly decided to change tack. She has put on a garish velvet dress, and her manner is equally elaborate and badly judged.

'Pete, Alice has told us so much about you. How lovely you've come to join our soiree,' she exclaims through a smile worthy of Luna Park, reaching out a hand in a pointedly languid manner. 'Especially after our little afternoon fiasco.'

Alan squirms, and Polly starts to delicately nibble at her fingernails. Her teeth seem surprisingly small.

'Please allow me to apologise on behalf of us all for the misunderstanding,' Xandrea continues. 'You see, Alice seemed to think it would be okay, so we hadn't anticipated any problems. She hadn't realised you'd left town – you can imagine how we felt, after such a long drive!' Her laughter is loud and mannered.

I have no wish to argue with this woman. 'Forget it,' I say.

'But I mean, there are degrees of unwelcome I've obviously yet to plunder. When you arrived with the police! But as I said, it was just a misunderstanding, on every side.' She laughs again, to demonstrate her jagged good nature.

Alice seems to be shrinking. Ignoring Xandrea, I reach out and squeeze her hand.

'How'd your exams go?'

She brightens and everyone seizes the opportunity to leave dangerous ground; the conversation turns general. Rob, like Alice, is studying architecture, Alan is in engineering and Polly, the finger gnawer, social sciences. Of the four, Alan seems the most focused. Xandrea, obviously not a student, is sidelined, and drags her most steadfast ally, the disconsolate Polly, into a discussion on energy levels.

Things remain pleasant while we order and eat. I avoid Xandrea's conversation as much as possible, and she is too vain to risk another rebuff from me. The meals are large and basic pub fare. After a huge feed and several well-deserved pints, I'm feeling relaxed and even starting to enjoy myself. Beside me Alice has fired up and is lively and entertaining, teasing Rob mercilessly. He responds with good-natured indulgence, which provokes her to accuse him of having the temperament of a Saint Bernard.

'Gina'd love you,' I respond.

'And Felix!' pipes Alice. She's quick enough to catch my look. 'What?'

'We lost Felix.'

'What?' Her gasp causes the others to stop talking and tune in. 'What do you mean?'

'There was a bit of confusion. He got left out.'

The faces around the table are a mixture of discomfort and disbelief. 'What do you mean "left out"?' asks Alan.

'I mean at night. With the mist.'

'And?' Xandrea is breathy, melodramatic.

'It ate him.'

Polly cringes, but Xandrea looks unconvinced. 'Surely that would have been wild dogs? I've read that ferals are a problem in Nebulah.'

'Feral dogs are not the problem. They're not into decorating with their leftovers.'

She looks at me for a beat, then pointedly shrugs. 'If you say so.'

'Is Milly okay?' Alice breaks in.

'Better now. She was pretty crushed. Blames herself, of course.'

'I didn't think you'd ever get her to leave.'

'Felix was the last straw. She could hardly argue she was safe from slipping up when that happened.'

'God,' mouths Polly, 'that's awful.'

Xandrea pulls a packet of cigarettes from the bag hanging on her chair and lights one up without asking if anyone minds. 'But you're safe as long as you're indoors?'

I don't bother to answer. She blows smoke. 'Isn't that correct? Otherwise you wouldn't be here with us, would you?'

'You're never truly safe,' I tell her, my jaw already working. 'It gets to you in other ways.'

'But if we'd been in the house, we'd have been okay. Like Alice was.' It's not a question.

'How would you have gotten in?'

She shrugs. 'We could easily have forced a window.'

'If you'd gone ahead as you'd planned you'd all be dead by now. Or still dying.'

Xandrea's not enjoying having her authority ambushed. She taps her ash into the dregs of her vodka glass and says quietly, 'I actually don't think we would be. Based on my past experience, and what Alice has told me of the mist's behaviour, it's a potent spiritual force, but not necessarily a violent one.'

'She's wrong.'

'She came back from Nebulah exhilarated, excited, not scared at all.'

Alice looks at me, embarrassed. 'It's true. That was my experience of it, I didn't feel it was malignant or evil at all. I really found it quite beautiful.'

'That's because it was manipulating you. That's what it does.'

Xandrea leapt. 'So you agree that it's capable of interaction?'

'I *agree* that it's cunning and manipulative. But let me

251

assure you, it would tear out your throat before you got through your neighbourly introductions.'

The others are listening keenly. For all her evident faults, Xandrea has a strong personality, an assurance in her own authority that lends her a certain credible charisma. It's obvious she is used to holding people's attention. She casually takes a final puff on her cigarette and drops the butt into her glass. 'I have come across these kinds of disturbances before, you know,' she says.

'I doubt that.'

'I've always found,' she continues, 'that it's dependent on the atmosphere, the approach used – that determines the response of the entity. You, for example, are clearly hostile, whereas Alice, who is less... inclined to be aggressive, had a completely different reaction and experience of it.'

'Are you saying that the people it's killed just had the wrong attitude?'

She frowns. 'Of course I'm not. It's simply a matter of experience, of knowing how to go about these things.'

'You're an idiot.' I've spoken too loud and people at nearby tables look over. Xandrea smirks, pleased to have finally made a mark.

'You see,' she says, 'if that's the way you tend to respond to people – friends, I might add – it's no wonder your experiences with something you don't understand are so fraught.'

'Fraught! It's killed my friends, our pets.'

'Why doesn't it kill the wild dogs?'

'What about the fucking wild dogs?'

'They're out in the mist, aren't they? Why aren't they hurt?'

'Sometimes they are. But fundamentally they have the same sort of nature, they hunt and kill, the mist isn't interested in them.'

'So it doesn't kill everything?'

'It would kill you. In a heartbeat. And I'll tell you straight that wouldn't bother me one little bit. But go on your own – don't drag along innocent people you've no hope of protecting.'

'Excuse me, my friends are all adults, they make their own decisions.'

Polly is now chewing on her ring finger in earnest. Beside her, Alan is folding his napkin into smaller and smaller shapes. Both Alice and Rob look deeply uncomfortable.

'Decisions led by you, when you have no idea what you're talking about. You pretend you know what you're doing and that they'd be safe, when you have no idea at all what you'd be up against. In reality, you're just a coward. You'd never go in there on your own.'

'You don't know me!'

'I think you're a crock of shit.'

People at the tables around us are now watching with open amusement, enjoying the spectacle. Rob stands up. 'Maybe we should call it a night. It's been a rough day, for everyone.'

'And you have a long drive home in the morning.' I stand and turn to Alice. 'I'll come say goodbye tomorrow.'

She nods and reaches up to give me a peck on the cheek, but her eyes are troubled and barely meet mine.

*

That night I'm too angry to sleep, and when I finally do I dream badly again. I'm driving through thick clouds like smoke, and I turn to find Polly in the passenger seat. She's chewing at her nails again, and as she does her teeth start to grow, until they're long and thin and jagged, and she starts to bite at her fingers, gnawing them into bloodied stumps. I throw open the door, and land with a thud on the ground, which starts to sway. I'm in a boat, surrounded by a sea of mist, which breaks into figures that rise like waves and hurtle towards me, building up momentum as they approach the boat, slamming into its sides, threatening to capsize it. I'm thrown from side to side, hanging on for all I'm worth, because I know that if I'm spilled overboard into the mist I'm done for. And then I realise that it's chanting to me, a gentle crooning like a lullaby. The words are dim and obscure at first, and then they become clearer, the bedtime rhyme: *When the bough breaks, the cradle will fall…*

I wake with a moan, disoriented and motion-sick. I lie gasping in the bed, trying to get clean air into my sour mouth, when the door, ajar, slowly starts to swing open.

I can't move, trying to work out where I am, with panic

curdling my guts, when Gina sticks her muzzle into the room, and peers towards me, looking worried. I must have called out and woken her. I call to her and she trots to my side and sits next to the bed, licking her lips. 'Good girl,' I croon, and realise with a start that I'm actually close to tears. And then I realise what day it is.

June the twenty-first. Solstice.

*

At the motel the next morning the wagon is loaded up in relative silence. Alan, Polly and Xandrea are clustered around it, ready to get going, while Alice and Rob finish paying for their room.

'Good morning,' Xandrea calls. 'Come to escort us out of town?'

'Yes.'

'You needn't worry. We'd hardly risk going back to Nebulah after what you said. We're not stupid. Besides,' she adds casually, 'there's no point. You'd just bring your mates out and have us arrested.'

'That's right. Unless you were on your own. Then you could stay as long as you liked, with my blessing. In fact, I'd give you a lift.'

She ignores this and turns to Rob and Alice, who are approaching. Rob stops and reaches out his hand. 'We appreciate everything you've done. Sorry we caused you so much hassle.'

'Come anytime. When we're settled, you'd be welcome.'

He nods, looking doubtful, and I get the impression there probably won't be a next time. I turn to Alice. She steps straight into me and hugs me tight. 'I'm sorry,' she says. 'I hope you understand.'

'I couldn't bear anything to happen to you. We should never have let you stay that night.' My hand against her head looks large and clumsy. 'Let me know when you get home.'

She nods. 'Will do.' When she stands back she keeps her eyes down and presses her hands together in front of her chest, giving me one of her deep, elegant bows. Then she turns and curls into the back seat.

I'm touched at the affection she's demonstrated, the huge hug. It isn't until much later that I realise she was simply trying to avoid my eyes.

*

The Eastern Highway, the meandering sole route to the road to Nebulah, is sixty-five kilometres north of Woodford. I don't intend to go further than that; there's no need to. To meet the Eastern and approach the Nebulah road from the other direction would involve a dogleg of close to 450 kilometres. I tail them about ten k's past the turn-off, then I drop back with a blast of the horn and chuck a U-ie.

I'm not stupid, though. Or rather, I just need to be sure. Peace of mind is never to be sneezed at. There's an open gravelly patch off the side of the road by the Eastern turn-off. I have my book with me, and my lunch. I wait for two hours, till I'm rigid with boredom and Gina looks ready to walk back to Woodford without me.

It's enough. It's solstice. And it's over.

I turn back to town.

PART
SIX

Over. It's a funny thing how people are always looking to compartmentalise their lives, drawing boundaries and edges as if to delineate befores and afters, like psychological picket fences. Before my marriage, my divorce, my retirement. Before my life turned upside down; before I lost everything; before I thought I had nothing more to lose.

Over. As if nothing lives on in thoughts or memories, doesn't keep churning, brewing. Fermenting.

The mind always knows, on some level. Outside the carefully erected barricades of the conscious, the seething still goes on. It's in the exiled depths, where the subconscious is sitting dealing cards with the sixth sense, that innate knowledge. Lying in wait. Like an insidious vine impossible to eradicate, they uncurl their tendrils, lassoing shoots into the slightest of cracks.

Thriving in the spaces we refuse to look.

When I get home, telling myself over and over that it's finished, that it's solstice and I'm safe, I find I can't settle. I end up pacing, flat and restless, and try to console myself that it's just the aftermath, a reaction to the stress of the last couple of days, weeks, months.

I should have known – I do know – when the relief I long to feel is so elusive, that *Over* is not a button you press to bring the curtains down. Show. Over.

I do know. While I pace and fret, unsettling Milly and unable to focus on the jigsaw or contemplate a book, I know. When I finally decide to give up and brave the chilly afternoon for a walk to the pub – a bit early, but just a quick one, a bit of company by the fire – I'm sure that in the depths of my mind I already know what I'm going to find.

*

She's huddled by the fire with a glass of something red and sickly, looking forlorn and utterly worn-out. She's gazing into the gas flicker of the replica log fire, chewing indifferently on a thumb, and so lost in her own thoughts she doesn't even notice me approaching until I sit opposite her.

'Polly.'

A rainbow of emotions rushes over her face: fear, dismay, regret and evasion. And the worst one of all, the one I expected but still hoped I wouldn't see: guilt.

'Shit.'

I'm overtaken by a fatigue that seems to leach the life out of my very bones.

'When?'

'Please, just leave them alone – they'll kill me.'

'How long ago did they leave?'

She squirms. 'An hour? Hour and a half? We waited a few hours up the road, so it was already… I dunno, two-ish?' Laughter from the pool table breaks into her pause. 'I couldn't cope cooped up in that room.' Her hands are clenched. 'I wouldn't go. They were pissed off, having to bring me back. I promised I wouldn't leave the motel. Shit.' It's getting on for three o'clock. On the shortest day of the year, which means it's too late.

So it's over, I think. *Soon*, unheard voices breathe around me. I don't want to know.

Polly is watching me, nervous. 'What are you going to do?'

I'm sagged with my hands between my legs. It takes all my energy to just raise my head. 'I don't know,' I tell her, and I'm so tired.

She keeps her hands clasped tightly together in her lap and begins to gnaw at her lip. 'Will they be okay?'

'No.'

One hand snakes to her mouth, unnoticed. Her words start to tumble. 'It was Xandrea, she was so determined to go, she kept saying it was winter solstice and the most powerful time of the year for a connection. She kept going on about what an amazing opportunity it was, like it was some kind of festival. And Alice wasn't sure, she felt guilty, but she did really want to go back, and Xandrea kept reminding her of how beautiful it was and she…'

Polly breaks off and breathes deeply. 'Rob didn't want to go, but he was worried about Alice. Alan, well, Alan lost most of his family and he doesn't say much. Alice told me once that the Khmer Rouge came to his father's village when his dad was just a small boy, and gathered everyone in the square and made them watch while they disembowelled the schoolteacher. He was squatting in the dirt, trying to hold his insides in his hands while the flies started to swarm, and the soldiers watched the villagers and anyone who cried or tried to look away was singled out for the same. So they had to watch and keep their faces impassive, and his father managed to escape with another family not long after, but I don't think Alan's had a very nice life. I don't know, he's usually pretty remote, but when Alice talked about the poetry he got really interested. Like it's a chance, a connection he missed.' She takes a breath and begins to wind down. 'Xandrea seems to know what she's talking about, though,' she hazards, subsiding.

'No. She has no idea.'

Polly nods, lowering her head and regarding her ravaged fingernails. 'She said that if I was scared of something like this I'd never make it as a Wiccan.' Her pudgy fingers flex. 'But shit, I never really believed all that crap. Spells and incantations – it was just fun.' She shrugs again. 'I always hated Sunday school.'

I can't muster up the energy to respond. A thick tear banks in the corner of her eye and slowly snakes down her face. 'I couldn't go. I had this dream last night that we were there and my teeth kept growing, they were like these long sharp tombstones. It was awful, I started eating my fingers and there was blood everywhere and I woke up and felt so sick.' She shudders and roughly swipes at the tear. 'I was determined never… but I couldn't, I just couldn't.'

There's another burst of laughter at the bar and she's at her nails again. I get up. Her head jerks. 'What are you going to do?'

I turn away.

'Please don't tell them I told you!' she calls after me. As if it still matters.

*

At the police station, Denham is arguing with a burly man whose fence has been graffitied again, who's insisting he knows who's behind it and can't seem to grasp the concept of evidence, thinks that kids swearing at him in the street is enough to prove guilt. Kath would have been better at dealing with him, she'd have assured the guy of his status as victim, which is really all he wants, and he would have left acknowledged, happily aggrieved. Denham is too officious to calm him, a brick wall, and the man, exasperated, moves on to his neighbour's barking dogs. Denham's eyes flicker towards me. He makes no move to wind things up. The utilitarian, endlessly reliable clock on the wall behind him seems to leer. I already know I'm wasting my time.

A few minutes into the incessant barking the man's mobile rings. He hesitates, torn, but like most people can't resist. Begrudgingly, he comes to a stop. As he pushes past me he is already building up to give his caller an earful.

At the counter Denham plays with a bundle of paper, keeping his eyes averted. I wait, calm and still; I am wasting my time. When he looks up, finally, his gaze is empty and cold. He is a busy man, it tells me. Nothing I have to tell him could be of interest.

'We have a problem,' I say.

His expression doesn't change. 'What can I do for you?'

'There's a group of kids in Nebulah, planning to stay overnight.'

Slowly, methodically, Denham starts to straighten the pile of forms in front of him. 'And?' he says.

'And they will be killed.'

He clicks in the nib of his biro and returns it to his pocket.

'How old are these "kids"?'

'Early twenties.'

He nods and meets my eye for the first time. 'Adults,' he says.

'Barely.'

'Legally. Old enough to take responsibility for themselves.'

'They will be killed.'

He shrugs. 'You don't know that.'

'They have no idea what they're doing, what they're in for.'

There it is, the faintest flash of aggression, a tinge of a smirk.

'I don't think I quite understand what it is you expect from the police department.'

I'm wasting my time. 'To get them out.'

'Under what jurisdiction?'

'Any!'

'They're not doing anything illegal.'

'You could still do something.'

'They're adults and they're not breaking the law.'

'They're going to die. You don't care.'

It's as though I've pushed a button, the sudden ignition.

'I'll tell you what I care about. People with nothing better to do, throwing their weight around and wasting police resources time and again. You act like you're some kind of veteran big shot. Sergeant Williams may humour your constant whims, but don't expect me to.'

'Denham, listen to me, this…'

'No, you listen to me. Didn't you hear what I just said? This stops now. Yesterday you dragged Constable Green out on a seven-hour personal mission, one of your vendettas again, and now she's under medical supervision, unlikely to return to work before she's had the baby. And now you come waltzing in here again, acting like some retired emperor, expecting me to drop everything and chase after this mob again, all because they committed the serious crime of not doing what you told them.'

'This isn't about me.'

Denham's face is ugly with hostility. 'Yes it is. You're too far up yourself to see it, you and your little power trips, acting like Sean's your personal bloody cop on call. If you'll excuse me, I've actually got more important things to attend to.'

'Like barking dogs.'

He smirks. 'Yes. Precisely.'

I'd known I was wasting my time, I'm not even angry. 'You're a pathetic excuse for a cop,' I tell him, nice and even. 'If Kath were here, even in her condition she'd make an attempt to save those people. She's worth a hundred of you. This isn't about me, it's about you being willing to let them die because you're a fucking coward.'

His face is draining to an anaemic shade of mist. 'You're all smoke,' I keep going, 'hiding behind your pile of forms. The truth is you're too fucking scared to go out there.'

'I don't get told what to do by a drunk.'

'No, you'll just let a drunk do your job for you.'

'My job doesn't involve bending over every time you get an urge. Out. Now.'

'You'll have blood on your hands for the rest of your life.'

The grin he gives me stretches over his teeth. 'I'll live,' he says. 'Now why don't you just fuck off.'

Denham turns away. Above him the clock oversees my departure, its implacable hands like a stop signal.

*

By the park I start to shake from the confrontation. Insults thrown so effortlessly; so much simpler to transfer guilt or hang-ups rather than face them. Wog, nip, homo: *you have to be the same as me or I won't matter.* Coward: *I'm terrified.*

I veer across the grass to lower myself onto a bench.

Nearby a group of kids on skateboards yell and clatter into the last of the day.

The last of the day. Already the sun is starting to wane. The only hope remaining is that they leave now, clear the town boundary before dark. Needless to say, Alice's phone is switched off.

One of the skateboarders, an older boy, is doing tricks, handstands on his board. He throws his legs, bent, into the air, then flips right over. Over and over he launches, the other boys trying unsuccessfully to follow suit. Their T-shirts flop over their heads, revealing long, lanky torsos, smooth and hairless. Not an ounce of fat on them; they'll probably go home shortly and eat their body weight in food, only to burn it up again by tomorrow's lunchtime.

One kid loses his balance and falls, only to spring up again, rubbing an elbow. The resilience of young bones, wrists and knees that can be depended upon, muscles that work without strain or effort.

A retired emperor. Not even that. Just old. Old and looking towards the dark and knowing that it can't be done. That I can't do it.

*

From its first appearance, even before we were aware of the danger it embodied, the mist emanated a palpable sense of threat. The disappearance of the unexplained convoy had everyone unnerved, so even before the mist enveloped the town people were already ill at ease. Sean and Napes had headed back to Woodford perplexed, unsure of how to go about the report they'd have to file.

There was a clutch of locals at the pub, Saturday regulars plus an extra posse who'd been spooked by the events at the cemetery and wanted to go over and over what had happened. For all the speculation and disbelief, it was otherwise a Saturday night like any other. The bain-marie lights were switched on at six, and Joanne Hayes started filling it with barely edible food shortly after: dried-out roast beef and salty gravy. The last race, televised from the east, was about to start, and the only real difference between this night and any other was that for once people actually had something to talk about. Within the space of a couple of hours, opinions had solidified into facts, and people had become experts on the visitors' origins and their purpose. Conversations would range around these certainties until someone would pipe up with the obvious: but where did they go?

And around it would go, again and again, like the horses being flogged on the Flemington circuit.

It was just getting on dark when Dave Jones and Nicco Schultz, both belligerent know-alls, started to blue. With neither of them able to definitively claim the upper hand in the arguments circulating over the men's disappearance, they soon resorted to personal attacks on each other, and things got nasty. When Jonesy punctuated an insult with a sharp jab to Nicco's shoulder, Earl reached over the bar and plucked his beer from the counter, pouring it swiftly down the sink.

'Come off it!'

'Bar's closed for you, Jonesy. See you tomorrow.'

'You're fucken joking? Come on, Earl, it ain't even seven.'

'You want to start manhandling other patrons, your time's up.'

'It was just a friggin tap!'

'Out, before it becomes a ban.'

Jonesy flashed a victim's scowl at Nicco, and muttering audibly, slammed the pub door behind him.

'Bloody prick,' sniffed Nicco.

'You're on shaky ground too,' rounded Earl. 'You're like a pair of bloody kids.' Nicco stared at Earl without flinching. Lowering himself slowly onto his stool, he drained his glass in one gulp, then lobbed it carelessly onto the floor behind the bar.

'Fuck you.' He turned to the door, scandalised murmurs swelling behind him. The outrage was palpable; this sort of aggression wasn't usual in Nebulah.

'Don't come back!' someone shouted at his back, but before he'd even had a chance to reach the door, it flew open and Jonesy, looking pale and wild, shoved his way back in.

'Oi!' Nicco started, but Jonesy had already turned his back to him, was hunched over trying to peer through the frosted glass panels of the door. 'Man, you gotta see this,' he said to no one in particular.

'I thought I…'

Earl broke off when Jonesy spun round, distraught. 'There's something weird out there. For fuck's sake, look at this.'

His fear was electrifying, and a small crowd moved to

the windows. Daryl Burcott gave a snort. 'Yeah, right, mate,' he grunted. 'It's foggy.' He turned back to the bar.

'It's got people in it!'

'Yeah, it has. It's called a street.'

'No!' Jonesy was starting to seem a bit demented. 'Not like…'

'Jesus!' someone at the window called. 'What the hell is that?'

It was like a gate crashing open, and spurred by the growing unease, people crammed to the windows to see what was going on.

'Oh my God.' Eva Wallis backed away from the window. I pushed my way into her space.

The street outside was dark and empty, save for a large cloud of fog gradually rolling towards us. At first it appeared to be merely smoke, or perhaps rain, approaching, but after a short while it became obvious that this fog wasn't drifting in the usual way. It seemed to be writhing, seething almost obscenely. As it neared, it became more distinct: a mass of hideous smoky figures emerged, gliding along the street towards us.

'The door! Lock the fucking door!' someone was yelling. Jonesy fell aside looking terrified. 'The back!' he yelled, whirling to Earl. 'Is the back locked up?' Earl and Joanne scurried out of sight as the windows of the pub were suddenly shrouded, and a smoky sea of leering faces peered in at us, almost in mockery, mimicking us all gaping out. As a group we fell back, away from the windows. The apparitions stretched their mouths into leering laughter and pressed long, splayed fingers to the panes of glass between us.

The silence was broken by Daryl Burcott. 'What kind of sick joke is this?'

'Shush!' hissed Maeve Summers.

'Come on, will you? What the fuck? Look at us cowering here. Someone's pissing in his pants at us right now.'

The mood shifted and the tension relaxed a fraction, as people moved from fear to confusion.

'You reckon?'

'Shit, there'll be a camera somewhere – a projector, with some arsehole laughing his ring out at what a pack of gullible shits we are. And he's fucking right!' Daryl started to laugh.

'Shhh!' I said. 'Listen.'

From outside came muted shrieks of laughter, as if blown from a distance on the wind. But another noise could be heard growing within it, a ghostly throb, like a chant. Slowly it became clearer: '*Little little little little little little little little little little little…*'

It made your blood run cold.

'It's just a…' started Daryl.

'Shut up!'

The chant suddenly changed, evolving without pause into another two, equally disturbing syllables. '*Come out come out come out come out come out come out…*' There was a guttural shriek, and the voices around the building intensified. It was like being trapped in a demented thunderstorm.

'Well, speaking for myself –' Earl cleared his throat '– I'm staying put.'

'There's no way I'm going out there again,' said Jonesy, shuddering.

'What if it gets in?'

'Oh God!'

'My vote is that door stays locked,' I said.

'What if we're here all night?'

'Then we'll be here in the morning, which is all I care about just now.'

'It might go away?'

The forms began to flit from window to window. Earl stared after them. 'Daryl might be right. This might be some kind of elaborate joke.'

'Don't open the door!' We turned as one to Jonesy, this large, blustering man not given to flights of fancy, shuddering like a child who's just been plunged underwater for the first time. 'Jesus, I was out there, it's not a hoax. It's freezing cold, you could feel it coming towards you. This fucking horrible chill. It's like nothing, it's like death.'

'That's got my vote,' said Wally. 'If it's a hoax I'm happy to laugh it off in the morning.'

Outside, suddenly, there was the sound of an engine. A car – someone was coming. People began to push towards the windows again, as close to them as they dared. The hazy figures seething on the other side seemed to freeze; then, as if a vacuum had suddenly been aimed at them, they wrenched away in a single mass.

Tentatively, we moved closer to the windows. Outside it was perfectly still.

'What is it?' asked Earl.

Daryl shrugged, squinting along the street. 'Nothing. I reckon it's gone. Like someone got a scare from the car coming and turned whatever it was off.' He turned away from the windows with a sneer.

The thud at the window behind him was like a bomb. There was no warning or approach, just the sudden impact, the swift view of the spread-eagled body of a man in a bloodstained yellow shirt, sliding quickly out of sight, leaving nothing but thin, opaque trails of blood on the window's clear pane.

Dave Jones started to retch.

*

I slept eventually, clutches of rest rather than a proper sleep, stretched on the floor near the pool table, after several generous serves from Earl's top shelf. Earl had offered us the few rooms the pub had available, but no one seemed inclined to leave the company of the group, and one by one we subsided on the hard chairs or the beer-scented carpet of the front bar.

Naturally enough, the small Woodford police station wasn't manned overnight, and the triple-0 operator who answered Earl's emergency call was less than impressed by his claim that fourteen local punters were under siege by a cloud of smoke that seemed to have people in it – trapped in the town's pub, no less. He showed a glimmer of interest when Earl told him that a man's body had been slammed against the building, but this quickly dimmed when Earl admitted he'd only glimpsed the alleged corpse, and had no idea who it was.

The operator grew increasingly placatory, assuring Earl of the frequency of such calls, and how easy it was to mistake a large bird flying unexpectedly into a window as something more substantial. Especially if you've been drinking, was clearly implied. It was likely that the bird was simply stunned and had since flown away. The details of the call would be recorded and passed on to the nearest jurisdiction in the morning, to be followed up when resources were available. But for the present, he suggested, perhaps it might be best if Earl stopped serving and everyone got themselves off home to bed.

*

The missing man's car was found parked around the corner from the pub, undisturbed. It contained his luggage and the remains of a McDonald's Happy Meal. There was no body and no blood, and no evidence at all of foul play; the thin strokes of blood on the pub's ornate windows appeared to have dissipated overnight. According to papers found in the glove box, the missing man was one Martin de Witt from the Gold Coast. A tourist. His status was established as Whereabouts Unknown, and unless his family reported him missing, there was no official concern. As it transpired that his only family was a son working in Kalgoorlie, who hadn't been in contact with his father for years, and an estranged brother in the Netherlands, it seemed unlikely that his disappearance would ever be taken further.

But Martin de Witt wasn't missing, anyway – he was back the following night, a gasping, bloodstained apparition in the heart of the swirling fog.

*

Unofficially, things progressed at a rapid rate. I spent the next few nights holed up at home, peacefully enough, but with a thin smear of smoke over the landscape, like a delicate gauze. My doors remained locked.

Daryl Burcott had soon followed up on his threat to reveal the 'hoax' by confronting the tricksters, and disappeared. The mates who'd goaded him on – but had stayed inside – were shamefaced and pale. They hadn't been able to see anything, but there'd been a fair amount of noise.

Daryl reappeared the next night.

Within days, people had changed their routines. Like an unspoken curfew, twilight became lock-and-key hour. A couple more people 'vanished', again with no signs of disturbance, so they became a phenomenon rather than a crime. As people started to lock themselves in, pets and livestock began to disappear. It was only a few days before people noticed that the birds were gone. It didn't take long for the town to begin emptying.

People who had no ties, or those with somewhere else to

go, started to clear out. It wasn't just the oppressive nights, the fear of the mist's appearance, it was the confusion, the unknown threat that shrouded the town completely, day and night.

There was a resurgence in church attendance, and the strengthened congregation swung into action, organising a religious protest in the form of a midnight mass. The minister, who resided in Woodford, came in specially to perform the service. He arrived before twilight, and was escorted to the local hall that served as the community church, where the congregation had gathered long before the ceremony was due to take place. The mass was performed with great dignity and formality, undisturbed. But at its conclusion, people noticed that the hall's windows were slowly being shrouded, isolating the worshippers from heaven's celestial reach.

There was an extended pause. The priest gulped, and then began shakily to pray. The defiantly unlocked doors were quickly bolted and secured.

The exodus began in earnest shortly after that.

*

I didn't experience the mist again myself until a couple of weeks after the first night. I stayed at home with my doors locked, and things remained relatively peaceful, albeit disturbing. I still dropped in to the pub, but earlier now, and generally the punters were all gone and the doors closed by nightfall. Earl was ageing noticeably; he openly admitted that if it kept up, he'd be out of business very shortly.

Takeaway liquor sales were certainly strong, but he hadn't become a publican to run a bottle shop, he sniffed.

My next encounter with the mist was at a crisis meeting called by Wesley Forrest and three other hobby farmers, who'd all lost their stock in recent nights. Wes had been a stalwart of the town for decades, its unofficial mayor and one of Earl and Wally's history society cronies. Most people referred to him (behind his back – Wes wasn't renowned for his sense of humour) as Alderman. Although he was now retired and had subdivided and sold off the bulk of his land, he'd held on to the best of his heritage breeding stock, and had established a lucrative arm in animal husbandry. His stud was purebred and worth a lot of money. And now it was gone.

Wes wasn't a man with a patient disposition. Arrogant at the best of times, he now offered us beers on his back porch with barely concealed fury. Gilda, his wife, had packed herself off to her sister's in Adelaide a week ago, after losing her beloved Siamese and her entire aviary. Wes meant business. A whiskey bottle stood a little to the right of his beer can. The day was only just starting to wane.

'What I want to know,' he was saying, 'is why the authorities are refusing to react. I've lost over eighty-thousand dollars' worth of almost pure bloodlines, almost irreplaceable breeding stock, which anywhere else would be considered a serious crime worthy of investigation. And all I'm getting is "no evidence" shrugs. Who gives a shit if there are no tyre tracks or footprints – it's their bloody job to investigate.'

'What's your insurance say?' croaked Fisher O'Toole through a mouthful of peanuts.

'Pending investigation. Pending the frigging police getting off their arses and doing their job. Doing something useful instead of cross-examining me and my family, speculating about my financial situation. Lazy bloody pricks.' He gulped at his beer, then reached over for the whiskey bottle.

'So what's your theory?' I asked him.

'My theory is that some shady arseholes snuck out here three nights ago with a stock truck and nicked four prime Hereford bulls and three of the best bloody breeding boars I've ever studded.'

'And you didn't hear a thing?'

He blanched, the briefest flinch. 'There was a bit of bellowing. I thought it was possums, or dogs.'

'You didn't investigate?'

'If I'd thought for a moment that some arsehole was making off with my livelihood, I would have been out of bed pretty bloody quickly, with a shotgun, I can assure you.'

'But you didn't hear a truck? Motorbikes? Dogs? Any sound of mustering?'

'Look, McIntosh, I've had enough bloody innuendo from your useless mates to last me a lifetime.'

'I'm just making a point. What would you think of a stockman whose entire herd disappeared from his pens, right under his nose, without him hearing a thing and with no signs of intrusion? You'll be lucky if your insurance coughs up a cent.'

Wes flashed and was about to tear into me, when Matt Johnson swore under his breath and pointedly cleared his throat. 'Sorry to interrupt, gents, but Wes, I think your bulls are back.'

Wes jerked around to face the fields. We followed the direction of his gaze, Matt's face strangely grey. The dusk had deepened while we'd been arguing, and in the settling dark a thick sea of fog was flowing over the fields towards us. Elongated figures seemed to cyclone around its edges, and at its dense core other forms pulsed and throbbed indistinctly. As the mist continued to deepen, the forms became more solid and recognisable. Standing out within the writhing centre were four enormous beasts, which would once have been hulking bulls, prizes of their species. Now their frames sagged, and they grunted forlornly, their huge carcasses stripped back to bones, with a few shreds of torn flesh hanging like rags. One raised his huge skull and bellowed, the ring audibly clattering in the bone shells of his nostrils.

Wes swore. The mist flowed on towards us, the skeletons of his cattle plodding in its midst.

'I'm out of here,' I said, and pushed back my chair. In unison, the others followed. To the side of the cloud, a large man in a bloodstained yellow shirt waved dislocated arms around like a grotesque, broken marionette.

'Wes,' Matt called from the doorway. 'Come on.'

'Matt's right, mate,' added Russell Simms. 'There's nothing you can do.' But Wes, a man who'd always fought – and usually won – his battles, stalked away from us, descending the back steps to the lawn and heading resolutely towards his fields.

'Wes!' called Fisher. 'For God's sake, man – come away!'

We'd all started yelling by then, but not one of us moved to go after him. We stood, shouting and imploring, until he reached the very edge of the mist, and began to yell into it, demanding an explanation for the desecration of his cattle.

At first the mist only swirled, while the grisly remains of the bulls slowly, mournfully moved to surround him, as if asking to be taken home. They brayed solemnly at first, and then their tails began to flick. Eyeless and unseeing, they nevertheless moved to arrange themselves so that they all faced Wes, enclosing him in their centre. He was surrounded. Beside me Fisher swore and began a furiously whispered prayer. One of the bulls gave a furious bellow, and they all began to stamp and paw at the ground, raising small puffs of dust to swirl among the mist. A low chant could be heard, arising from the smoky cloud and building like an audible wall around the scene.

'Wes!' Larry yelled, 'for shit's sake, run!', but at the same moment the largest of the bulls lowered its massive skull and charged, lifting the big man and tossing him into the centre of the cloud. The others stampeded, with sickening thuds that were soon drowned out by the shrieks of laughter coming from within the mist. Frozen on the back porch, we could just make out the writhing figure beneath the stamping hoofs, being pulverised into his own field.

As the mist eddied around the scene, three smaller

loping skeletons with blunt snouts and long curved tusks broke from its borders and galloped towards the house.

There was no pride, no decorum. Paddy Lynch was sick before we'd even finished bolting the door.

We hit the freak-show circuit shortly after that. We waited and fought for an official response to our situation, the disappearances, but were treated with tongue-in-cheek condescension or outright hostility. Nebulah did not match any existing bureaucratic criteria for evacuation or relocation, and no government department was willing to introduce any that officially recognised unexplained haunting as a finding on disputed fatalities or a basis for social assistance. Politicians from all parties recognised a political minefield that could sink a credible career in a few words, and steered well clear. They all adopted an aggressive, face-saving ambiguity towards the 'question' of strange happenings in our small country town – or downright open cynicism, suggesting we were bludgers after compensation from the hard-working taxpayer. We became leper-like, all eyes averted from us. Best to be ignored and avoided. Files were closed, or misplaced.

Tourists and looters proliferated as the townspeople left, and a police patrol was begrudgingly established – at the road into town. Then suddenly, one day, we discovered that all the road signs had been tampered with: all reference to Nebulah had been quietly removed. By the Eastern Highway stood a denuded pole, testament to a town that had ceased to exist. On the state highway signs there were patches of clumsily matched green swipes where our town's name used to be. We were 215 kilometres down the road and a whole other world away.

*

There's a disturbance from the direction of the skateboarders. The older one has misjudged a jump and rolled badly. He tosses his board with an expression of childlike fury. It lies impotent, blameless, on the ground. It's signalled the end of the session and the others gather to leave, boards under their arms.

Two of the smaller boys remain behind. Without the intimidation of the other boys' presence, they launch into attempts at the older one's tricks. The smaller of the two, a wiry, dark-skinned boy, released from his self-consciousness, throws his legs high, finally executing the flip he was so desperate to achieve. When he lands upright and stands, his face is bright with the redemption of triumph, lit with youthful joy.

How quickly we lose joy. I'm struck by a memory of Julie, at one of the primary school sports days I so rarely attended, suddenly realising at the end of the egg-and-spoon race that she'd won. Her concentration had been so focused on not dropping her egg that she'd blinkered out the other competitors. The effect of her realisation was instant and transformative, and on receiving a blue ribbon her face lit with unfettered happiness and pride. It was the same face Gina had lifted to me when I was finally allowed into the maternity ward to find her nursing our newborn daughter, a face that immediately crumpled into tears, overwhelmed by the intensity of her joy.

Had I ever been overwhelmed like that? Difficult to recall a single instance. The birth of Julie, yes, but that was fleeting, tinged with anxiety, a sense of responsibility I found almost crushing. Instead of abating, this sense grew over the years, as Julie grew from fragility to vulnerability, and then, almost worse, to independence. My role in her existence lessened, but the anxiety of responsibility deepened, accompanied by an increasing sense of powerlessness.

*

I experience that same draining sense of powerlessness when Alice's phone swerves straight to message bank yet again.

At home I find a note: Milly is at the supermarket.

Gina watches me anxiously as I load the gun into the car. I have to think for a long time before I open the passenger door for her. Before I lock the house I try Alice one last time. I'm just disconnecting from her message service when the landline starts to ring. I don't know what it is that stops me just as I am about to pick it up. I hover, waiting for the answering machine.

There is a long-drawn breath, a harried voice. 'Pete,' says the voice. 'I know you're there. Please, Pete, please. Listen to me. Stay.'

It's Alex. Ringing me on a number I've never given her. It's the first time I feel close to losing control. She stays on the line, saying nothing for a long time. I stand by the phone, still and silent as if somehow any movement would reveal my presence. We stay suspended like that, both of us hoping that the other will reach out, until finally she gives a deep sigh and says, simply, 'Don't.' At the click of the call's disconnection I feel grief overwhelm me like a fierce wind. She's told me nothing I don't already know.

*

Once, very early in my career, I had to attend the suicide of a young girl. She was fourteen years old and sixteen weeks pregnant, at the stage where it could no longer be hidden. Charges were subsequently laid against her father, but that was little help to her. The time for helping her, her eyes conveyed, was long over. I remember her eyes more than the terrible damage she'd so inexpertly done to her body. They were clear and focused, and beyond. They told you that no one had come when she'd needed them, and anyone who was here now to do the right thing was administering empty justice. Her eyes were blue, the colour of the sky.

*

With my foot down, I make Nebulah in just over two hours. I drive like I have demons after me – ironic under the circumstances. The risks I take are frightening, but somehow the die-trying mentality kicked in the instant my decision was made. From that moment, everything is risk. Every screech round every tight bend is a thread of that decision; the barrier to caution has been removed and now all is instinct. With any luck a patrol will see me, pursue me into Nebulah. I wonder if they'd follow the pursuit through once they realised where I was heading, or if they'd back away and just wait to pick me up the next morning. Assuming a next morning.

But despite a small handful of shocked or outraged faces on the rural highway, nothing steers me from my course, and it is still light when I pass the denuded pole that used to signpost our town. It is pre-dusk, just. The time of evening I'd be having my last smoke. I have, at the very most, about half an hour.

There's a stillness in the town that is alive with menace. It's like that frozen gasp that precedes a scream, the catch of breath. The setting sun is like a gaping, shimmering mouth; the open, leering clown mouth of my dreams, announcing, 'Solstice!' Wisps of cloud spread from it like threads of laughter.

At Li's they've hidden the car, but the curtains are open. The flickering light of a gas lantern is visible, even though they've gone to the trouble of placing it out of sight behind the couch. All our house keys are still intact on my ring, and I let myself straight in the locked front door.

Alice has come out into the hall and is waiting for me. When she sees the gun she looks suddenly old, shrunken. 'I…' she starts. I walk straight past her into the lounge. Rob stands by the door, and Alan and Xandrea are still in position in dim corners to the side of the front window.

Xandrea's lip curls when she sees the rifle. 'Is that a threat?'

'If need be.'

'You're too late. It's already practically dark. We can't risk leaving now, so it looks like we're stuck here.' She gives an elaborate smirk and twines her hands, swinging her arms back and forth like a celebrating child.

I turn to the others. Alice has followed me into the room and grips her arms tightly round her chest.

'There may just be time to get out, but we need to go now. Leave your stuff.' They stare at me, bewildered. 'It's the only chance.'

'Excuse me,' snorts Xandrea, swinging to the centre of the room. 'Our *best* chance, if the mist is as fearful as you insist, is to stay right where we are, don't you think? Surely that's the obvious course?'

'You can stay, but I want the others out. Now.'

They are still hesitating, confused, but now that the sky is dimming the menace in the air is palpable, and the potential reality of their situation is unnerving them.

'Surely we'd be mad to leave now?' Rob hazards.

'If you stay here you'll die. I promise you.'

'You watch too much telly,' laughs Xandrea. 'We're quite safe here, even without you and your arsenal.'

'We don't have time. We need to go now,' I say to Rob and Alice.

Rob's getting scared. He squints towards the window at the darkening sky. 'But is that wise?'

'No, but it's all very heroic,' Xandrea begins, but I cut across her.

'How did you get in?' I ask. Rob's shamefaced look is the only answer I need. 'We'll fix it,' he mutters.

'You won't fix anything. You'll be dead. Don't you understand that with a broken window it'll be able to get in?'

'We've blocked it, of course.' Xandrea's voice has lost a shade of its arrogance.

'It. Can. Get. In.' They stand, frozen as if stunned. 'It's probably too late already. But here, with a broken window, we're just sitting ducks.'

The dynamics change as the impact of my words finally sparks. Alan grabs his pack from the floor and Rob wraps his arm around Alice and starts to push her towards the door. She looks over her shoulder. 'Xandrea?' It's almost a wail.

'You go if you're scared. The window's been blocked.' With a grand gesture she sits back on the couch, tucking her legs under her and reaching for her cigarettes as if she's settling in for a night of TV. I push the others out in front of me. I don't look back.

When we get outside the air is charged, it seems to bristle. The light is almost gone. Gina barks at us from the Land Cruiser, as if telling us to hurry. As they cram clumsily into the back seat, I glance at the sky and acknowledge the shortest day. It's already too late.

I don't bother to reverse, just drive straight over the kerb and the garden, swerving through the gate at full pelt, barely in control. The others fumble at seatbelts. My panic is infectious.

'How long do we have?' shouts Rob.

'We don't. I'll try for Milly's, it's closest.' I can't stop checking the mirror.

In the last of the light Alice's eyes are huge pools of fear and confusion. 'She'll be okay, won't she?' she says, peering back. Snail tracks glisten on her cheeks.

'It's not up to you whether she's all right. Her choice.'

I mount the kerb turning into Main Street. Ahead of us the night is deepening. I floor the gas for one more block, but it's useless, it's already coming, seething towards us along the street. I skid to a stop in front of the pub. The huge cloud is a cacophony of shrieks and moans. Alice is staring at it in horror. An Asian man shifts from the side of the mass, his face impassive, his arms outstretched. In his hands he clutches his flyblown insides. There will be no poetry tonight.

The pub door is locked. I have keys – Earl gave me a set when he left, so I could keep an eye on the place. There's a deadlock and a security latch and the mist is bearing down on us. My fingers are like sausages as I fumble with the key ring, getting tangled. Behind me Gina is at attention, facing towards the mist, barking ferociously. I raise the gun.

The wood shatters and Rob and I shoulder the splintered doors open and herd everyone into the building. The shrieks behind us are bloodcurdling.

'The cellar!' I don't stop running. The trapdoor entrance to the cellar is in the taproom behind the bar. As we stumble around the counter, tentacles of mist are snaking around the remains of the outer door of the building. Alice slips and goes down the cellar stairs on her knees, Rob on his arse. Alan takes the first steps three at a time, then falls the remaining distance. I bolt the door behind me and snap the huge padlock in place, not bothering to check whether I have a key for it.

And then I think of Gina.

*

The cellar is a large and well-insulated space. The lights are out, but small windows spaced at intervals along the top of the outer wall look out onto the footpath, letting in small postcards of light. Two old straight-backed chairs near a dusty desk are the only furniture beyond the empty shelving lining the walls. Pipes protrude from the brickwork, lifeless without kegs to milk.

Alan sits bent over on one of the chairs, his arms tightly wrapped around his torso as if holding himself together against a great force. His eyes are screwed shut. Alice and Rob kneel on the floor near him, unmoving. I'm sprawled across the small landing at the top of the stairs, winded and trying unsuccessfully to steady myself. Branded into the forefront of my mind is the stance of a German shepherd, positioned between us and the approaching mist. The rifle clatters down the steps to land on the concrete, pointing at Alan. The safety catch is off. The irony of accidentally shooting him now almost makes me laugh.

Milky fingers of cloud swirl over the row of windows, dimming the moonlit view of the night outside. A low moaning drones on, with an occasional screech, like the piercing cry of a hunting owl. Alan puts his hands over his ears and begins to rock.

'Sorry,' I say. 'I'm gonna smoke.' I start to roll, hoping the smooth action will steady my hands.

'Can you do me one too?' croaks Rob.

I drape the paper from my lip; it hangs forlornly like a sail without a steering wind. Fingernails scratch at the small windows. There are no curtains to shield us from what's outside.

'It'll be a bad night,' I say, lighting up and passing Rob the lit smoke. 'Solstice. We'll just have to pray they won't be able to get in.'

'Oh Jesus, Xandrea!' sobs Alice, and she curls into a foetal position, burying her head in her arms. Above us there is a shriek from the mist, and then it suddenly peels from the windows as if it's being sucked away. The view to the bright moonlit night is unimpeded. The silence grows until it almost throbs.

'It's gone?' asks Rob. I shake my head at him quickly, emphatically, before the others look up. He knits his brow, failing to understand what I mean: that if the mist isn't with us, it's because it's found other quarry. It's gone somewhere else to play. This is something they really don't need to know.

*

They find out soon enough. It stays away for a few blessed hours, allowing us to start to unwind a bit, to get drowsy. It's close to midnight when the light from the windows is suddenly shadowed. The face of Xandrea, wide-eyed and terrified, peers down at us. 'Are you there?' she calls, squinting into the darkened space. 'Alice? Alan? Anyone?' The last is a sob and Xandrea starts to cry quietly and hastily, peering impotently into the stillness. Alice stands. The face at the window gives a gasp. 'Oh, thank God. Thank God, thank God. Alice! Oh, thank God, Alice, let me in.'

Alice spins to me, her face expectant. She stalls at my stillness, my expression.

'Pete?' I do not move. Alice is quickly at my side. 'Pete, you can't.' Her eyes are ancient, appalled. 'You have to.' She spins to Rob, who is looking at me, lost. She turns back to me. 'You can't leave her out there. It's murder. You couldn't.'

Xandrea starts to thump her open palm on the window's smeared glass. 'Please!' she sobs. 'I'm sorry, I'm so sorry.'

'Pete!' Alice screams.

'She's already dead. That's not her.'

Alice spins to the window, to the terrified face crying messily on the other side. 'Xandrea!' she calls, 'it's okay, come round to the door.'

Xandrea registers, giving a quick nod, and disappears from view. Alice positions herself in front of me. 'Open the door.'

I'm quiet. 'No.'

'You have to!' Alice is wailing now, tears flowing unchecked down her face.

'Alice, Xandrea is dead.'

'She's here!'

'She's not. That's the mist.'

293

'You can't be sure of that.'

'Sure enough to know not to open the door.'

Alice's scream is that of someone losing control. Rob moves over to her and tries to hold her, but she pushes him away and launches herself at me. 'You can't do this!' she shrieks.

A weak knocking starts at the cellar door. A muffled voice can be heard, calling to Alice. I walk away from the others, sit myself in a far corner. Alice looks after me in horror, then runs clumsily up the steps to the locked door, starts pulling at the bolt.

'Just hang on, hang on, Xandrea.'

'Hurry!' the voice calls. Alice tears and slaps at the door, then spins around to face the room. 'Pete!' she wails. Rob and Alan stare at me. 'Could it...?' begins Rob.

'No. She's long gone.'

'Can you be sure?' says Alan quietly. Behind him Alice clambers down the steps towards us.

'No.' I say.

'God, if there's any chance, shouldn't we...'

'No.'

Alice's face is twisted. 'Just because someone makes a mistake, you can't let them die. It's... inhuman.'

'Alice, we used to go through this every night. Milly's husband, Gavin, outside, begging us to let him in, to save him. It nearly killed Milly. He'd been dead for nearly ten years.' I stand rigid just to the side of a patch of light. 'I'm not risking us all. The chance of her being real is minuscule.

Where do you think the mist has been all this time? I'm not opening that door till morning. It's the only chance we'll stay alive.'

'Oh God.' Alice dashes back up the stairs to whisper furiously at the door. On the other side the sobs grow in volume, increasingly panicked. Alice wrestles with the padlock in desperate fury. 'Rob, for God's sake!'

With his head down, Rob makes his way slowly across the room and shuffles up the stairs. He lifts the padlock briefly, then lets it fall. 'There's no way without a key.' He is barely audible.

Alice howls. 'Then help me!'

Rob plonks down on the stairs and buries his head in his hands.

'Please!' calls the disembodied voice. 'Rob, please!'

'I don't know,' mutters Rob to his feet, from under the shield of his arms. Below, Alan is still sitting perfectly rigid, with his hands clasping his knees and his eyes closed. He looks as though he's made of stone.

In the pause that follows we become aware of distant noise. The echo of shrieks. The mist is on its way.

Alice clatters down the stairs again and stands in front of me. 'I'll break a window.'

'Then we all die, not just Xandrea.'

'I can't just leave her out there!'

'You already have. Alice, she's already gone.'

Outside, the distant shrieks are getting slowly closer. Alice sobs and tries to grab at my pocket for the keys. I hardly have the strength to hold her off. 'You have to!' she keeps howling.

'Alice!' the voice at the door screams. 'Alice, hurry!' Alice scratches at my face and our fight begins in earnest. In his chair, Alan flinches but otherwise remains immobile. Rob moves in, horrified, but stops just out of reach. At first I simply try to ward off Alice's blows, but then she makes a sudden grab for the gun, and I shove her savagely backwards. She lands heavily on the concrete floor but is immediately up again, tearing at my jacket, her hands everywhere, a dervish. We wrestle, grunting like Neanderthals. 'Shoot me!' she starts to bellow. 'You'll have to shoot me, I won't let you do this!'

Outside, voices are all around the building. At the door Xandrea starts to shriek.

'Alice!' she cries, over and over, and the voices of the mist pick up and echo her scream, until an army of voices begging for Alice is a crescendo around us, and in the midst of all this Xandrea's screams skyrocket, cries of pure torment. Alice wails and collapses; frozen on his chair, Alan starts to move his lips in silent prayer and suddenly pulls his shirt over his head as if to shield himself, his arms pressed against his ears. Rob crawls over to Alice and wraps himself around her. They huddle together, Alice's body convulsing in violent shudders, almost in fits.

I move to the other chair. I'm familiar with the noises outside. Acclimatised, you could say. Xandrea's cries slowly fade, then die off completely. At the bottom of my soul I pray with everything I have that she was already dead.

*

Solstice was one of the areas Milly researched when the mist first appeared. She came home well versed in the various cultural interpretations and rituals associated with it, but with nothing remotely of any use. Except as allegory – the arrival of the longest night, the winter months, signalling the beginning of an extended period of famine. The slaughter of livestock and the fermenting of alcohol sound dionysian, celebratory or debauched, but it was largely self-protection: nothing would survive the season ahead.

Except, of course, those who were already accustomed to starvation, already conditioned to survive on little. Constitutionally suited to it.

Acclimatised.

I keep my back to the flitting horrors at the windows and try not to smoke too much. The straight chair makes my back ache, but I don't want to disturb the others by walking around. They're quiet now, huddled together in the darkness on the other side of the room, as far from the windows as possible, curled like kittens.

We've pulled the desk over to a dark corner and turned it over to form a partition of sorts, as a pathetic excuse for a toilet, and we've all taken advantage of it. The smell adds to the overwhelming sense of degradation, as opaque and suffocating as the darkness.

It has already been one of the longest nights of my life.

'Alice!' Xandrea calls playfully, peering through the windows. 'Al-ice.' As if calling her out to play. 'I wasn't dead,

Alice. Before. It's all your fault, you know – you told me it was beautiful, then left me out here for it.' She begins to giggle, and the mist surrounding her chuckles in chorus. 'Do you know what it did to me, Alice? What you let it do? Come out, Alice, come out and talk to me. You owe me that much. You owe me.'

On the floor, Alice curls up tighter, her arms wrapped around her head, her face completely hidden.

'Murderer,' the mist is crooning. 'Come out, come out.'

'You murdered me, Alice,' sings Xandrea. 'My death is yours.'

Alice gives a twitch and rolls to face the apparition pressed against the window. 'I didn't,' she chokes. 'I didn't.' Her finger snakes out and points crookedly across the room, as if exhausted. It points at me. 'It was him.'

'He killed all of us,' adds Wesley Forrest, kneeling down beside Xandrea and peering into the cellar. Around him the mist swirls and murmurs. 'He'd never take risks, he only ever looked after himself.'

'Ask Li,' hisses Monica Lambert, one of the first to disappear when the mist began.

'Ask Li,' echoes Xandrea, and it becomes a chant, rising and receding like an incoming tide.

And then there is Li, kneeling, raising her eyes to the window and nodding silently.

'But Alice,' Xandrea breaks in, calling over the top of the voices, 'you're as bad as him. You're dripping with my blood.'

And Alice, rolling back into a tight little ball, begins to wail.

Rob is pale, even in the lack of light. 'Can't you make it stop?' he hisses at me.

I ignore him.

'Fuck!' He pushes himself up off the floor, standing to face the sea of ghouls peering down at us. 'Can't you just fuck off?' he shouts. 'You can't get in, just fucking leave us alone.' He sounds like a whining child.

The faces at the window distort. 'Leave us alone!' they howl, their laughter even worse than their screams.

Rob's defiance shrivels. 'You can't hurt us,' he tries lamely. This produces another round of laughter, and a new chant begins. 'Can. Can. Can. Can. Can.'

'For God's sake!' Rob suddenly kneels, clasping his hands before his chest and closing his eyes. 'Our Father, who art in heaven...'

The mist seething around the windows explodes. 'Hallowed be thy name!' it shrieks, 'Thy Kingdom come; thy will be done.' Its laughter howls around the words.

Rob's hands lower. He seems hunched, aged beyond time. 'What are you?' he whispers, as if to himself.

The mist explodes into howling again. 'We. Are. You.'

'You. You. You. You. You.'

'Al-ice! Al-an! You need to come out here, you need to be part of this.' At the window Xandrea's face is starting to melt. 'This is solstice, it's your last chance. Your last chance to atone. To understand, Alan, everything. Come out. Or you'll have me forever.'

On the floor, still curled into a ball, Alice begins to

rock. Rob crawls over and wraps his arms around her. After a moment, Alan shuffles over and presses himself into their huddle. Like kittens, left out in a storm. I stay to the side of the room, in the darkness. Above me the mist whispers. *Coward.*

If it had waved a bottle of whiskey at me, I would have opened the door.

*

They talk about your life flashing before you when you die, in which case I seem to be pretty safe. My review of everything I've ever done wrong takes an eternity.

On the floor nearby, Alice is curled with her back to me, wishing me into non-existence. I can recall Julie and Gina in the same posture, curled up in the same protective ball; Gina in the days before I realised she was seriously ill and required careful handling. I used to stay away from home as much as possible, to avoid behaviour I viewed as petulant and shamefully self-indulgent. When she sobbed I read the paper, when she yelled I left the room – or the house. I was repulsed by her slothfulness, the glasses of sickly cask wine that were always at her elbow, and by her bewildering and destructive lies. I'd think: *lazy, selfish, manipulative.* I'd even called her a nutter, but to my shame it never occurred to me that she was actually genuinely unwell.

The Gina I met and married was shy, creative, plump and happy. When I think of her then, I think of colour, paint and books, bottles of red wine and bowls of cashew nuts, and weekend suburban barbecues, where people gathered together and ate and laughed. And sure, they drank too much and talked and argued about mundanities like the football and recipes, but that was the point. It was escapism, a chance to relax and just float on the surface for a while.

It was good. But no one ever came along to the parties and Sunday drinks and said what they really felt. We argued over football and no one ever stood up and said: *I never imagined that saying 'till death do us part' meant watching someone get fatter and duller and more selfish by the year,* or: *When my baby cries constantly through the night I just want to kill it, I'm so tired,* or: *When I drive to work in the morning the pressure of responsibility is like a worm, chewing at the walls of my stomach, maker it harder and harder to stand upright.*

Instead, we rolled sausages around and charred steaks, and talked about TV shows as if they were real and bloody boat people as if they weren't. And when the cheap veneer of our social framework started to buckle and warp we were horrified, shocked. In our parents' day happiness was an aside, something that was accepted without drama or acknowledgement – like being asked about the wallpaper pattern in a room you use every day and realising that you don't even know the colour.

When the framework started crumbling, we could only stare at the wreckage in bewilderment. When wives started to divorce drunken, bloated and unfaithful husbands, and men were caught with their fingers in the till, or in the other, divorced wives, and children were found to be selfish turds and not the reincarnation of goodness itself, then the cracks that opened were too vast, too confronting. We watched the disintegration, and we *understood* it, and once our social safety net had been slashed with the recognition of the inevitable, we went into freefall ourselves.

My inappropriate choice of career became more apparent every day as I was thrown into situations of conflict, but I hated my father so much that I refused to give him any grounds to scorn me. So I remained in a world that scared and repulsed me, a world full of hate and deceit and deliberately inflicted pain, and I coped by barricading myself in. It was as if a wall had been constructed two feet in front of me that kept me removed, kept me from registering. At first my wall kept me sheltered from the turbulence of my work, and then increasingly from everything else as well. As Gina, in her escalating unhappiness and confusion, flailed and hammered at my detachment, I reinforced it with increasing amounts of scotch and beer before I even contemplated going home.

Even after all this time, I haven't forgiven Gina for turning our daughter against me, but in one sense Julie is quite right. Gina needed help and all I gave her was indifference. Yet my hiding place was so closed in and devoid of light that I came to consider myself the victimised one, unfairly imprisoned, and my calculated callousness towards her felt entirely justified. It's no wonder Julie blames me for her mother's collapse.

*

It has been quieter for a while now. Feet skip regularly past the windows, snatches of schoolyard rhymes float through the night. Every now and then the rhymes break into the chanting poetry first used to seduce Alice, but now it's harsh and mocking, like the worm-ridden inside of a beautiful crisp red apple. Alice moans and Alan wraps his arms around his head, burying his face.

The night is slowly drifting towards morning. If we can survive another couple of hours, we will be safe. Thinking this relaxes me a little, and a sudden movement at the window startles me. It is Gavin, peering fixedly across at me.

'Pete!' he calls. 'Aloha!' I look away, try not to register the dirt that clings to him, the wriggling. He breaks into his completely unselfconscious, delighted laugh, the one that made him a favourite wherever he went.

'Milly and I were so happy Pete, you know that. You knew that and yet here I am, and there you are. It should never have been me, Pete. You're the miserable fuck should have been mashed into that tree.'

I know this isn't my friend Gavin, it's just some horrible apparition of the mist, but I can't help thinking that this, like Julie with her arrows of blame, is right on target. There is movement in the mist around Gavin, and a clutch of figures break from it and squat to peer through the cellar windows, seeking me out. Women.

At first not all the faces are familiar, but I begin to recognise them: the young girl beside Li is my pregnant teenage suicide, the anxious woman beside Gina is Marylou

Shanks, who'd rung me scared to death during one of the first nights of the mist and hasn't been heard from since. Julie is there, and Milly, Liz and Alex, and a few old callgirls who used to work the fringes of my eastern beat. Xandrea. They all peer down at me, not saying a word, but they don't have to. Everything is there, draped and flowing from what isn't being said, hanging in the silence between us.

From the last of the night outside comes a rhythmical drum, which I suddenly identify as the sound of marching, hundreds of marching feet, heading towards us. There is a shuffle of movement and Alex lifts her head to look beyond my gaze. 'Goodbye, Pete,' she says, and raises her hands to press against the window. The other women follow suit, and then they disintegrate, one by one crumbling into nothingness as the marching feet appear as a swarm of children, who press up against the windows until the panes are a sea of tiny faces.

'Come out to play,' they call, whining, petulant, and then their faces start to elongate, melting into moonlit rivers of blood. A gurgling red tide flows against the windowpanes, pooling along the bottom ledges. There is a gasp, the smallest of sighs, and on the other side of this red curtain appears the first tiny crack of dawn.

And I can't help it, it's instinctual; like an involuntary tic the first word that comes to mind at the glimpse of light is: *Over*.

PART
SEVEN

Dawn. The beginning of a new day; the end of a night. How do you tell which is which when the distinction between the end and the beginning is blurred, is essentially the same thing?

Without a *Snap!* how do you tell who's won, and who, when the echoes of the cheers have faded, has lost everything in their hand?

The key to the cellar lock is only the second one I try; the ease of getting out is like a further ricochet of silent accusation. Another brick in the wall that's solidifying around me.

We emerge into a peaceful dawn, a morning softened by a light but consistent drizzle. The street smells damp and clean after the stale confinement of the cellar, with its unavoidable human stenches. The freshness of the air seems infinite; it's so free from pollution it is as though it's completely empty, like an unblemished slate. A new beginning.

Or the beginning of the end?

On the Land Cruiser's dashboard my phone shows eight missed calls. Alex. The same message, over and over, increasingly panicked: 'Pete? Please don't be there, please don't. Ring me, please, please call me.'

And then suddenly, at the end of the stream of Alex's desperation, there is Milly, quiet and calm. 'I got your note; I don't need to tell you that I'm worried. Can you give me a call when you can, let me know you're okay? There is a pause. 'Pete? Soon? If…'

Then the phone is overcome by static, and anything after Milly's *If* is obliterated.

When I try to ring home there is nothing, just silence, a void like the emptiness of a street washed clean by the persistence of morning rain.

*

My house is closest to town and to Li's. There is no milk and the few remaining teabags are stale, but there are lemons on the tree out the back, so we make do. The musty cold of the closed house is tomb-like. I leave the doors wide, throw open the windows along the front. The fresh morning air seeps over the threshold.

Rob manoeuvres Alice from the car into the house, his gentle pressure overpowering her obvious reluctance. She is grey and expressionless, and she flinches when I reach to touch her, try to put my hand on her arm. She refuses to look at me, staring off to the side. The taste in my mouth is the residue of old smoke.

The towels I find are remnants, threadbare, but we need showers, need to wash off the clinging odour from the night before. I dig out old sheets and show a wan and silent Alan to the spare room, while Rob makes up my room for Alice. By the time he joins me at the table, the tea has overbrewed and tastes both bitter and musty. I roll him a cigarette without asking and he takes it without comment. We both know what's ahead.

*

We continue our silence throughout the drive to Li's.

When we get to Li's gate, I find I have to stop for a moment. The long driveway seems like a portal, as if it's a crossing to a new dimension. It's probably lack of sleep, and shock from the drawn-out foulness of the previous night, but turning in to the driveway seems somehow momentous; it looms like an open mouth. I have to flex my shoulders in an effort to release the tension collected in my shoulderblades. It doesn't work.

Li's garden has become overgrown in the short time since we left town, already wilting under an air of desertion. The pang I feel at the sight of the neglect is physical; Li would turn in her grave, I start to think, but the thought makes me shudder. It's a turn of phrase we tend to avoid.

Rob's hands are tight fists in his lap; my delaying isn't helping. He gives me a quick glance. His hair has transformed from rumpled curls to unkempt tendrils, lank and unattractive. He's unshaven and there's an edge to him beyond sheer exhaustion. He's aged, considerably and irreversibly. I think of Alice, the change in her overnight, her

309

grey skin and surface emptiness. Her lifelessness.

Our eyes meet only briefly before we both look away. I put the car into gear.

The house stands empty and passive. The front door is wide open. There is no sign of any disturbance. I park further along by the shed and open the car door without killing the engine. Rob pauses for a long breath, then follows me out of the car.

Instinctively I pause, awaiting the arrival of a dog. The morning is completely silent: there are no birds or cicadas, not a breath of breeze. It's like entering a movie set, lifeless, empty, as if filming has just concluded or is waiting to begin. The stillness is challenging; it's not a comforting silence. The winter sunshine is weak but also strangely charged. Rob zips up his jacket, but his self-conscious movements suggest that it's more for distraction, something to do, than for warmth. A similar urge has me reaching to my pocket, but I change my mind. I'll need a smoke soon enough.

Our footsteps on the porch seem unnaturally loud. At the front door we both hesitate, neither one of us wants courtesy to be interpreted as cowardice. We're avoiding each other's eyes now.

Rob follows me into the house.

In the lounge room the disarray from our hurried departure is the only sign of disruption. The packs lie open against the wall, spilling their contents. Hands of cards are fanned upon the table. Xandrea's cigarettes and lighter are there too, and the ashtray holds a number of butts. Some spilled ash is streaked across the table top where it fell short. I go over to the lantern, which is out. When I shake it, it is empty.

Rob scans the room restlessly, continuing to avoid my eyes. I head to the back of the house. In the laundry the air is chill. The window they broke to get in is exposed, the cardboard they'd jammed over the broken pane lies on the floor beneath it. It's impossible to tell whether it has simply blown off.

There's no indication that anything happened here at all. It's a thought that chills my blood.

When I get back to the lounge room Rob is zipping shut the last of the packs. 'I'll bring the car round, if you like,' he says, but instead he stands staring at a large tie-dyed carryall, lying on its side with a black shawl hanging out of it. He looks at me for the first time. 'I have to ask,' he says.

'I have no idea,' I tell him.

He expels his breath in a long sigh through his teeth. 'It'd be good to know.'

'Would it?'

He shrugs, lets the pack he's holding drop to the floor. I can't offer him anything.

At the car we load the packs and sleeping bags in silence. We leave the coloured carryall on the floor where it is.

*

It's almost noon before they're ready to leave. Rob lets Alan and Alice sleep, not waking them till eleven. Alice

311

emerges looking greyer and more withdrawn than before. She won't look at me at all, pushes her lunch of tinned salmon and beetroot around with her fork. When she does raise a small amount to her mouth, she winces and lowers it to her plate again.

Alan's remoteness is so profound it's starting to seem catatonic. He eats methodically, pale and cryptic behind his glasses.

I'm sitting outside in the cold having a smoke, when Rob comes out and slumps onto the step beside me. I grind my cigarette butt under my heel.

He clears his throat. 'The police,' he says. 'We've agreed to say that we couldn't find the key to the cellar in the dark, that we couldn't let her in.'

I stay motionless, sagged on the porch steps. I don't think I could move even if I wanted to.

There is a small noise from the direction of the front door. The tiniest flash of movement tells me that Alice has turned back over the threshold and closed the door behind her.

*

The silence once they've gone is familiar, but it also feels unnatural, overwhelming, because now it is internal as well as surrounding me. The station wagon's engine has faded into the day, everyone has gone, and Gina is lost. There is only me, and I am crushed, a husk as devoid of life as the deserted trees around me.

I slump backwards and lie spread-eagled on the porch,

staring at the sky with my arms outstretched and my legs sprawled down the steps. Like a crucified scarecrow.

A locum constable had answered Rob's call to Woodford. Obviously only vaguely familiar with the history of Nebulah, he'd been unimpressed at Rob's wild story, remaining noncommittal about Xandrea's alleged disappearance. Eventually he told Rob they'd need to come in to the station to make a statement.

I told Rob to drive slowly and carefully. By the time they get to town Denham should be back on duty. They were unnerved when I said I wouldn't be going with them.

I'm guessing there'll be hell to pay.

The lightest of breezes has sprung up, a cool, gentle caress. I'm so exhausted that I barely notice it as I crash into sleep.

*

The hospital where they took Gina had once been fairly modern, but was already run-down, showing unmistakable signs of distress. I've always held a belief that buildings channel emotional energy: you can always tell a business that's not doing so well from its lifelessness, the frozen garishness of its fittings; or the truth behind the 'family holiday' pretext offered by the deserted father, seeping from the silent walls of his empty home.

The hospital corridors were like journeys in themselves: long and tortuous, endless, exhausting turnings. Warrens of doors and exits suggested the many directions your situation might take. And then the sudden, unobtrusive barricade beyond the swinging doors at the ward's entrance, with its busy day room. A locked sliding window beside the heavy door, where casually dressed but hard-faced staff shuffled medication charts, oblivious to the buzzer, pretending they couldn't see you waiting to cross into their world.

The scanned security card and then the begrudgingly pressed green button, which released the door with a humming clank, like a ship's hull swinging open to swallow something. The world on the other side of that door was muffled, as if you were now underwater, in an open space full of shuffling, feet too heavy to lift from the ground, eyes and mouths sinking under the weight of the ritual sedatives. In the corner, canned laughter from a television blared into the muted atmosphere. Dressing gowns hung on wasted limbs, revealing arms snaked with bruises and burns, labyrinths of scars, the long-healed layered with the recent.

I waited with Julie for the doctor, Gina's bed between us. As she explained her mother's sudden decline, Gina would interrupt with disconnected sentences and disturbing giggles that were more like rasping than laughter.

She was isolated from the other patients. In the silence that fell between us while we waited, the locked door handle of the room shook and rattled. 'I have to go in there,' an unknown voice wailed. I found myself rigid with disgust for this hideous but necessary place, with its stench of release and sterilisation, the dampened pain ricocheting off its walls. Gina's incoherence contrasted with the glittering comprehension in Julie's eyes as she registered my discomfort, and my disinterest.

Her mother perhaps, but no longer my wife. 'Over,' I said to the doctor, 'our marriage ended well over two years ago, I don't consider I have any jurisdiction over her treatment.' And I felt rather than saw the heat of outrage burning from my daughter.

The doctor shrugged 'We can administer the electrotherapy under our own authority in the absence of consent, if the family declines to intervene and we feel it's in the patient's best interests.'

Gina's mother was still alive, but had been withering from dementia in a nursing home for the last five years, and was beyond consenting to bowel movements, let alone electric shock treatment on her mentally shattered daughter.

'I'm happy for the hospital to assume responsibility for treatment under the circumstances,' I told the doctor as he scribbled notes. 'I've been estranged from my wife for some time now; it doesn't seem appropriate for me to yield that kind of authority over her treatment. Do whatever you think is necessary under the circumstances.'

Seventeen-year-old Julie burst from her seat like a bomb going off. 'You fucking coward,' she hissed and slammed out of the room, leaving an acrid trail of hatred like smouldering gunpowder. The doctor, impassive behind the barrier of his clipboard, explained the procedure and the forms for surrendering consent, while the woman who used to be my wife lay bloated and dislocated between us, singing, 'Fuck-ing cow-ard, fuck-ing cow-ard, fuck-ing cow-ard.'

I monitored Gina's slow progress, and eventual incomplete recovery, by phone, but I never visited the hospital again. It was years before Julie would speak to me again, and then it was only because she'd met the Toad, whose obsession with the protocol of appearances meant that he wanted to formally request my permission for her hand in marriage. Again, I declined to exercise any authority over the lives of the women supposedly under 'my protection', a stance that was seen as 'shirking my duties' by the Toad, and as bloody typical by Julie.

'The choice is Julie's,' I'd told the Toad, who was bloated up with self-importance, expecting to be welcomed with open arms. 'I don't see that my opinion has any bearing on decisions she chooses to make.' A response that was interpreted by them – correctly – as lukewarm and not very encouraging. I attended the wedding in the same spirit that the invitation was issued, going through the motions, and loathed the groom's parents as much as they despised me, although I did end up making a night of it, getting brutally drunk at a pub up the road with an uncle of the Toad's, a large bloodshot man it was difficult to say no to.

I seem to have spent an entire life doing the wrong thing by trying to do things right. Or, more accurately, by trying to avoid doing anything at all.

*

I'm so lost in sleep that it takes a while for me to register the noise that's breaking through my slumber. The dim recognition that it's my mobile, abandoned as useless on the kitchen bench, drags me back to the outside world. The phone switches through to message bank as my eyes flicker open.

It's late. I must have been asleep for hours; the sun is perched not far above the treetops to the west. Sleeping on your back on a concrete porch in midwinter is not to be recommended, and I have to lie still a moment longer, gently reviving my joints. Sleeping during the day is dazing, too, especially such a deep, undisturbed and dreamless sleep. I'm disorientated, confused by a sense that something is not quite as it should be, that something fundamental has shifted.

I'm pondering the significance of this feeling when I remember that my mobile has been dead since it was left out in the mist over solstice, petering into static in the midst of Milly's message. I stretch carefully, testing each limb before slowly raising myself up to sitting position, and the other noise that's been teasing me suddenly comes into focus, winding me with the force of an unexpected blow to the solar plexus.

Birdsong. The bushes beside the porch shiver; a tiny form wheels out of them. There are two finches in the grevillea near me. They swerve across to the branches of the large gum, twittering to the sinking sun. I feel life flooding back into me like a surge of blood, and battle the pins and needles in my feet to stagger inside to the phone.

The message is from Woodford police station: Denham, cold and crisp with officially suppressed fury. He informs me that my attendance is required immediately, for questioning in regard to allegations made about the abduction and possible homicide of one Xandrea Collison, reported missing by her companions. I have twenty-four hours to present myself for an interview, before a call will go out for my apprehension. How like Denham, to hide behind protocol, following due process within the safe, strong boundaries of his little police station, instead of venturing out into the unknowns of Nebulah to investigate.

He would be shitting himself over the repercussions of my testimony, the public exposure of my warning and his official cowardice the day before. I doubt he'd be in any hurry to locate me.

I try to ring home again but the answering machine kicks in. I'm wondering whether there's anything to eat besides the remains of the beetroot and salmon from lunch when there is a sudden eruption from the garden, and a screech scares me out of my skin.

A corella. In the gum where the finches were, shuffling his way along a branch about midway up the tree, looking as cheeky as all get-out. He regards me with an amused brown eye, as if to say, *What?* I stare back in amazement, as if to say, *How?* He opens his beak and lets out another terrible screech, just as the phone begins to ring again.

I check the number first, in case it's Denham. But it's not.

'Thank God!' Alex says the second I answer the phone,

and then she bursts into great hiccoughs of sobs. 'I've been ringing all night and all day, the phone seemed to be dead. I thought you were too.'

'I tried to ring, but I left the phone out last night and it's been stuffed – it's only just come back to life.'

'Where are you?'

'Home.'

'In Woodford?'

'No. Nebulah. But it's okay,' I add quickly, sensing her panic.

Her quick intake of breath is the prelude to a launch. 'Of course it's not okay, what the hell are you doing there?'

'It's a long story. We got trapped here last night.'

'We? Not Milly?'

'No, Milly was in Woodford. I was trying to get a group of kids out. They wanted to be here for the solstice.'

'You're joking?'

'A psychic told them it'd be great.'

Alex utters a disgusted expletive. 'No one with an ounce of ability would go anywhere near there at such a time. She had no idea.'

'Yeah. Well, she paid for it.'

There is silence on the other end of the phone. 'Shit,' Alex finally says. 'Anyone else?'

'No. They've got a bit to get over, but they got out.' I take a breath, try to form the words without a hitch. 'It was bad. Really bad.' I breathe. 'I lost Gina.'

'No!'

'It was my fault. It almost got us – I was in such a panic I shut her out.'

'Are you okay?'

'Sort of. Numb, really. Shock, I guess. I keep looking for her, expecting her to come trotting up.' I take a careful breath. 'At least it didn't drag it out, make me watch. It's what I would have expected.' I try not to think about Xandrea's desperate entreaties.

'Could she have gotten away?'

A thin veil of hope, but it's possible. The question hovers in the cooling air, and the temptation of it is almost within grasp. 'The wild dogs often get left alone – I suppose she could have escaped. It was too busy with us, and if it had got her, I reckon we'd have known about it.'

I break off, my focus broken by a burst of twittering. 'Did you hear that?' I ask Alex.

'What?'

'Birds. The birds are back.'

There is silence at the other end of the line. Finally, Alex gives a short 'Really?' Her tone is loaded with scepticism.

'I've seen a corella and some pairs of finches. All in the last hour.'

There's another short silence. 'You're planning to stay, aren't you?'

The sun is on its way to the treetops. If I'm going to go, it'll have to be very soon.

'Pete?'

I almost say, 'Yeah I reckon I might,' but I think better

of it. 'Nah, I've got to get back to Woodford. Denham's on the rampage about the missing girl and Milly'll be worried. But what do you reckon about the birds?'

'I honestly don't know. It's an interesting sign.'

'Could solstice have been the Last Supper?' Immediately as I say it, I have terrible visions of Xandrea outside in the mist, and I recoil.

'Well, I suppose. If it was D-day it would explain why the messages were so strong and so insistent. You're so lucky to be alive.'

'Amen. It feels different now. Nothing I can put my finger on, but it feels… clean.'

'Pete…'

'No, I'm off.' I glance at the sky. 'In fact, I'd better make a move.'

'Call me, let me know you got back safe?'

'No worries. Just relax. Did you sleep last night?'

'Major bad vibes. Far too many frigging old men in this world.'

'I'm safe. Rest.'

'I will when I hear you're back. Drive carefully.'

Alex rings off. I stand looking at the fading sky. In town, Denham would be on the warpath. I pick up the phone again.

'Hi, this is Alice,' a laughing voice answers. 'Please leave me a message.' There is a long pause, then the message bank's shrill beep. The tone is like a divide: her, then me. Her laughing voice, so removed from the traumatised young woman who'd refused to even look at me that morning. Until they left, when I'd held open her car door and leant in over her, insisting that she meet my eye. And she turned on me a look that withered everything I've ever managed to value about myself. A look of bewilderment rather than hatred, her eyes bright with fear and disgust. A look that turned me to dust.

In the grevillea, the sweet, mournful cry of a wattlebird as the sun dims towards another ending.

*

Denham rings again just as I'm easing myself into the Land Cruiser. I don't exactly know what surges through me, probably anger. No, fury. I find myself answering quickly, before there's time to think clearly and avoid him.

'Pete McIntosh.'

'You're an evasive man, Mr McIntosh.' Denham's restraint is in line with my own. 'Constable Denham. We require you to attend the Woodford police station immediately for a formal interview.'

'Check your records. I was there last night. You weren't interested.'

'You had nothing of interest to say last night.'

'So it seems. But now, suddenly I'm worth listening to.'

'We've had some serious allegations made about your involvement with the disappearance of a young woman, last seen in your company. We require you to respond to those allegations.'

'What are the allegations?'

'I'm not at liberty to say at this point of the investigation.'

'You're not at liberty to say. Is your involvement in her disappearance being investigated as well?'

There was a sharp pause. 'I have no involvement in her disappearance.'

'Not yet. But you will. You could have saved her.'

'By arresting you on suspicion of intent to commit a crime, I certainly could have. I regret that. Deeply.'

'Then they all would have died. How did they look, Denham? Shattered? All because of you.'

'If you do not voluntarily present yourself at Woodford station for questioning before noon tomorrow, a warrant will be issued for your arrest. Do you understand that?'

'When I make my statement everyone will know you're a coward, Denham.'

'Please provide your current whereabouts.'

'Do you think I'm curled up in fucking bed? You know where I am, Denham. How about I wait for you here?'

'And Millicent Pryor?'

'What?'

'The current whereabouts of Milly Pryor?'

'Why?'

'She is a known associate of yours with a close involvement in your affairs, and she also cannot be located. When she reappears we'll need a statement and an alibi.'

'Then you'd better get off your fucking metrosexual arse and find her.'

I disconnect the call. After all that, it had done nothing at all to abate my fury.

*

It is just on dusk when I pull up at Milly's. I try home and her mobile again and again, but I can only get the answering machine at Sean's, and her mobile is dead. I regret now the anguish I've caused Alex, stirring her for not sleeping.

There is no sign of anyone at Milly's, only the disarray of abandonment. By the gum tree along the side, the mound that is Felix's resting place is already overgrown. There are no tyre marks or footprints. The house is closed and dark, the curtains drawn over windows cold and empty. The only noticeable difference is the shrieking of corellas, off in the direction of the dam. They break into the evening stillness, adding a dimension of normality to a scene that should have made me feel threatened. In the dimming evening I circle cautiously to the back of the house, examining doors and windows, and the ground for traces of trespass. There is nothing.

The light has almost completely faded. It's a time of day I'd usually be cowering inside with every door locked, listening to the first sounds of the mist's arrival. But somehow the evening seems peaceful, empty. The sunset screeches of the corellas have brought back memories of the priceless serenity of living out of town, the secluded, tranquil evenings.

I bring myself back to earth. This is dangerous thinking and I need to be on my guard. I need to get inside, to safety, quickly. Just in case. I make my way up the verandah steps, searching through my bunch of keys in the dim night. I am just fitting the key into the front door when I realise I've left the gun in the car.

I turn away from the house to face the twilight, which is a hovering charcoal grey, almost but not quite completely dark. The Land Cruiser isn't far away, less than fifty metres. It would be a matter of minutes to retrieve the gun from under the seat and get inside. I hesitate for only a second; there is no time to waste on indecision. At the car I wrestle to get the gun clear of the seat, clumsy in my haste. I finally have it free, but as I turn back to the house, which seems to be squatting as if holding its breath with trepidation, the bushes beside me rustle violently and a shape leaps out, between me and the front door.

In panic I raise the gun, but just as I'm reaching for the trigger the form moves towards me with a yelp, and I realise that it's Gina. She gives another yelp and I almost cry with joy. I can barely see her in the dark, but don't waste time, just yell, 'Come on!', and she sprints beside me to the waiting house.

I don't stop to get my breath back once I've closed the door and bolted it behind me. I still need to be sure that the house is secure. Starting with the back door, I run from room to room, checking every window. Gina pads down the hallway after me, panting and every now and then giving a whine, as if to say, *What about me?*

I finish in the bathroom. Everything is fine. Back in the lounge I peer warily through the curtains, but the stillness outside belies my panic. There is no sign of mist, just the beginnings of a dim, cloudy night. I switch on the light.

Gina's waiting by the couch, and when I turn to her, her tail begins to thump the floor and she shuffles from foot to foot with excitement. I kneel in front of her and she whines and gives a series of little yelps. I rub her chops; one of her ears is badly torn, and as I run my hands over her flanks she yelps in a different way and flinches. When I examine her side, there is a very nasty ragged slash that runs the length of her body. It needs to be seen to as soon as possible. Her fur is matted with twigs and grass seeds; she must have come home through the cover of the bush. It's possible these injuries are just from other dogs. I'll get her straight to the vet in the morning; it's so good to see her I could cry.

In the kitchen the only food is a few broken remnants in the bottom of a sack of dog food, too few to bother packing when we left. They're stale and awful now, but Gina is obviously famished, and chomps into them with forbearance. 'Tomorrow,' I tell her, 'tomorrow we'll celebrate big time. A meat pie each. And yep, you can have sauce.' I ruffle her undamaged ear and she leans her head back into my hand, her mouth stretched into a grin of contentment.

I take another look at her side – the bottom half of her coat is dark and matted with blood. I'll have to try to clean the wound, ascertain whether it needs stitches. She hates baths.

But first, I pull out my phone and key in Alex's number. I need to share the news of Gina's survival, the one joy in an ongoing sequence of disasters. But the phone has gone dead again; instead of a dial tone there is only that same faint, snowy static. I sink onto the couch with frustration. There's no chance of the landline still being connected, but I pick it up anyway, just to be sure. There's the same snowy, distant crackle. I'm just pondering it when I hear the noise outside. The sound of an approaching car.

No. Not car. Cars.

I grab the rifle and throw myself full-length onto the floor, sidling on my belly to the large window. I use the gun barrel to shift the curtain minimally on one side, creating a tiny slit. It enables me to see the driveway, which is awash with the approaching beams of headlights.

I realise that I'm not breathing and take in a large gasp of air. I can feel my blood pumping manically. The logical explanation is that Denham has come after me, bringing reinforcements. He'd never come on his own. If they think I'm going to come out, they're going to have a long night. I'm only beginning to register what this could mean when the vehicles come into view.

There are five. All grey, all tinted so it's impossible to see within, all with their powerful engines humming slowly. One by one the oversized 4WDs turn slowly in front of Milly's house and glide to form a line out the front. The effect on my bowels is instant, and the knuckles clutching the gun are almost pure bone. But I'm inside, locked in. *I'm safe*, I keep telling myself as I struggle to keep my breath slow and deep.

The cars sit idling outside the window, in no obvious hurry to do anything. None of the engines stop and the doors remain closed, the tinted windows impenetrable. It's like watching a huge, coiled predator.

The cars have been there so long I've started to cramp across my shoulderblades when without signal or warning the first car begins to move slowly forward, closely followed by the rest of the convoy. Each vehicle turns at the side of the house and continues at funeral speed around to the back.

Seriously frightened, I scramble to my feet and stumble into the back bedroom. Using the gun's barrel again, I shift the curtain just enough to give me a view of the vehicles. God only knows what they are up to.

Or where they are. They've gone. Between the front and the back of the house, the five cars have vanished.

Just like the last time.

I wheel back to the front room and kill the light, taking up position at the window with the gun cocked and ready. The adrenaline rush has well and truly kicked in now and I don't have to fight to control my breathing anymore; it's slow, measured and rhythmical. I'm geared up and utterly, utterly calm.

As it is outside. The faintest of breezes has sprung up and the trees are gently rustling, as if expecting rain. The peacefulness of the night is mesmerising, the sort of night it wouldn't surprise you if fairies appeared, dancing delicate circles in the overgrown grass. The air has the charge of magic, extenuated by the appearance and disappearance of the strange uniform convoy. I'm intoxicated with the gentle emptiness of the scene outside, the thought that it could – maybe, possibly – finally be over.

Unwilling to be lulled into letting my guard down, I loop back to the bedroom. It's always possible the mist could be luring me, seducing me at the front of the house. I stand to attention to the side of the bedroom window, my back to the wall, watching carefully. And I have the feeling that something is out there.

I'm only in position for a short time when I pinpoint the source of my suspicion. A clump of native grass is swaying, jerking in a way unnatural for wind. I'm wondering what on earth the mist is up to when the grass splits to the side, and the shambling form of a tiny echidna waddles into view. It pauses, its snout twitching, before carefully making its clumsy way along the side of the garden bed, snuffling into patches of foliage before finding something of interest and crashing back into the undergrowth.

It's hard to describe the feeling that washes over me at the sight of the little creature. It's almost religious – or how I would imagine a religious experience to be. The wave of wonder and pure joy – that's the only word I can think of – is engulfing. It is over. I am sure of it now. I feel as though I'm floating, released into a realm distinct from hard reality, one touched by celestial beams.

The scratching noise that reaches me as I peer into the night, elated, is coming from the back. By the time I reach the kitchen it's stopped. The key to the back door is lying on the floor and the door is wide, open to the night. Gina is sitting to attention beside the table, facing me. She is skeletal now, her fur matted and filthy: a beast rather than a dog. She is staring at me attentively, through burning yellow eyes that are both glowing and vacant at the same time. Her tongue is lolling as she pants, the sharp points of twisted teeth just visible. She emits a long, low snarl that is beyond feral, it's more like a rumble from the depths of the earth than something from a living being. Her claws sprawl from her paws, grotesque against the linoleum.

I grab at the kitchen door and wrench it closed just as she springs. The thud of her body against it is tremendous, like that of a large wild animal. There is no key to the kitchen door, and the thought of the open back door scares me witless. I retreat into the lounge, jamming the sideboard against the door. I just need to calm down and get my bearings. I leave the light off and cross to the windows. The car isn't that far away, I could get out the larger window easily enough, and then it would only be a short sprint to the Land Cruiser.

But then what? I'd still have to get out of Nebulah. Or to somewhere I could lock myself in. One thing is for sure, I can hardly stay here. And I don't have time to make plans.

And then I see it. Milly's ute, parked right up against the Land Cruiser, so close it would be impossible to get to the driver's door. It had arrived with no sound at all.

I sense the two figures seated on the couch before my eyes adjust to the gloom and their outlines become distinct. Milly and Gavin are holding hands. Like reunited lovers.

'I came to find you. Yesterday. I gambled.' Milly's voice is a gurgle. 'But I was too late, I didn't get very far. But I did distract the mist for a while, gave you time to get to the pub.'

Beside her Gavin has started to giggle. He raises her hand and kisses it. 'I reckon he owes you,' he chuckles.

'Huge. Debt,' she croons back.

As they launch from the couch, I raise the gun to my mouth and pray that I am in time.

ACKNOWLEDGEMENTS

I owe huge thanks to Arts Tasmania and the University of Tasmania for awarding *Soon* the UTAS Prize for Best Unpublished Manuscript in the Tasmanian Premier's Awards in 2015. Thank you to the judges Kate Gordon, Chris Gallagher and Hamish Maxwell-Stewart for their enthusiasm for the book, which was unexpected and tremendously encouraging. Acknowledgement must be made, too, of the support of the Tasmanian Writers' Centre and in particular the efforts of Chris Gallagher, who was instrumental in seeing the book come to print.

Major kudos is owed to Barry Scott and the team at Transit Lounge, who are a blessing to new writers and a much-needed addition to Australian publishing. Penelope Goodes, as editor, was a pleasure to work with, zealous cliché exterminator. I hope Transit Lounge get the next Harry Potter.

Personally, the divinely beret-ed Vanessa Russell has been nagger extraordinaire, recently dragging the equally divinely shod Winnie Salamon into the Get Your Arse Into Gear stakes. Thank you to both for the encouragement/shame.

Family of course, and in particular Adam, who has always challenged me to keep working, and celebrated any success so buoyantly, transforming trepidation into excitement. Christine Murphy's opinion and support have always greatly mattered, in that particular way of sisters who shoot from the hip, and I would give anything to have her here to share in this.

Lois Murphy has travelled widely, most recently spending six years exploring Australia in a homemade 4WD truck, working mainly in small or remote towns, before settling in Darwin for a number of years. She has won a handful of prizes for her writing, including the Northern Territory Literary Award and the Sisters in Crime Best New Talent Prize. The majority of *Soon*, her first novel, was written while living in a caravan park in Carnarvon. Lois currently lives in Melbourne, Victoria.

More at https://loismurphy.wordpress.com/

SEALED
NAOMI BOOTH

Heavily pregnant Alice and her partner Pete are done with the city, haunted by rumors of a skin-sealing epidemic infecting the urban population. Alice hopes their new house will offer safety. But the mountains hold a different danger. When violence erupts, Alice is faced with the unthinkable as she fights to protect her unborn child.

Timely and suspenseful, *Sealed* is a gripping fable on motherhood, a terrifying portrait of people under threat from their own bodies and from the world around them.

"What a delicate, provoking balance of apocalyptic vision and personal journey *Sealed* is. I loved it"
Aliya Whiteley, author of *The Beauty*

"A brilliant dystopian distillation of just about all the ecological fears a young parent can suffer from"
The White Review

TITANBOOKS.COM

THE CABIN AT THE END OF THE WORLD

PAUL TREMBLAY

Seven-year-old Wen and her parents, Eric and Andrew, are vacationing at a remote cabin on a quiet New Hampshire lake. As Wen catches grasshoppers in the front yard, a stranger unexpectedly appears in the driveway. Leonard is the largest man Wen has ever seen but he is young and friendly. Leonard and Wen talk and play until Leonard abruptly apologises and tells Wen, "None of what's going to happen is your fault."

So begins an unbearably tense, gripping tale of paranoia, sacrifice, apocalypse, and survival that escalates to a shattering conclusion, one in which the fate of a loving family and quite possibly all of humanity are intertwined.

"A tremendous book – thought-provoking and terrifying, with tension that winds up like a chain… Tremblay's personal best. It's that good"
Stephen King

For more fantastic fiction, author events,
exclusive excerpts, competitions, limited editions and more

VISIT OUR WEBSITE
titanbooks.com

LIKE US ON FACEBOOK
facebook.com/titanbooks

FOLLOW US ON TWITTER AND INSTAGRAM
@TitanBooks

EMAIL US
readerfeedback@titanemail.com